Mozart's S

'It is fascinating. It is learned, touching and funny. It is so well written.
The picture of the family which emerges is passionate, strong and in
period. I loved it.'
— Mike Shaw of Curtis Brown

'This book constitutes a remarkable act of sympathetic restitution. By
amplifying the scattered facts with imaginative fantasy, A. M. Bauld
brings the personality of Mozart's too-little considered sister vividly
back to life while offering an intriguing hypothesis about Mozart's end.'
— Bayan Northcott, composer and writer

'The interweaving of fact and fiction is compulsive in this novel.
A. M. Bauld brings eighteenth century Salzburg to life through letters,
conversation and a beautifully composed narrative.'
— Heather Birchall, Curator, Tate Britain

'This imaginatively constructed fictionalised biography contains both
powerful imagery and a strong sense of place and period. As the narrative unfolds from several viewpoints, the reader is given a convincing
portrayal of the shadowy family behind the genius of Mozart. The
appendix detailing the known facts of Nannerl Mozart's life is an
unexpected bonus.'
— Natasha McEnroe, Curator, Dr Johnson's House, London

A. M. Bauld was born in 1944 in Sydney. A piano student of Alexander Sverjensky at the Conservatorium of NSW, she later studied acting at the National Institute of Dramatic Art, touring in Shakespearian productions before completing a Bachelor of Music degree at the University of Sydney.

She came to England on a university scholarship in 1969. After studying composition in her first two years in London with Elisabeth Lutyens and Hans Keller, she completed a doctorate in composition at the University of York in 1974.

Her music, almost all of a theatrical genre, has won international prizes and is regularly performed in concerts and broadcasts throughout Europe, the USA and Australia.

A.M. BAULD

Mozart's Sister

A NOVEL

ALCINA PRESS

LONDON

First published in the United Kingdom in 2005 by Alcina Press.

ISBN 0–9550713–0–5

Set in Warnock Pro
Printed and bound by Lightning Source
www.lightningsource.com

Cover image shows a detail from a painting by the author.
www.alisonbauld.com

Alcina Press
9 Stanbridge Road
Putney, London
SW15 1DX
United Kingdom
www.alcinapress.com

Contents

Chapter 1

Coach Journey from Vienna to Salzburg
Early morning, 7th December, 1791

Inside the coach was the coffin, wedged in by a bale of hay and a Goliath of a man with hair the colour of the surrounding straw. All seats had been removed to allow space for the cargo and from the beginning to the end of the journey he rarely moved from his corner, arms draped like a yew in a travelling graveyard. If he stirred at all, it was because the coach was sliding down or staggering up in a perpendicular climb and he would seize the brass handles of the coffin, slapping his thumbs hard against the metal, relaxing his hold only when the coach was again on level ground.

PRELUDE

Karlsbad, 29th June, 1844

I am like an old man sitting at a table with several bottles of wine in front of him. Each bottle is different and I intend to savour them all, one after the other, though not necessarily in any obvious order. I am longing to confide my secret knowledge. It is the caprice of someone with enough time to confess, for I will not die until the middle of this summer.

Through an act of will, I am able to exist before my birth as a spider in the corner of the ceiling that has always been there, a witness from beginning to end. This will be the story of what happened to my Aunt Nannerl, the forgotten sister of a genius. It is a story contained in a set of Chinese boxes describing the stages of a fantastical journey – a fugue by coach that takes place in the dead of night with its cargo, a coffin guarded by a silent giant and his peculiar retinue. Who lies within must remain a secret until my aunt's tale is spun. It is the reason why the grisly outer layers are exposed in fits and starts.

1

Allemande

Salzburg, 14th July, 1829

'Why should I complain? I am seventy-eight years of age and not dead yet.' My Aunt Nannerl is half under the covers in her invalid's bed. She reminds me of a doll without its stuffing, a husk that will blow away if I blink.

'So many memories my darling boy, the thoughts run like vomit from an old dog. They run all over the place because I remember everything. You, Franzel, and good, kind Joseph Metzger, are the only ones who understand how I feel and hear – how I even see a little.' Metzger is my aunt's fellow lodger and unpaid companion.

'Forget what other people say about me. I can see if I choose.' She closes sightless eyes. 'I want to tell you about the lace caps and ribbons, the hours of scales with a stick stuck up my back, the longings that I carried in my head or in my thighs – how I practised my galanteries and how such precision was greatly praised. Your father said a woman of talent plays with more sensitivity than a man. How strange. I just thought it was me.'

On her head there is a bird's nest of dull, curled hair. As for her eyes, they are without colour and covered with fine skin like a sausage.

'You can see how I look.' Her voice, though faint, is sharp. 'Even with my widow's stoop, if your father were still alive, I'd be the taller of the two and my coffin longer. My fingers always ache if I try to play his minuet from Don Giovanni with my good hand, which is annoying. It ends up sounding like a lame donkey. Hee-haw.'

She laughs, or at least I think she laughs. There are these small panting noises when her head wobbles on the pillow.

'Of course, my dear Franzel, it destroys the spell for those who can remember that I was the better pianist of the two. But then, I was.'

She is relying on me not to interrupt, blinking in the direction of my shadow.

'Your father, my very own Jack Pudding, was so thin, pale and plain, people thought him younger than he was, whereas I always looked my age. This is such a disadvantage for a prodigy.'

My aunt is very vain and very old but because she's lived so long and so intensely, has a wider range of feelings than I will ever know. I believe what stirred me to listen to her repeated tales, was not so much that she was a lovable woman, but the instant impression she gave of truth and intelligence in details of family history.

'I have had my share of admirers. I don't remember exactly when they started to arrive but there was the Baron Von Mölk in particular – a poetic man with a passion for sleigh drives. I tried to imagine what he found interesting in me, although I was hardly drawn to him in any other way than this.

'My Papa, your grandfather, saw it all from a different point of view. He believed my increasing height and swelling body were symptoms of my destiny from which I would never escape. He regularly predicted my death in childbirth, or worse, my life as a fat, beribboned female with no time for the pleasures of counterpoint and modulation. The idea of my obscurity repelled him because it was the inevitable rebuttal of his will and he hated to let go of a bone. It is why Papa would grieve or moan aloud whenever my performance reached perfection – this man, my father, whom I loved and who loved me. It was not that he underestimated my talent you understand, more he feared that I would never have the recognition I deserved.'

I am certain her English visitors, who know no German, cannot possibly interpret her grunts as they remain on their window seat, waiting for me to translate her words from beginning to end. There is a misleading vagueness in her expression when she accurately recalls a letter that my grandfather wrote to his old friend, Hagenauer. Its piety and vehemence have the stamp of Leopold Mozart and its contents is not distorted by repetition. It is perfect with practice.

'Though my daughter lives, I almost lost her. Should she die, she will die content. If God spares her, then I pray he will let her go to a much later death, as innocent and blessed as she is now . . . God has unbalanced my plans and it is obvious that my daughter's health matters more. Any rational human being can see that if God decides she will survive, I cannot expose her to the rigours of a sudden journey. It is quite obvious that I have taken no advantage from these circumstances, but on the contrary, have experienced only great loss.'

'Yes, yes. Papa called it The Divine Will when that particular fever passed on and I surprisingly did not. It was the Divine Will when poor Wolfie suffered from the same illness but took longer to recover.'

She makes little sucking noises with her lips and I murmur in moderate sympathy. This is all she needs to give her more wind.

'It was not the Divine Will when Von Molk wept and whispered to my brother that he would swallow a whole ounce of tartar if I refused to share a sleigh drive with him. As for Wolfie's assumption that I must have felt a tweak down there, it was a nonsense, which only he and Papa would believe, since it made them both feel better about leaving me behind in Salzburg with our martyred Mama.

'In my nineteenth year, they left for Italy without us. I practised my scales until I ached all over and then I realised it was really toothache, not heartache or finger-ache or arse-ache, and my whole face swelled up so that Mama was provoked into saying I really looked like the trumpeting angel. In all this terrible pain, I could see a future in which my brother's name would be enshrined and mine would be forgotten, so I carefully placed all my compositions in the bottom drawer of my father's desk. *Aut Caesar, aut nihil.* It was inevitable that I felt I was nothing, despite Jack Pudding's encouragement.'

My aunt and I have always felt like this, but we hope that there has been something original about our attempts, unlike my own dear mama, who writes no music, has worshipped Mozart at our expense and is unable to understand the pressure of such blood ties. Auntie has become quite agitated, determined to recall a compositional triumph as clearly as she can without many teeth.

Rome, 7ᵗʰ July, 1770

'Cara Sorella Mia!

You compose so well. In short, the song is beautiful. More of this please and do send me the other six minuets by Haydn. Addio,

— *Wolfgang Mozart*

P.S. My regards to all our dear friends and please kiss Mama's hand. Mademoiselle, I have the privilège d'être votre serviteur modest et frère.

— *Chevalier de Mozart*

Goodbye and good health. Shit in your bed with a loud crash. Make a mess of it.'

As she speaks it seems she can see such is the force of her expression, although the eyes remind me of milk jellies on a plate. It is not because they move in any particular direction, either up or down or side to side, but because when they do want to search for something, the whole head has to turn to accommodate the stare. She presses the fingers of one hand into the crack of her lips before they fall onto the coverlet to signal she has said enough. I push back the wisps of hair on either side of her face and hold my breath in case I weep.

Herr Vincent and Frau Mary Novello, her English visitors, have not moved an inch from their window seat. They are like twin porcelain figures, an incongruous luxury in this bare room. They may hope for a complete translation of what my aunt has said, but they must recognise that I also need to protect her privacy. It is why I am silent for as long as I can be without rudeness and why Frau Novello twitches her skirt to show she is alive.

'Frau Sonnenburg must rest now.' I try to deter their questions, which they have prepared in advance. 'Perhaps we could discuss her recollections some other time?' I wonder how it will all end as I watch the china gentleman caress his chin with delicate, contemplative strokes. When he speaks, his voice is as deep as Sarastro.

'My dear sir, we await your aunt's convenience in this matter. My wife and I would be happy to return at any time, although we are expected in Vienna within the next two or three days.'

I know he is saying one thing but meaning another, poor fellow. Vincent Novello is a music publisher and reveres the memory of my father. I can hear his disappointment and see defeat in the sharp manner with which his wife closes her fan, her face softening unexpectedly as she comes closer to my aunt. She bends down and kisses the skeletal hand on the coverlet in a gesture caught between ritual and common impulse. I think they recognise that this will be their last time with her and the simple action is both her farewell and homage.

Herr Novello moves from the window seat to examine the painting by Della Croce, hanging near her bed. It shows my father and aunt in a duet on the clavier with an overlarge portrait of my grandmother above the instrument. My grandfather peers from the corner with his Mittenwald violin in one hand, but for all the detail, the painting is stiff and lacking in proportion. Herr Novello appears enthralled and his wife curls one smooth arm around his with exactly the sort of spontaneity that is absent from the picture. I suspect they might ask for it on the spot, so I stare pointedly at the door, coughing in the way you do when you want to change the subject and are planning to leave as quickly as possible without causing offence. I may not admire the painting, but it is my family up there, not his, and I understand these hero worshippers. They'll take the shroud if they're allowed.

Auntie is quiet at last and dreaming in her bed, although the visitors have made no attempt to leave. I can tell by the flicker of her eyelids that she is lost in another world.

> *Too late to turn back.*
> *Lingering*
> *like the winter fly*
> *caught in half-spun web,*
> *I shudder*
> *at the base of an unseasonable womb*
> *and lie outstretched*
> *with thoughts of you,*
> *the ancient cause of my involuntary quakes.*
> *Since I do not want to give them up,*
> *I think of no one else*
> *but servilely feed my addiction*
> *until exhausted by a ceaseless ecstasy,*
> *I sleep.*

Who in Heaven's name is she dreaming about now? Oh auntie. It was never easy being the sister. It's quite bad enough being the son and I ask you, who would be his match?

INTERMEZZO

The English publisher and his wife, Vincent and Mary Novello, have come to pay a visit and have brought a gift of money from her admirers in England. It is an act of practical compassion and respect. I only hope she lives long enough to enjoy their generosity. In return, they want to know the cut of his cravat, what he ate for breakfast and the shape of his skull on the basis of a hat. I know all this because I understand the avarice of worshippers, being one myself. We walk up and down the street outside the house where he was born, pausing at the entrance and staring up at the windows, hoping for his ghost to appear. It is why I am unable to control the conflict between filial pride and my own spiteful disregard for vulgar adulation. It is a reluctant complicity.

I will let the Novellos know enough to satisfy their lust for extra-musical tit-bits but no more for the moment. Certain memories are locked inside my aunt's head and as the one who interprets, I have the key to both their revelation and their ornament. It is her tune with my orchestration. Believe me. My hands are related to hers and her life is at the tip of my fingers, as I will write on her gravestone when the time comes:

'Here lies in obscurity beneath the nettles, the skeleton of Nannerl von Berchtold zu Sonnenburg, born Mozart.'

Or better still, I will carve the following on a red marble slab, just to stir the shit a bit:

'Here lies the dust of Freyfrau Maria Anna Walburga Ignatia von Berchtold zu Sonnenburg, the sister of a genius.'

It is true I am embarrassed to see Auntie's room through the eyes of others. The walls have a skin disease. Damp bumps erupt through the striped paper, weeping, twisting like liquorice sticks in a distorting glass. There is a smell of stale urine in the air, which is a smell of old age, not poverty.

Vincent and Mary Novello behave as if oblivious because they are romantics. I can tell this by their permanent smiles and artistic dress, a look not touched by the dreariness of wear and tear. I see them examine the white sharps and flats of the instrument on which my aunt used to play duets with my father. I suppose they find the dust on its case is romantic as well. When Herr Novello presses one of the ebony keys, it sounds more like a fortepiano than a clavichord but nothing is said about its pinging qualities. I observe them pass the iron stove at the other end of the room. This is carved with the twists and swirls of a Viennese pastry but lies empty in the summer.

I am worried that my aunt, being so thin, will catch a chill on a day like today. I really must ask Metzger if he will order some more fuel, but again,

I'm relieved that the Novellos show no signs of discomfort. Perhaps their well-bred English martyrdom allows them to ignore the cold. As for myself, I can feel my toes curl inside my shoes and I am cross that today of all days I am wearing my thinnest stockings.

Auntie receives few visitors, rarely moving from her pillows unless to attempt her toilet in front of a small hand mirror, which I give to her reluctantly. It is a good thing she is almost completely blind, or she would have to turn away from the sight of her poor slipped face. I think she was pleased to have our company today and we only leave the room when she begins to snore.

Chapter 2

TARANTELLA

What I failed to tell the Novellos, or anybody else for that matter, was that once alone, I would spin myself back in time and become the spider I described, hanging from a ceiling in the apartment of the Mozart family more than half a century ago. My perception of the past is no guesswork for I'm able to observe almost everything that is visible, sometimes invading my aunt's mind and those of others who were close to her without distorting real time or influencing events, which is just as well, or endings would have to be changed.

At the beginning of a long, frost-bound winter, my Aunt Nannerl was nineteen years of age and composing busily. Her musical, spiritual and physical yearnings were confused. Her yearnings were caught up in dreams and such dreams were important because they had no restraint, transforming the banalities of her life into something bearable.

There she sat, not like Rapunzel, trapped in a tower with her witch by day and her prince by night, but by her own destiny in a middle sized, comfortable apartment in the centre of an archbishop's heaven, Salzburg.

There she lived, supported by an indulgent mother and a superfluity of churches, with a foreseen mixture of music, archery, religious worship, sleigh drives and soirées.

Her feelings for her father and her brother were increased by their remaining in Italy for the past three months and by the probability of more. There was no apparent cause for discontent, except that can be a reason in itself. My aunt's fantasies were always moments of redeeming disquiet to be dreamt away again if they proved uncomfortable. These were the acceptable vagaries of a woman.

On this day, the stove in the corner of the music room had been burning so fiercely, Nannerl removed her fichu and stroked the moistness at the back of her neck. I am too connected to her image to judge its beauty. Her nose, by its length, reminded me of a horse. Her mouth turned upwards at each corner before she laughed. Perfect for an oboist except she was a keyboard player who wanted to be liked. As for her hands, they were unexpectedly small with prominent knuckles and spatula fingertips, the nails bitten unevenly across the top. She fiddled with one hand against the folds of her dress as if playing a clavier. With the other, she stroked the point of a feather quill. I was curious to know what she was going to write.

Dearest,
    Hold me now in case there is no next week.
                        — *Nannerl*

The words rang out like a bell. I think she was trying to catch their sound on paper as part of her next composition. She curled her tongue delicately against her upper lip and her drumming fingers became an absent-minded mannerism that revealed she was serious. Listing her deficiencies aloud was a personal ritual that would free her to compose.

'I disgust myself. I really do. Am I incapable of restraint? Do I wish to see him every day? I do when he's not there, but I'm afraid I might not if he were. Dear God, I am perverse.'

The drops of sweat on her neck had turned into an irritating trickle, which every now and then she would try to wipe away. The text at this point was unintelligible, although she would hum to guide her thoughts while the lips remained closed. The sound came from somewhere at the back of her throat whenever she started a new line. Humming or grunting, it had little to do with the music she was writing or what she was thinking.

'Wolfgang says when I am serious I could terrify an army. Since my letter is both serious and fantastic I'll tear it up immediately.'

One hand closed quickly around the letter, which had been pushed to one side, away from the pages of manuscript. For a minute or two, fingers opened and closed, crushing its parchment into a puckered ball as she rose from the desk and walked slowly to the window.

'By not going to the Mirabell Gardens, we would miss each other. It would be the same if I stayed late for confession. I would be miserable and Mama would insist I take the waters to improve my spleen.' She was staring at the square below but her eyes saw nothing outside the windowpane.

'I could distract myself by studying more Italian madrigals with Signor

Martinelli. Or, I could sing my latest song to Herr Hofmann when he next visits Mama, and send a copy of it to Wolfie to show my composition has improved.'

Her fingers slowly tore at the paper ball in her hands. She watched as the narrow, uneven strips slipped from her fingers, then twist and blacken inside the glittering orange mouth of the stove. She picked up her quill for the second time and sat down to compose at her father's desk. Although she wrote quickly, there was a curious sense of languor in her body. I would have liked to say aloud, if you think something is real, it is probably real in its consequences. But of course I said nothing at all as I dangled from my thread and struggled to read the words she had scribbled underneath the notes.

NON VO'PIÙ AMARE	NO MORE OF LOVE
Non voglio amare	I do not want to love
per non penare,	because I do not wish to suffer —
ch'amor seguendo	for the soul,
di duol sen va	when bound by love,
l'alma struggendo	is gnawed at by grief,
di pene amare.	and swallowed by pain.
Non vo' più amare,	I wish no more to love,
no, no, no, no.	no, no, no, no.
Chi vive amando,	How can I live with love,
s'è cieco amore?	if Love is blind?
S'è cieco amore,	And if Love is blind,
come ch'egli è,	as it is,
il mio dolore	then it cannot see
non può mirare.	my misery.
Non vo' più amare,	I wish no more to love,
no, no, no, no.	no, no, no, no.
Fuggir vogl'io	I would like to run away
quest'empio e rio	from this spite-ridden force;
s'amor è crudo,	if Love, this naked child,
come ch'egli è,	is as cruel
fanciullo ignudo,	as that,

che mi può dare?	what can it give me?
Non vo' più amare	I wish to love no more,
no, no, no, no.	no, no, no, no.

She covered the manuscript in front of her with quick, sloping strokes that sprang from a flurry of dots. After several hours without any distractions other than the refilling of an inkwell and the silent dismissal of her mother by ignoring her when she came into the room, composition and text were finished. She stretched both arms above her head, cooling her cheeks with the palms of her hands. After a minute or two, she noticed the fire in the stove was no longer burning. She gathered up the pages of manuscript, ordered them, blowing across the last sheet to dry the ink. Her dress was so long it dragged behind her as she walked towards the clavier on the other side of the room.

Fingers ran from the bottom of the keyboard to the top and back again in a faultless arpeggio. This was not what she had written and she laughed at the incongruity. Both hands pounced on the middle keys, opening out with thumbs that became blurred in a flamboyant trill. What next, I thought.

'No more. No more.' This time it was her voice that smothered the room and startled the dog, asleep in a fragile patch of sunlight by a window. It was Miss Pimperl, my father's dog as well as my aunt's.

'Nannerl, my dear,' declared Frau Mozart, hovering at the door. 'Marianne,' she insisted with a force to match Nannerl's, my grandmother being the daughter of the finest tenor in Saint Gilgen and knowing a thing or two about throwing her voice.

'Herr Hofmann has arrived. Indeed, he is at the entrance below, but I have asked him to come upstairs to this room.' She continued on the same breath, afraid any hesitation would allow Nannerl time for another arpeggio. 'He has brought with him a large box, my petal. It is filled with the most delightful objects. Oh I'll not be able to resist a single one.'

She remained in the entrance, stroking her own stomach as a plump person does when excited by the thought of food. My grandmother obeyed her instincts because they served her well, which is why she prattled.

'There are lace caps from Vienna, all manner of trimmings, at least six different coloured shawls and I saw several packets of the needles I so admired when we were in London.'

Nannerl leapt from her seat, bit her lip and hugged Miss Pimperl distractedly many times. 'I am not ready,' she replied, tasting a trickle of blood at the corner of her mouth and wiping it away with her tongue. 'I never will be,' she thought.

'Not ready my dear? Not ready? Only yesterday, I remember you said it was time for one of Herr Hofmann's visits. If he didn't come you said, we would have to go and find him ourselves in the market. You did my dear, you did.' Frau Mozart was so ruffled and indignant that she failed to understand her daughter's distress.

'I meant I'm not yet ready for a visitor, Mama.'

'When will you ever be, my dove, my love?'

The dog was trying to lick his mistress's throat. Since they both had rusty hair and long noses, I thought they were devoted to one another because of what they had in common. Frau Mozart fanned her face with a page of blank manuscript and rolled her eyes to the ceiling. A man in grey stepped into the room as Nannerl returned Miss Pimperl to the floor. She rubbed her shoes together underneath her skirt so she could appear calm elsewhere.

'Good afternoon Fräulein.' The draper moved into the fading light next to the dog and accepted her extended hand. The curve of his shoulders was habitual, made worse by the way he read each night, slumped in his bed over books. The cummerbund underneath his frock coat was grey and the ringlets that spilled onto his lapels caught the flecks of twilight. On his head was a small silk cap, so pale that it looked like a bald spot. The toes of his boots had been highly buffed, reflecting his chin as he bowed and the general effect of his appearance was a conspicuous denial of the need for any colour.

'I do not wish to interrupt, Fräulein Mozart.' His voice and manner were hesitant. Nannerl bowed so low she was able to examine the cracks between the floorboards, relying on her mother's chatter to cover any silence.

'Nonsense, nonsense, Herr Hofmann. Pray do bring in the box. Indeed we have been expecting you. Marianne was working at her composition all morning and I must apologise for . . . for . . . Will you please . . . Maria Anna, will you please make room for our dear friend who has made a special effort to come and see us?'

Frau Mozart waved her arms in the direction of a box outside the door and pushed her daughter to one side. Her tone was so ecstatic that if I could have done so without spoiling the scene, I would have accompanied her right there and then on the clavier. *Dum-de-dum-de-dum.* Quick recitative followed by very long aria.

'I am drawn to the silk shawls and the needles, particularly the needles.' Hofmann lifted his box from a small trolley, carrying it across the threshold and placing it at the feet of the older woman. 'I have no more packets of the English variety, Herr Hofmann, which have the very finest points I am sure. What is more, they do not rust so quickly. I should like to buy a dozen of this kind.'

It was a mustard yellow trunk with large scratches scored across the top, revealing different coloured paints underneath. There was an elaborate brass lock with the star of David engraved upon its hasp, a single redemption from straightforward ugliness. He placed it beside the window seat and signalled to Frau Mozart to turn the key. Nannerl remained detached in her corner, so her mother could abandon herself to an Aladdin's treasure.

Out tumbled the multi-coloured shawls, lace collars, several caps and nightgowns of a fine, woven cotton, numerous packets of pins and needles, silk hose and spools of thread, all of which had Frau Mozart making small gasping noises of delight. Beneath this sumptuousness, lay a bole of wrinkled velvet, black in its deepest crevices, garnet red on top.

'Oh schätzl, schätzl, do come and look!' Frau Mozart remained solidly in front of her daughter. 'Here at last is a length of velvet in your favourite colour. It is quite enough to make you a dress with a bonnet and cape when you play for the Archbishop.'

'I don't need to wear a bonnet or a cape when I'm playing, Mama.' Nannerl plucked at her mother's sleeve affectionately and stretched an arm around her waist until she was able to reach the fabric. It was as soft as Miss Pimperl's hair.

'Do you like it?' Hofmann's voice came to them from behind while Nannerl stroked the material.

'Quite beautiful,' she replied without turning.

'I will buy it for you my pumpernickel. Say no more. Your father gave me instructions to find you something suitable. This is perfect. Indeed, Herr Hofmann, I would like to buy everything in the box, but please excuse me for a moment while I do my reckoning.'

The mother stood on her toes to whisper in the daughter's ear. 'Something is biting me schätzl. Do come and scratch me,' and with a backward glance at Hofmann as she left the room, added loudly, 'I will return directly.' Nannerl thought she heard Hofmann ask, 'Will you play your composition for me Fräulein?' But she wasn't sure.

The dog settled its full weight on the draper's shoes and remained there contentedly. Nannerl wanted to say: 'I wrote you a letter, expressing all the things I cannot express when we are together, but I burnt it this morning.' The words she formed were meaningless as she swayed slightly from the effort of trying to be still. 'Ah . . . by . . . um . . . t . . . mm . . . ' My poor besotted aunt.

Unselfconsciously and naturally he moved closer to her, bending his head lower until it was level with her face in an attempt to hear her speak. Whatever she said was inaudible, which was just as well. The dog felt the movement of his body through his shoes and rolled over before rising reluctantly to find comfort elsewhere under the clavier.

'What were you saying, Fräulein? Forgive me. I am confused.' His fingertips briefly cupped themselves around her chin and Nannerl was afraid she would lose balance from the strain of such intimacy.

FUGUE 2

'Karl,' came the whisper from the back of the coach.

'What do you think of it then?'

Karl was sitting on top of his wooden box, examining the ends of whips and putting to one side those that were in need of mending.

'Not much,' he replied as the vapour wrapped round him in streaks.

'Do we know who lies within?'

'We do not.'

'Or why we must deliver?'

'We do not.'

'I thought as much,' said the whisper after a minute or two. It had moved to the front of the coach and was now closer to the horses, who understood his demands. The wheels lurched or rolled through ditches and when the lead horse stumbled, the rest had to follow.

Chapter 3

GAVOTTE

Nannerl would have liked Herr Hofmann to take her in his arms, wildly or even discreetly as would happen in a novel. She hid her disappointment when he did neither, by crouching next to the clavier and persuading the dog to come out from underneath it.

'There has been no time to correct the composition.' She was trying to control the tremor in her feet as he closed the lid on his box. My aunt was hiccoughing from the effort of stooping to lure the dog away from the pedals. Her feet stopped shaking and the hiccoughs only subsided when he turned towards her with such gentleness and bent down so that the floor became their ceiling and Miss Pimperl thought they had decided to become dogs.

'What is the song about?' He summoned the surprised animal to his side with a click of his tongue.

'All love, which is hopeless.' She frowned. Her sense of the absurd had been limited by her own intensity and it was a struggle to remember what she had composed. They regarded each other with upside down eyes for several moments before they straightened out as partners unfolding from a bizarre bow or curtsey. The dog left the room in disgust and Nannerl arranged herself before her instrument, patting the sides of her chair and stroking her lap to remove the sweat from her fingers.

I could see from where I swung upon my thread that he cared for her in exactly the same way as she cared for him. The trouble was that neither could express their feelings directly and so one was a witness to some elaborate, fraudulent dance where steps were designed like a maze to divert and confuse.

'The words are in Italian and it begins with an extravagant cadenza which is followed by a simple lament. I will perform it for you if you like.'

Hofmann closed his eyes to listen, standing near to the curved edge of her clavier but not touching it. She watched him for the first time without shyness, freed by the sounds her fingers made on the keys. She shook her head, the tip of her tongue visible through her lips, sucking it noiselessly back into a narrow funnel. The moment she sang, the voice was clear . . . *'Non voglio amare per non penare . . . '*

I was sure he desired her. The colour had drained from his cheeks and a muscle jumped behind one of his eyelids making a thin corrugation in the skin like an infinitely small worm. It was a betrayal of tension that took time to slip back into its original smoothness, his lips moving without sound after hers, not in imitation, but in a private expression of his thoughts while he listened to her play. At the beginning of a sudden modulation he found his elbow collided with a sharp corner of the instrument's lid and she stopped as he opened his eyes with surprise and pain.

'Go on,' she thought he had said.

'Ch'amor seguendo . . . '

He felt a tightness in his head from feelings of responsibility he would rather not have had.

'Non vo' più amare, no, no, no, no.' A wisp of thread from her dress floated onto one of the white sharps and slipped into the crack between the keys. At this point, I would like to write that:

Hofmann thought the composition was operatic but never meandering. It was declamatory but not clamorous. It was the divine marriage of an Italian voice and a Viennese keyboard. Modulations were as adventurous as they were skilful. Not one ornament obscured the ideas and their effect seemed as tightly wrought as a motet by Padre Martini. But here, I am obliged by a respect for accuracy to record that the song was none of these things. Its performance was as dazzling as the content was mediocre. From the first to the last note, it was like any one of my own concerts. What would my father say if he heard? 'Pilfered stuff like chopsticks.' It was an expression he liked to use.

'Well . . . Thank you, thank you Fräulein Mozart,' is all Hofmann said in the silence after she finished.

Nannerl sat with fingertips entwined across her lap and studied her friend. She had a look of youthful earnestness on her face but she expected more enthusiasm than this. As he raised his arms and slowly stretched them above his head, I was certain she expected him to tell the whole of Salzburg to be quiet in the company of such talent. I was afraid the draper would knock me off my web in his expansiveness as I had spun myself dangerously close to the tail of the clavier. Fortunately he missed me by a thread and I scrambled back unnoticed to the ceiling where I crawled inside the heart of a plaster rose.

'My dear . . . I am surprised.'

'Why surprised? Am I so very different from my brother whose compositions you admire greatly? Are we not from the same pod?'

Hofmann replied that he did not eat peas. The fraudulent dance had begun again so I knew the draper was drowning in a sea of his own infatuation, complicated by his desire to tell the truth in all matters. I knew he wanted to draw my aunt into his arms at that moment and reassure her that her mediocrity as a composer was irrelevant to his feelings of regard for her. You could see the man was struggling to contain his emotions by the exaggerated way he now folded his arms against the front of his frock coat, digging deeply and painfully into the cummerbund around his waist. But instead of talking as a lover, freely, intimately and without awkwardness, he began, tongue tied by his place in history as much as anything else.

'I was impressed by the courage of your performance.'

'Courage?' Nannerl pounced on the word. She could smell nit-picking in his next breath. 'How strange you should find courage where I see truth.'

'When an idea is expressed and there is no way of knowing how it will be received, I see that as courageous.'

'Are you saying my composition is unpalatable?'

Hofmann fiddled with the edge of the clavier, horrified at the twisting of his words, uncertain what to say next.

'You misunderstand me, Fräulein Maria Anna. I would like to hear the song again. I have passed no judgment. You only think I have.'

Ah, I thought, spinning back into my rose. A trifle pompous, but this is more like it. He cannot bring himself to tell her the song is bad, so he asks her to sing it again. I know the ploy. I have tried it out myself on my own students. It gives one time to think and sometimes, mercifully, to revise an original opinion. I might then concoct a sweetener, or grapple with the consequences of one of my nastier perceptions. 'Herr Müller,' I would say, 'you reveal a skill that could be encouraged,' or, 'Herr Dobrowolski, where is the music?' And to think I believed the man's infatuation had affected his taste. My dear Auntie. She is about to be devastated I'm sure.

'Will you sing it again for me Fräulein? '

'Now?'

'If you are willing.'

'Yes.'

'Please.'

'Very well.'

The performance, second time, lacked the edge of the first. Errors of composition seemed more exposed than before. Where there should have been variation, there was plain repetition. Such decoration as occurred merely served to emphasise the emptiness of ideas that had all the woolliness of improvisation and none of the spontaneity. Style was more apparent than content, which at best, might be suitable as an accompaniment to the hubbub of a ball for the deaf. In short, it rambled.

My aunt looked at Hofmann before the final cadence and missed the last chord. She understood there would be no spoken verdict. His concern, though she had longed for it, was humiliating in its silence. She had assumed a gift by divine right of blood. Quite clearly, not so. Where before she may have believed her talent was overlooked, now, she believed she had none.

'Marianne! Anna Maria! Nannerl!'

Her mother was calling her from the bottom of the stairs, persistently and without effect. My aunt was so distressed she could only hear the unwanted thoughts inside her head.

Was it always to be so? You begin with an idea you are struggling to convey; you are convinced of its worth and so you write it down and as soon as it is played, it has as much life as a dead hedgehog.

She hoped Hofmann would miss her tears. He missed nothing. In his own struggle to be calm, his face became another bed of twitches, especially where the nose was pinched in on either side of his nostrils until the rims started to quiver. They turned from blue to white as he stood with his arms folded, fingers still digging into the embroidered cummerbund and his mouth no more than a crease. If this suggests ugliness or deformity then I have painted the wrong portrait. His expression was distorted simply by the effort of concealing everything he felt.

'Child!' Frau Mozart filled the doorway with arms outstretched towards Nannerl while the litany of woe continued inside my aunt's tormented head.

Am I deaf? The song is a screeching hotchpotch – a vulgar muddle – no more than that. He knows it. I know it.

She raised another hand to her face and shielded her eyes as a child does when it wants to hide. An immense longing for rest and oblivion swept over her.

'Can you come, Schätzl? There is something . . . ' Frau Mozart paused to scratch the back of her head, her shrewd, miniature eyes fixed on her daughter, who now rose from her instrument with such fierceness that the swish of her dress knocked over the stool. Hofmann moved closer, so close that Nannerl's tears splashed onto his hands when they knelt to pick up the chair in the long and embarrassed silence which followed.

'I must go,' is what she managed to say as she turned from Hofmann, at the same time drawing her mother away from the entrance to the music room.

'Go, Fräulein Maria Anna?'

'Go. Just go.' For a moment she forgot that she was meant to be the one who was departing, her mouth opening and shutting like a freshly stoned mullet. The better words, the words that could describe the way she felt were locked up in another person's head. 'I will ask Mama to make my excuses,' she thought. Miss Pimperl, who had been skulking unhappily in the hall ever since her exit from the music room, hurled herself enthusiastically at her mistress who collapsed against the wall under the weight.

'Wretched dog! Out, OUT!' she howled on one breath and pushed the startled animal to one side as she struggled to her feet.

Her mother on the landing and the draper who was still standing next to the clavier, flinched independently of each other. Frau Mozart forgot the itch at the back of her neck and gathering up her skirt, followed her disappearing daughter down the stairs and into the courtyard. There were still patches of frost on the cobbles and on windowsills, which had not melted from the night before. Nannerl leant against the arched doorway and surveyed the menacing glitter of rows of icy, polished stones. She kicked her slippers from her feet and lay down on the ground, soaking up the wetness with her body. Frau Mozart was appalled.

'Marianne. My love. What can you be thinking of? Herr Hofmann. The cold. Come inside.'

The older woman pulled and nudged the younger back through the door and up the stairs with a bland patter of disconnected phrases that years of mothering had perfected.

'There my flower. I'll make your apologies to Herr Hofmann. It is that stove again. It gets too hot. I'll have to tell your father we'd prefer a smaller one. It's not good for the instruments I'm sure.' She guided her daughter past the music room, past Miss Pimperl who was whimpering under the clavier, past Herr Hofmann, who was unhappily removing the contents of his box and struggling to make sense of his own unhappiness, past all other rooms until they reached Nannerl's. She soothed her with a kindly barrage of words which on other occasions would have driven Nannerl to distraction but which now served to keep her quiet.

'Sleep well now, Schätzl. A little sleep. That's all. So, Herr Hofmann did not like your composition. So, you are upset Schätzl because you also think it is a mess. Well. Maybe it is. So Schätzl, you'll write another and it will be perfect. I am optimistic.'

Hofmann waited alone for quite some time. He locked the box, having carefully laid its contents, piece by piece in rows on the window bench. He left without formal farewell, taking the empty box and trolley with him. He spent the rest of the afternoon standing by the bridge or walking along the side of the river with his box turned on its side and dangling from one arm and then the other. He was listening to the water as it splashed against the banks, ignoring the frost in the air, the ache in both arms and the chilblains that tickled his ears.

'Good afternoon, Herr Hofmann.'

'Greetings, Herr Hofmann.'

'Is it market day tomorrow, Herr Hofmann?'

'Good Day, Herr Hofmann. How cold it is.'

He was not capable of deliberately ignoring anyone, but he only half heard the passing pleasantries or half acknowledged each one with a mournful smile and eyes that saw nobody. He walked by the river for some distance, following the direction of the current and it was dark before he thought about making the long journey home.

Chaconne

My aunt, who had always been so fastidious, now spent entire days without getting dressed, preferring to put on her thinnest nightgown, opening the windows when it was snowing and complaining that she felt stifled by the heat of the stove. A wilful perversity settled on her as if this contrariness in life were her only remaining pleasure. She would ask her mother to bring her some hot milk, only to insist on drinking chilled water the moment it arrived. With letters from her father and brother, she would complain if there were none, but when there were, displayed no interest in reading them or in hearing their news. When asked to explain her capriciousness, she would deny that it was so and take to her bed for mornings and afternoons of mutinous silence which served to make herself, her mother, Miss Pimperl and the servants even more miserable.

A doctor was summoned to scratch his head and prescribe steaming bowls of camphor and a trip to Gastein for the waters, both of which my aunt refused. She grew pale with boredom and her own physical lassitude. Neither she nor Frau Mozart made any mention of Herr Hofmann or his cornucopia of haberdashery. A servant would take the dejected Miss Pimperl for her daily walks in the Mirabell and for three weeks, the clavier remained unopened.

When not in bed, she sat by the window of her bedroom and stared down at the courtyard swallowed up in fog, watching the vapour as it swirled around the edges of the building and across the stone ground, sometimes so thickly it was as if she were peering into a bottomless well whose walls did not belong to the house in which she lived. It was protecting her from an outside world she did not want to see and made her look at herself instead.

She knew her behaviour was disturbed but did nothing to change it. She had cast herself as the heroine of an implausible romance and had gone and buried her song and her lover in the haze. The memory of how it was became confused with how it should have been, while a list of self-recriminations turned into a chant: the draper was an invention to ease her loneliness – just a fancy, no more than that. Her vanity was the real problem – and as for her conceit, was it not conceit, which drove her to think she could compose in the first place? What of that? What possessed her to believe she could do more than shit in her bed, make a mess of it? The thought of her father? Jack Pudding? Perhaps. Was it, she thought self-pityingly and with no irony, a relative merit, like two peas in a pod? Or boredom? Boredom with primping, frizzling, powdering, perfecting minuets? Boredom with target practice, music practice, sleigh rides, soirées and such admirers as she had?

Again the unearthly wail when she thought more of her absent brother and less of Herr Hofmann, or when she tried to think more of her music and less of her heart, although she suspected one fed the other. Visitors to the house, who heard her cry, might have thought a storm was on its way. Bitternesss consumed her for the remaining winter days. She forgot how to be amused or amusing but despaired instead. It was the pleasure of pain and melodrama. It would pass. 'Soon please,' hoped her mother, who remained sane despite the aggravations. And it did pass – although there was no obvious reason for Nannerl's spirits to improve.

One day the sky outside her room lifted above her head and a clear yellow light streamed in through the windows. The promise of spring may have helped. At the end of the third week, with no more thoughts of growing old, my aunt awoke one morning and startled my long-suffering grandmother by singing in the music room. Frau Mozart heard the animation in her daughter's voice and made no comment in case Nannerl denied that all was well. Instead, to herself or the dog, she mused on the healing benefits of time to the stone wall that was in front of her. She continued her household duties, praying this time her daughter's happiness would last.

Scales flew up and down the clavier in the music room, followed by a set of complicated studies, which Frau Mozart recognised as ones her husband had written for Nannerl to practise in his absence. Sound stopped abruptly when the door was unexpectedly opened. With an instinct for knowing where her mother would be at any time, Nannerl ran straight to the balustrade, lunged wildly across its rail and demanded a fresh supply of quills. Just like that. As if possessed by demons, she sat down to write – very fast with lots of careless flourishes. Only the words she used were controlled.

Dear Friend,
    I may not hope you will excuse my strange behaviour when last we met, although I pray you will believe I regret my rudeness to you

as profoundly as I regret the inadequacies of my song. Since I have resolved to mend the composition, I wish to do the same to our friendship by offering my earnest apology.

— *Maria Anna Mozart*

Having once written the letter, Nannerl re-read it three times for pleasure before she tore it apart from the centre, cleanly from top to bottom of the page, tearing the resulting two halves from their centres, placing four strips neatly, one on top of the other, tearing them apart and dropping every single quivering shred into the furnace, again for her pleasure. It was as if the act of writing, as much as the content of what she wrote or its consignment to a symbolic inferno had helped subdue her feelings of remorse, anger and unhappiness. In one leap, she had reached the bottom of the stairs and laughing loudly, snatched a bundle of quills and fresh manuscript from her mother's arms before bounding all the way up again. It was an edgy, uncontrolled laugh, which she expressed with the same childish intensity as she did her grief. The hysteria was always there underneath.

But again my aunt worked with her head bent over the manuscript and covering it with those characteristic sloping stems. Occasionally she would rise from her father's desk and move to the clavier, nibbling on the point of her quill, oblivious to the ink that was seeping into the corners of her mouth. With her spare hand, she would lightly finger a sequence of notes, pause and appear to be listening to their echo in the silence that followed. When satisfied, she would return to the desk and write some more. If displeased, she would pound her keyboard and remould the offending passage. Oh the care and passion which she lavished on this song. At last.

At last? I think I am saying it is hard to remain interested in a heroine who is withdrawn from everyone else for such a long time. She becomes unsympathetic. So far, I have portrayed my aunt as querulous, fanciful, selfish and turbulent. She seems riven with self-doubt one minute or with an arrogant self-regard the next. But she was also capable of being generous and companionable. When not posing as a Queen of Sorrows, she could occasionally be fun. The trouble for Nannerl is that a heroine is rarely described as learned. Clever is different. She may be charming or teasing in a light, sardonic way, but generally heroines are a prey to tears and fainting fits; they are the playthings of the other sex; they have little else to occupy their minds apart from matrimony and amusement. They do not seem to feel lust for its own sake. When they grow old and a man no longer looks at them with a lascivious eye, they are consoled by reflections on a life devoted to the home. Rather than catch their withering image in a glass, they appear content with the narrow vision of their own domestic affairs and pride themselves on having been good mothers. A heroine is not expected to behave consequentially for twenty-four hours in succession. And yet, what if she has been encouraged to believe in her own worth? My poor, muddled aunt, who was midnight's child.

FUGUE 3

Land and sky looked cut from the same cloth, they were both dark. A light wind from the north had failed to blow away the mist as coach and horses smashed their way through yesterday's mud. From the animal's hooves to the three cornered hats of the four coachmen they were splattered in it. Sometimes they would stop briefly to allow one of them to climb down and inspect the wheels. Sometimes they just stopped to rest the horses who were nearly spent. The pants and snorts seemed twice as loud in the early morning stillness and at such moments, the men drew closer for companionship and to talk quietly amongst themselves.

Chapter 4

RIGAUDON

Nannerl awoke in the morning to the sound of voices coming from the square. There was a crowd on its way to the market and above the hullabaloo, she heard someone shouting 'Herr Hofmann' several times in an excited manner. The reply was drowned by a child's crying and as that was all she could hear through the general din, she dressed quickly, snatching up her bonnet with a fringe of coral beads to join the crowd.

As she was about to leave, her mother called, 'Maria Anna! Schätzl!' It was typical of my grandmother to announce herself by addressing the members of her family from afar whenever she wanted their attention. It was irrepressible but frustrating when the message, which invariably followed was lost in the distance. Leopold despaired of correcting the habit and neither Nannerl nor Wolfgang paid any attention. To them, this was their mother; an impatient enthusiast with a sense of occasion who practised daily rituals as the rest of her family practised scales, diligently. She wished her house to be in order and was as sensible as she was frivolous but always according to demand. She behaved as a small and commanding bird, fluttering into her daughter's room and reaching out to draw the curtains with a continuous flapping of her wings. She would be slightly out of breath whenever she did it and today she was puffing more than usual. Her cheeks blew in and out rhythmically like small bellows until she began to speak, at which point the heaving subsided when she got the better of her agitation. In common with her son, she enjoyed the sound of her own voice and could not bear to be still.

'Herr Hofmann is here. At least he was here, and he's coming back directly. My dear, he came without his box, and I did wonder for a moment if he'd forgotten your father is still in Italy. But it seems he wants to speak with you in particular.'

'Indeed Mama,' replied Nannerl, pleased.

Frau Mozart leant lovingly against her daughter for a moment, savouring this apparent tranquillity, then abruptly pulled herself inwards, which was difficult because she was so tightly laced. The gasping noises returned and as they did, her mood changed to one of anxiety.

'So you are not vexed, Schätzl?' She studied her daughter's face with care but missed the point. A horde of images, all equally unpleasant, crowded into her motherly head and made the poor woman feel ill. Nannerl – lying on her bed by day, a portrait of lassitude. Nannerl walking up and down her room by night, a portrait of misery. Nannerl weeping. Nannerl – not eating. Nannerl wasting. She was so thin, no man would ever look at her. The clavier would be closed again. Her husband would return and find his daughter dying. The dog would be howling at the bottom of the stairs and refusing to move. Wolfgang would be unable to write another note. Oh my dove, my love. My poor, bruised petal.

'Vexed, Mama? Why should I be vexed? I'm delighted he'll be able to see my finished song. You know that Papa has the greatest respect for Herr Hofmann's judgment.'

She untied the strings of her bonnet and turned to her mother, taking her by the arm and steering her towards the music room as she murmured soothingly over the top of her mother's wig.

'But I think the song is perfect already, Schätzl,' interrupted Frau Mozart, becoming more agitated with every murmur. 'Do not change another note. That's my advice.' Her upper lip was compressed so tightly against her teeth it disappeared and Nannerl, seeing her mother taut and alarmed, stroked her gently on the sleeve and hummed a ridiculous tune that made both women laugh and relaxed the mother in spite of her instincts. Hofmann had already been shown into the music room by Berthe.

Berthe was the Mozarts' elderly housekeeper, who cost little on account of her age. Berthe succeeded in reigning tyranically over all other servants who came and mostly went in Hannibal Platz. My father, my aunt and my grandfather were all afraid of her but my grandmother, who was not, would not hear a word against her.

'Thank you Berthe, you may go and remove the drips of tallow from the candlesticks in the hall.'

Frau Mozart remained hovering next to her daughter, discussing such important matters as the size of thimbles and ladies' wigs with Herr Hofmann. Why, she exclaimed, a draper could never have too many of either. Could he not, she enquired, obtain some stuffing to enlarge their coiffures? Of course it was fashionable to pad the ladies' wigs but unfortunately her husband had complained in his last letter that the coaches would have to be made taller to allow room for their heads.

Hofmann smiled tactfully and promised he would bring various samples on his next visit while my grandmother, satisfied Nannerl was not going to have another crise over differences in musical taste, swept from the room, declaring at the top of her remarkable voice that the chamber pots had still to be emptied into the Salsach.

Alone with Hofmann, Nannerl could see he was wearing a wig with hair that was coarser than his own. A yellow armband had been added to his left sleeve to signify a Jew. It was the law, although quite often he did not seem to be wearing it. She observed these facts with detachment and accepted them as unexceptional, although of course they were not, since Jews were as rare as Andalusians in Salzburg.

'I blame myself for what happened last time we met,' laughed Nannerl, stretching out her hands towards him before withdrawing both of them in a self-mocking gesture that left Hofmann feeling quite confused. 'My feelings of remorse will pass soon enough. I have no doubt.'

Hofmann would have replied but Nannerl was unstoppable. Frenzied chatter was still a part of her liveliness as well as a family characteristic and she would only falter when out of breath or interrupted. It was a nervous, bubbling monologue that was fed by the draper's silence as she noticed the small pinkish rings of pressure at the base of his nose that had been white as bone when she first entered the room.

'Herr Hofmann.' Nannerl tapped her forehead, trying to remember the sense of what she had written and then burnt. 'I'm ashamed – I'm so very ashamed of my behaviour when we last met. I cannot excuse it and nor must you. I expected lavish praise for a feeble little song and you gave me tactful circumspection instead. I desired your good opinion because I was uncertain of my own. I've tried to mend the song. I've tried so many times and now I think I have succeeded. But please, my dear Herr Hofmann, I would like to repair our friendship.'

Words tumbled out so fast that understanding followed sound. The pillage from her letter was abandoned and at last there was a silence long enough in which to regard him without distraction and which provoked from him an intimacy of thoughts, which was unprecedented.

'Maria Anna. What are you saying?' By accident, he brushed the hair on her forehead with his fingers.

'Listen to me. None of this makes sense. What can I say? That yes, the song was feeble, or no, perhaps you misunderstood my response? Why should you apologise to me, my dear? You were not rude. You were naturally distressed and I – I failed to convey what I really felt.' This time, he deliberately caressed the fuzz of hair as she lowered her face to conceal herself but his hand remained suspended above her head as if he were about to instruct.

'I am your friend, Marianne, and I hope that it is you who will forgive me. I'm your father's pupil and your mother's draper. I beg you to remember this when you are considering the worth of my opinion.'

'I value it highly,' she said quickly and at that moment I could see past her tongue all the way to the back of her throat. Its pink pod of flesh was dangling from the roof of a cave, tempting me to explore further until I realised that that would be the end of me.

Hofmann edged closer to the window overlooking the square. From where he stood, he could cast his professional eye onto the last of the stragglers from the crowd. A small boy was running in circles around his parents who were trying to ignore him, two priests walked side by side in silence like a pair of clockwork toys, while a tall, thin woman in widow's weeds lifted her skirts carefully over the cobbles and an orange-haired family carried empty bags in the direction of what he hoped would be his stall. The hope was as automatic as it was compulsive and from the look of profound woe on his face, I realised he felt doomed to spend the rest of his life consumed by the importance of his business at the expense of his heart.

'I must leave now or I will be late for the market.' He hesitated before adding softly, 'I am in Salzburg until quite late and would like to return before I leave for Frankfurt.'

He spoke without turning from the window and Nannerl, not shifting her gaze from the top of her bodice, said simply: 'My mother and I will be here in the afternoon.'

Hofmann bowed. 'I will return at four.' He left as Nannerl sat down at the clavier, pausing for a moment or two before she fingered a scale with such deliberation that there was time for a dozen thoughts between each note.

'I speak.'

'He speaks.'

'We appear to have separate conversations.'

'I'm glad he's promised to return.'

'He didn't say why he came in the first place.'

'I wonder.'

'Why he came.'

I could have told her, but as I said before, it's not in my power to alter these events. The draper had spoken as boldly as he dared. He could not say more without her encouragement and he was fairly certain he would not do so even then. He knew well enough that Leopold Mozart would be appalled by any understanding that might exist between his daughter and a Jewish peddler with a fiddle, a box of hose, despite a predilection for philosophy. These were ante-revolutionary days when the aristocracy was esteemed, the church revered, the poor expected to be oppressed, lords were meant to be proud and underlings were content to be plebeian or obscure and each remained with his own. Those who were caught in the middle admired those above and looked disdainfully on those below. My family sat somewhere in the middle with dreams of elevation. The archbishop's musician with his periwigged splendour fancied himself a jot above trade.

Not that Leopold would willingly be disloyal to his pupil. Hofmann's intellect was admired as much as his business acumen, while his musicianship was the greatest leveller of all. But there was the question of Nannerl's recent admirer, von Mölk. Frau Mozart, in the way of mothers, dreamed that her daughter's life would be inextricably bound up with the son of a man who was the court chancellor. This would suit my grandfather, my grandmother, the court chancellor's son and just possibly the court chancellor himself.

The flesh around Hofmann's nostrils was the pale, almost translucent blue of a corpse when he walked out of Hannibal Platz. What he really wanted to say to my aunt was unthinkable, but because he spent so much time in a state of agonising thoughtfulness, he could hardly drive these ideas out of his head. Nor could she, despite her father, her music, her religion and her sex. She would shock no canon of taste in a society where the talk would more commonly be of diarrhoea than the analysis of inner feelings. Lust, unlike quotidian bodily functions, was not always boisterously admitted, (my father and my grandmother, his mother, being something of an exception in this). Excrement, a useful metaphor in family letters, was being poured daily into the Salzach but more profound emotions were generally buried until the wedding night when the husband rewarded his wife for her virginity in gold. Nannerl chose to obey the laws while Hofmann, because of his rootless wanderings and his concealed desires, was equally constrained.

'Fräulein Mozart. Fräulein Anna Maria.' It was Berthe with her bonnet on her head and an empty basket in each hand. Sunlight had caught the weave of her dress. It glittered on the outside folds of her skirt as she leant against the open door with a grim expression on her face and eyebrows as black as crow's wings. Berthe was a spinster with the heart of one. It had never been broken, although every other part of her body was so brittle and dried up it was a wonder she remained intact.

'Frau Mozart, Miss Pimperl and all of Salzburg have left for the market. I should like your permission to go now or everything will be sold before we arrive.' Her eyelids were fluttering so uncontrollably, they revealed the whites underneath and Nannerl wondered if their maid had eyes in the back of her head.

'Wait Berthe. I want to go with you but first, I must find my purse.'

'Well Miss. That's not the way I understand it. You don't want to go with me and I don't want to go with you, but I daresay we'll leave together. Now that is the facts, God knows it.' Berthe leant on her good leg for support, gave her bottom a furtive scratch and waited in silent thought and bad grace for her younger mistress to return with a pouch of coins. Berthe venerated God's wisdom at all times. She would frequently stop in the middle of scrubbing a floor or making beds or washing linen to get down on her knees, if she was not already on them, and pray. She was only comfortable with facts and had a strong mistrust of ideas that did not relate directly to God. She made an exaggerated effort to correct other people's untruths in case God noticed the deceit and ended up punishing those who were guilty and her own self for good measure. Market day was one of her few unholy passions and God, she was sure, would punish those who thwarted her pleasure.

The square was empty when the two women hurried diagonally across it, Berthe, painfully, and Nannerl, with ease, on account of her desire to catch up with Hofmann.

'I hadn't realised Mama had gone,' said Nannerl to soften the servant's mutinous look. 'Don't be cross with me, Berthe or I'll leave you in front of the apothecary to find a cure for your crossness. Besides, we're nearly there.'

Before they even turned the corner and saw the rows of stalls stretching downhill towards the Mirabell, they could smell the produce and hear the din of bargains being struck. People swarmed in their market best, examining the bottled wares, the buckets of flowers and the dead chickens with broken necks and startled eyes, the live ones, squabbling in their narrow cages. Men paraded in frockcoats with velvet collars and long flapping coattails. Women walked demurely at their side in dresses that spread out from their waists like toadstools, cluttering the narrow paths between the stalls. There was a haze of dust in the air that occurs wherever there is a market or wherever the earth is kicked and churned by a thousand passing feet. It was particularly dense that morning and since dust invariably makes me want to sneeze, I took refuge from it in the fringe of Nannerl's shawl. My aunt had already seen Hofmann's head above the crowd in the distance and was hurrying towards him.

'I'll leave you now Fraülein Maria Anna if you please and God's willing,' announced Berthe, still sulking as they drew closer to Hofmann's stall.

Nannerl was worried the servant might flop down onto her knees and pray in front of the whole of Salzburg. Certainly her head was lowered ominously towards the ground as it always was when Berthe felt moved by spiritual needs. Instead, she quietly limped away towards a stall selling remedies for every ailment known to man and my dear aunt could not believe her luck. For the first time that morning there was no one left to disturb her fantasies. Her mother was lost somewhere in the crowd and she was aware of Hofmann studying her as she drew near. 'You followed me,' his eyes were saying with surprise.

She understood that he might be uncomfortable seeing her in front of his stall instead of at her clavier, and as she was indulging this delicacy of feeling, a woman dressed in black moved between them to select a flimsy and foxed piece of card from a tray of buttons. It had been strung with a dozen twisted, luminous fragments of mother of pearl. She held it in the flat of her palm to ask how much, listening to Hofmann's reply with such gravity that Nannerl felt a witness to a significant moment in a play, which she must not interrupt.

Hofmann recognised the widow he had seen through the window in Hannibal Platz. She made no attempt to bargain with him, instead, moving away in the opposite direction as Nannerl watched and considered whether she had the right to call the woman back, at the same time, fingering the coins in her purse. Hofmann merely shrugged his shoulders, pulled at the ends of his wig with a fidgety reluctance and puckered up his mouth to show disinterest in what was a common enough moment in market life. The draper was not reckoning with my sentimental aunt who shared her mother's talent for interfering.

'Dear friend.' Her confidence grew with the sense of novelty about what was happening and her tone was self-righteous. 'It would . . . I am certain it would be a great kindness if, perhaps, you could sell them for a little less.'

'I see you are telling me which way to conduct my affairs, Fräulein Maria Anna.' How could a Mozart begin to understand his world, the idea never occurring to him that he might not be able to understand hers?

Nannerl held the card at arm's length, admiring the beauty of the buttons, searching for an argument to make him change his mind.

'If we were discussing a composition, I would expect you to offer your opinion. Is it not the same for me with what you sell?'

'By all means, tell me what you think, but don't expect me to listen in this particular case, because I can see what is happening.'

Hofmann was chuckling as he drained a bag of coral beads into an empty tray and observed the widow approaching from behind once more. He stirred at the beads, creating a pink spiral with his thumb as she paused beside Nannerl. The woman was clasping and unclasping her gloved hands in an agitated manner and her mouth kept opening and shutting, either rehearsing what she wanted to say or because she was hesitant about saying it.

'Sir, I have thirty-seven kreuzer in my purse, of which half a gulden must be set aside for rent. That leaves me six kreuzer to buy food and medicine for my sick child. I am not bargaining. I am not begging. I only wish to admire certain buttons before they are sold, if that isn't too much trouble.' She touched her lips quickly with one hand the way people do when they want to stop themselves from saying more, while Hofmann and Nannerl in one of those unintentional comic moments, did the same and the card fluttered to the ground, landing near the widow's feet in front of the stall.

'I'm so sorry. How clumsy of me.' Nannerl stooped, retrieved and presented it to the widow with a bow.

Hofmann alone could see how the matter would end.

'I cannot alter the price, since these buttons were a gift to me – do you understand my dilemma? They have the value of a gift. But let me cut the card and I will give each of you one half.'

Nannerl was about to ask why the buttons were on sale in the first place, but was silenced by his frown as he pinched and sliced the card in two with a large pair of scissors, so the pieces curled upwards in the widow's hand. There was an intimacy about the act of cutting, which made Nannerl uneasy. She was mortified by his assumption that she shared the same degree of moral obtuseness as this woman or that their desire for pretty things was at someone else's expense. Hofmann returned the scissors to a hook in a corner of the stall.

'The matter is resolved,' he thought to himself, 'and the judgment is fair. It's in my interest to be generous,' at the same time, curling his fist into a ball, regretting his cynicism.

The widow somehow managed to give Nannerl her share without a single glance in her direction. She slipped the other half into the reticule dangling at her waist and with a brief nod to Hofmann, hurried away. My aunt glimpsed her in the distance, talking to an orange-haired man with several orange-haired children, who were alternately tugging at his knees and her skirt. If Hofmann saw the same, he gave no sign of it, busying himself with the next customer and choosing to ignore Nannerl as she tucked her fragile booty into her purse.

'They are not mine,' she decided and 'I shall return them later if he refuses payment.' She stepped aside to avoid some elderly matrons, jostling one another for the finest scraps. Her meddling had disrupted at least three sales so far and she whispered her excuses above their heads before moving onto the next stall. Hofmann was cutting from a bolt of lace; although he saw her go, he did not ask her to stay.

With bright colours and strong smells, the next stall was selling birds in cages, strapped to a set of poles. They were hanging in a chaotic pile of flying feathers and as Nannerl examined each one, she tugged at the knot on her shawl, uncertain which to buy. Since this was just at the point where I was hiding, I dropped a thread into her purse and landed on top of the buttons. Within minutes, she had dislodged me yet again with her search for coins and her purchase of a canary. It was pale yellow and plump, from the top of the heap – a particularly noisy bird, too fresh to its cage to be cowed. Nannerl held it high and stood on her toes, searching for Berthe or her mother in the hope they would take it away. An old friend discovered her instead.

'Anna Maria! Wait there! Wait for me please!' Katharina Gilowska was a friend at such moments when my aunt had the time, which was not as often as was good for her.

'What is this my darling? A canary in a cage? Will you warble together?'

'Hmm. Would you rather I kept it in a goldfish bowl?'

'Of course.'

They laughed, although Nannerl was not clear in her mind if she was pleased by her friend's arrival. The uncertainty made her waspish inside and the sting of her thoughts often cut through a type of blandness when she tried to be nice. Katharina continued to laugh with such straightforward pleasure and without a hint of resentment that the bird whistled back at her, batting its wings against the bars and flapping in circles around the cage, each as artless as the other.

'There. I knew it. All canaries can sing! I'm afraid my cat would disapprove if I were to bring a bird into our house.'

Most of her attempts at original conversation were like this. They had a tinny ring to them because she believed the main purpose in friendship is to either hear or give the gossip that the other person craves. Nannerl understood this, and whether out of guilt at being a reluctant friend or fear that she would be without one when she was most in need, made an effort to show interest when she had none.

'Come home with me. Come now while everyone is still at the fair and we can talk as much as we like without interruption.'

The promise of any intimacy was a gift to Katharina, who pushed or dragged my aunt through the crowds until they reached the last row of stalls. Nannerl suddenly stopped, a finger raised for silence, as she recognised a voice coming from behind them.

'I have thirty-seven kreuzer in my purse, of which half a gulden must be set aside for rent, the rest to buy food and medicine for my sick child. But I was admiring that copper kettle on your shelf and would like to take a closer look, if that's not too much trouble.'

Nannerl turned as little as she could without being observed and saw the tinker select the largest copper kettle from his bench, present it to the widow, their exchange inaudible as Katharina was hissing into her ear.

'Why have we stopped Anna Maria?'

'It's nothing. I thought I recognised someone, but I was wrong. Later Katherl. We'll talk later.'

She spoke roughly, knowing she would have to satisfy her friend's curiosity with some concocted tittle-tattle when there was nothing to tell. At least, nothing that she felt she could reveal.

'Haberdashery. We must discuss our costumes for the next municipal ball,' said Nannerl with relief in her voice as later they climbed the stairs to the apartment in Hannibal Platz. Dancing was a passion that she shared with my father and the pleasures of dressing up for it came a close second.

'Yes, yes. Of course we must.' Her friend wore the look of someone who has received a bad hand in cards, but Nannerl showed no pity as she resolved to steer clear of anything of consequence or mystery.

COURANTE 1

Salzburg, 1841

This is a brief leap forward in time. I need my human form to write under the shade of the trellised vines in my mother's garden as I wait for lunch to be served. My dear mama, Constanze, married a Norwegian count after the death of my father and lives halfway up a mountain that is named after nuns. If I look down, I see people the size of ants on both sides of the Salzach and if I look up and across, I catch a streak of cloud that has coiled itself around the tops of mountains in a white wreath. For a brief while I am content to be alone.

Without these moments of serenity, I feel I'm hurrying to nowhere.

I wake up in the morning and wonder if I am back in Poland with my beloved Josephine, or here in Salzburg. (I am not prepared to digress with a description of the woman I have loved for many years and cannot marry because she is already another man's wife. It is an unfinished story and since I am a direct protagonist, I'll not be the one who tells it. History will record my life with Josephine as a footnote I've no doubt. I feel the same way about any discussion of my mother, who may have been called Constanze by name, but was lacking in its virtue. Someone else will have to tell her tale, not me.)

Unfortunately I suffer from bouts of melancholy and sometimes I wish the day would disappear without my knowing that it had ever happened. I'm hurrying my life away like the carriages below, which appear to be locked in a perpetual and pointless motion. Then perhaps it is just that I'm caught in my own web. Since it is understood I am sometimes a spider in the corner of the ceiling, spinning through space, I will explain that although I have seen certain events before in another time, I cannot alter them for any person's comfort. Certainly not for my own.

The effect of all this – my being a witness I mean – is that I begin to think and talk like those I'm watching. It would seem possible if not logical, if I can be like them, they can be like me. Do I end up inhabiting each one and reflecting their characteristics or do they reflect mine? I'll have to think about this later, although it is simpler to believe that the minds of my Aunt, Hofmann or anyone else in this tale, belong to themselves. It is the same with the scales on a fish. Each one is both different and yet similar. Looked at closely, I suppose we are distinguishable from one another but is the degree of difference a matter for the observed or the observing? In bitter moments, I think there can be no originality about anything. Even my father pillaged from himself.

That consoles me for the moment and besides it is time for Jakob Hofmann to give his point of view. As I have already explained, I must be discreet until everyone is dead, which means I will try to avoid a frank discussion of those who are living, my aunt excepted since she is dying. I will say little, even if charming people like the Novellos would go to Hades and back for such knowledge. Explanation has to come at the end or there is no climax. This is a novel I am weaving, not a short story. Also it is true my aunt foresaw little and expected much. Certain affairs might have been handled differently, but who can say to what advantage? It is important for me to keep on reminding myself she was not always blind or paralysed, and as she says herself, she can still taste, remember and smell. I will bring her some roses from my mother's garden when I've finished today's chapter. Now back to Herr Hofmann.

Chapter 5

HOFMANN'S TALE

Departure is a time of loneliness or regret, discontent or adventure and sometimes relief and hope. Each time I begin a journey, I plan my return to ease the uncertainty and try to make a few different homes along the way that I can either go back to or leave. Packing and unpacking, telling myself I'll move on only when I've made my mark in a particular place. The draper's box and his fiddle. It's always been so.

It is not the detail of this that matters but the principle. People have left their land behind in despair or great unhappiness or restlessness, but it has never stopped them from going. They've accepted the delays and the slowness of human travel, the waiting for the right weather, the right wind or a change of carriage or of horse. It is sensible that we should know about such things. If we understand, we let in hope.

I called at Hannibal Platz at four o'clock that afternoon as promised. I left my wig, which smelt of the market, on top of my box and trolley in a corner of the hall downstairs. When she opened the door and I saw her friend standing behind her, I was angry with myself for bothering to come at all.

'Good evening, Fräulein Mozart . . . and Fräulein Gilowska, I see.' Berthe Salz had already removed my coat and I was obliged to stay though I wanted to escape. There was also the matter of my promise to Maria Anna. I had said I would come but Katharina Gilowska was bobbing up and down like a demented parrot from behind her friend's shoulder and I knew my worst fears were justified.

'Teach me. Amuse me. Disturb me. Make me think. Show me how I should be.' Quite impossible demands. That's how it always was with Fräulein Gilowska and it would always be so. Like picking up bits of knowledge on the way and putting them in storage. She had no ideas of her own but had the sense to know who would give her some. If I opened up her skull, I am sure I'd find a collection of other people's thoughts laid out neatly in a basket. They'd be covered in dust of course. Useful or unused, you had to admire her cheek and at the back of my mind, is a vague awareness that there must be something more to her or Maria Anna would not be her friend.

'Good Evening, Herr Hofmann.'

'Why, Herr Hofmann, what a delightful surprise.'

Fräulein Gilowska definitely seeks gossip to exist and without it, feels deprived. Her vivacity, I can tell by the way it waxes and wanes, relies on the intimate knowledge of other people's flaws. She is not handsome. The nose belongs to another face. Her hair is the same colour as her skin and one eye has a habit of looking at you while the other wanders. The head is too large for a childlike body, but she owns rather like Berthe, the maid, such distinctive, thick eyebrows, they give the impression of strength. Her look is eager because she doesn't want to miss a thing, although she often does because she only understands what is obvious. The Fräulein is redeemed by her sweet temper and unlike Berthe Saltz, is not at all devout. As for my darling girl, she seems flattered by the devotion of a slave, which is natural under the circumstances. They have one common interest, fashion, and they enjoy dressing up for other people's parties in fancy dress. Please note. It is my fancy dress.

'Have you brought your violin with you or your box?'

'Katharina intends to become my father's pupil – as you are, Herr Hofmann,' Nannerl was pulling me further into the room, showing me by her ease that I should not mind her friend's insensitivity. But of course I did.

We sat there, the three of us, with Fräulein Gilowska doing most of the talking. There was a canary in a cage by the window, which seemed interested in what she had to say. Between them there was such a counterpoint of twittering that I found myself wishing for the dog's growls to add depth. Miss Pimperl had wisely left the room already.

'I need your help, Herr Hofmann. I would like to dress as an exotic bird at the next municipal ball and I require some feathers. Do you have a pheasant tucked away in the bottom of your box? Or perhaps one of those exotic birds with bright red and green feathers?'

'You mean a parrot,' laughed Nannerl. My dear, sweet friend was so amused that neither she nor Katharina Gilowska could see I was still annoyed by the Fräulein's presence.

'A macaw,' I snapped.

'Yes, yes, of course! One of those birds which talks all the time.' She stroked the length of her nose as she would were her own pet. 'However, I would prefer something more feathery for dramatic effect. Have you Herr Hofmann, have you such a bird?'

'There's not a single stuffed bird in my box, Fräulein,' I sat down on the empty seat, pausing just long enough for her to feel disappointed. 'But between the silk ribbons and the velvet you may find a dozen ostrich feathers and of course a tiger's head with a tail attached if you change your mind about costume.'

Katharina Gilowska rolled her eyes in disbelief. She was clearly as good-natured as I am not, appeared willing to be friends, which I was not, and made me regret my gruffness as soon as I saw Nannerl frowning at the floorboards in disapproval of what I said; or was it the way in which I said it?

'A dozen ostrich feathers would be perfect, Herr Hofmann – and of course you may forget the tiger. Do you know that Maria Anna intends to dress as a statue? I keep telling her she should be a goddess with a sword and a helmet.'

'You are mistaken, Katharina. I've changed my mind.' Nannerl jumped up from her chair and was determinedly steering her friend towards the door. 'I've decided to dress up as a gondola,' she said with perfect pronunciation.

'Surely you mean a gondolier my dear?' Katharina slid from out of Nannerl's arms and glided in my direction to show how perverse she was prepared to be. Without hesitation, Nannerl twirled her back again.

'Ah, but a gondolier must exert himself and a gondola floats. I prefer to float.'

'Then how do you dress as a boat? You're not serious, Anna Maria. Herr Hofmann, please tell her she'd be much prettier as a goddess.'

'Please do not, Herr Hofmann. I forbid it. My dear Katherl, have you forgotten Mama would like to see you? She's somewhere I believe with the Abbé Bullinger, but I insist you interrupt their plans to reform the church. Herr Hofmann has come to judge my composition, not my costume, and

I promise you'd be bored if you were a witness to it.'

Fräulein Gilowska tugged at the pale hair that hung like a carpet fringe from the top of her forehead and which stopped short of her eyebrows. She seemed more amused than insulted by her friend's sharpness, more curious about my feelings for Nannerl or Nannerl's feelings for me. But as I watched the tap-tap tapping of her nose with her fan, I hoped nothing would be said when I had gone that would embarrass, shame or ridicule me. Small comfort in knowing I would never know, and all the while the strange ritual of tapping persisted. Perhaps she was summoning me from the other side of the door, for she bowed with such an outrageous display of petticoats I really did wonder if she was sending me a message. And yet the Fräulein is never so obscure. She thrives on bungled complicities. There was and is no subtlety in her bones, no obvious sign of intelligence.

'Remember the feathers, Herr Hofmann. Marianne and I have had such a delightful time planning our costumes. I'll come to ask you for my bits and bobs in an hour from now.' This was not so much a threat as a tidy promise since she seemed to have no idea that she was being driven from the room. And yet the moment she had left, I found I could like her so much more, which is my failure I admit, not hers.

'Jakob.'

With just one small word, Nannerl offered me a moment of intimacy. My darling placed one encouraging hand on my arm and flapped a sheaf of manuscript under my chin with the other. How was I to explain to this divine person that I was loath to give her my advice? Should I refuse outright?

'Dear, dear Jakob. It would be better if you read this music without my having to perform it. I would then be forced to imagine what you think. Your eyes, you see. They would tell me everything I need and possibly everything I do not want to know. There.'

She forced the pages into my hands and sat down in front of me as I stood. I could have cried but instead I blushed. I blushed because I was nervous or because I was disturbed by the strength of my feelings, which had nothing to do with her music and everything else to do with Nannerl. I tried to read, but it was hopeless. I forgot what the original time signature had been, which key we were meant to be in because the keys kept changing, which sections were repetitions and which were variations on the original idea. I had let her down abominably. How could I admit that all the while my head was bobbing dutifully up and down the page, I saw nothing but a splash of black dots with tails? I tried to console myself that such lack of comprehension happens to everyone at some time, even Leopold, Nannerl or . . . maybe not Wolfgang. I will start again, I told myself.

Good God! She is watching me I am sure. She has guessed the truth. I am a fraud and she is appalled by her discovery.

'Jakob.'

I swear I shall be undone by such intimacy.

'Herr Jakob, you've turned two pages at the same time.'

Ah. Herr Jacob. Now she knows I'm a sham. It serves me right. She believes I can't read music. I play blind, like the gypsy.

'My leap was deliberate Fräulein. I had to know what it would be like if you were to skip the passage in between.' My knees were swaying. 'I think it works better without that particular section because the line which begins: 'for the soul when bound by love, is gnawed at by grief,' can then be followed by 'I would like to run away from this spite-ridden force.'

She was studying me with interest and I felt encouraged to go on.

'The middle stanza is left out from where it was originally meant to be but suddenly, it's heard for the first time in the repeat. The change makes it stronger don't you think? More economical. Do you agree?'

So smooth was I. So oiled and almost plausible. I was beginning to convince myself as well, since my eyes and brain had by now adjusted to what they saw. The missed page, I realised, meant one less modulation and might I argued, be a benefit. But I had said enough. I was determined not to upset her any more than I had already.

NANNERL: Jakob.

ME: Fräulein?

I couldn't bring myself to say aloud, Maria Anna. Anna Maria. Nannerl.

NANNERL: Why did you come?

Clearly she was not afraid of anything.

ME: I came for your composition.

I was not afraid of that. Not when I gave myself enough time to think.

Nannerl: But can you bear to hear it again?

Perhaps she, on the other hand, was a little afraid.

Me: You said you would try to mend the song. I remember your words exactly.

I forget nothing.

Nannerl: You said you would return at four; your words.

She also forgets nothing.

Me: So I returned as promised.

Why are we arguing? Can I be truly lovesick?

Nannerl: I didn't ask you to look at my song when you called here this morning.

Now that's not what she told Fräulein Gilowska.

Me: Would you rather I called because I wanted to come?

I'm trying so hard to please, I drop the pages of manuscript to the floor in my anxiety. Nannerl picks them up before I can.

'Yes,' she says, placing each page in order on the music stand.

It worked – my trying so hard, not my clumsiness. If she stood up and walked towards the window, I'd follow her just like Miss Pimperl, stand next to her, touch her on the tip of one of those small bumps that run down the back of her neck, even smell her skin, for we would be so close. If she remained sitting in the chair I would be unable to hide my feelings and all would be up! Now the room was stifling. The stove next to the music cabinet had a malevolent will of its own. It always burned more fiercely when it was least required to do so. I felt dizzy and was afraid I might vomit in front of her. I remember covering my mouth with both hands. I think I must have stopped breathing. It is just my way of avoiding more trouble.

'Herr Hofmann, what has happened?'

'Dear friend, are you all right?'

'Good God. Is he dead?'

Such ridiculous questions. I looked up to see the faces of Nannerl, the Abbé Bullinger and Frau Mozart bending over me. Thank God, no Katharina. Their eyes and mouths were blurred, grotesquely magnified because they were so close, while suddenly I could hear rather than see the whirr of Fräulein Gilowska's fan above my head. Miss Pimperl was howling somewhere close by and it was still unbearably hot. I lay on the floor, trying to remember if I had slithered off my chair or tumbled forward. Too difficult. I not only felt sick, my head was banging like a cuckoo clock with the combined shrieks of three women, an Abbé, a dog and a canary. An absurd menagerie. Nannerl, send them all away – instantly, for I am dying most unhappily of love for you.

That is what I thought but is not what I said. Spasms ran from one end of my body to the other and because I could see both arms flailing about in the air, I tried to roll over and trap them underneath me. Except that I couldn't move at will. I was rigid everywhere apart from the legs and arms when my dear Nannerl leant closer to unbutton my collar. Even in my miserable state, I could imagine this was heaven and despite my revolting gripes, I managed to count the hairs that sprouted featherlike from a mole at the side of her chin. There were three, one black, two gold.

'Herr Jakob – am I hurting you?' Nannerl arched backwards as my left arm hit her by mistake.

'Aaaach.' This infantile moan slipped out without permission when what I really wanted to say was, 'Not at all.'

'I think perhaps he is having a fit of some sort,' said Fräulein Gilowska, pleased she could offer a diagnosis and not reckoning for a minute that I could hear.

'Katharina, fetch Herr Brummer immediately. The apothecary will be quicker than the doctor. And Berthe. I must find Berthe. She will know what to do.' Frau Mozart was in command, her voice soaring effortlessly above the gibberish of Fräulein Gilowska. Miss Pimperl became tangled up inside the Fräulein's skirts. I saw the Abbé hesitating before he made the sign of the cross, bow and leave the room. There were more raucous shrieks until Nannerl firmly shut the door on the chaos. She, who was the cause of my fits, appeared quite calm. I remember thinking I must not dribble under any circumstances or allow my nose to twitch and I remember admiring a blood pink light behind the eyelids, which I wanted to paint if I ever had control of my limbs again.

'Jakob, Jakob, Jakob, Jakob.'

Where was this hissing, missing sound which spun and dived around my ears like wind? It persevered, then stopped. I forget what happened next and have no idea how I came to be sleeping on a couch in the music room, which is where I found myself the next morning when I should have been travelling by coach to Frankfurt. I do know that what I heard from my makeshift bed was a revelation that changed my life completely. I lay there half-dreaming, a solitary audience for the real recitative and aria which followed, although a small, common house spider had crawled out of my hair and down the side of my face and neck, burying itself inside my shirt so that I forgot about it for a while.

Someone kept walking restlessly around the room and I suspected it was Nannerl, but I decided to keep my eyes shut in case it was someone else. At about the hundredth step, yesterday's whispering began again; exactly the same swishing noise that had called my name before. This time, I discovered I could hide any part of me, which stirred under the blankets. As for the spider, it had begun to scurry back and forth across the buttons of my shirt for no apparent reason before it finally tired and settled in a fold of my sleeve.

Chapter 6

RECITATIVE & ARIA

by Nannerl Mozart

Recitative:

'Jakob . . . Asleep? I am constantly begging for your good opinion and I have discovered I prefer the idea of begging to reward. The more I beg, the more I wish to remain hungry. The moment something is mine, I no longer want it. You see I've developed an insatiable appetite. It's so predictable, it ceases to be perverse, which is why I beg you to find fault with me now so you can avoid disappointment later.

'I need you to pick out the errors in my composition so I can defend them against all common sense. Of course I realise you are asleep and I know you can't hear me, because otherwise you'd have to reply. But sometimes, when I look at you, I think I made you up inside my head.'

Aria:

My dear Jakob, how do I begin or have I begun already? I am unhinged by love filched from an Italian madrigal. The trouble is it cannot be expressed between us or it would cease to be. I am therefore writing about it in a letter, although I am determined you will never read its contents. It excites me to confide about such feelings and I know that the excitement improves my composition. My counterpoint fits together upside down or back to front with the ease of Jack Pudding. Perhaps this is the reason he writes without apparent effort. My brother lives in a constant state of sublime agitation.

It's true I recognise I am only half alive when my existence is ordered, calm and predictable. Composition becomes a poor copy of my brother's scraps when I lose the excitement in my belly, or is it in my womb, behind the cherry? No matter. I do not care which part of the anatomy it is, as long as the feeling is there. I'm too afraid to explore any further and so I press the tops of my legs together very firmly to hold in the satisfaction, as if it were my monthly cloth. At that exact point of pleasure, I begin to feel alarmed or perhaps ashamed, but I am so afraid of losing it again and feeling dull.

I submit and seek confession. I am so very respectable. Regular prayers and practice, concerts in the archbishop's palace, mass on Wednesdays, Saturdays and Sundays and sometimes other times besides; a pious, disciplined life, soothed by my fervent attempts at expiation.

'Father, forgive me for I have sinned.' I rehearse the words before I step inside the box. My eyes wander to a plump cherub on the ceiling as I imagine the priest's reply from behind his grill. I know he is somewhere there beyond the folds of velvet that are stiff with ancient dust and puffed out by the heads they have concealed.

'Is it a sin of the flesh my child?'

'It is,' say I, 'the sin of lust which offends my conscience.'

I listen to him sneeze onto the stone flagged floor underneath our feet. I count three slow bars of four beats each before I return to the pink and white cherub who is beckoning me and flying nowhere after all these years of being stuck up there. I promise all sorts of atonement and pray with yet more quivers inside my belly. I silently give into them, hoping they will pass. I count another ten bars for penance. *Largissimo*. Finally, I draw the curtains to confess.

I can't explain any of this to anyone else. Wolfgang believes in my seriousness and would be shocked to discover how much like him I might be. Besides, he is too young and I wouldn't dare mention it to Papa, who is of course in Rome with Wolfgang. Papa would simply believe his worst suspicions were confirmed. As for Mama, she would try to be practical once she had recovered from the shock of knowing that I feel a longing in my loins. She would insist I take the waters, which I don't mind doing, except they're not going to change anything, especially since I don't want to be cured of feelings that have such a good effect on my composition. If anything, I'm trying to develop them further. If only I could explain all this to my father – that when I stop feeling and start thinking, I lose not only the ideas, but also the desire to put them down on paper. They are best when they come in a rush. They come when I'm hungry. Artists must be hungry, mustn't they? We are not all Wolfgangs. Besides, I can't afford to be self-critical. I leave that to you, Jakob or Papa. When the work is finished, I am no longer interested in changing what I've done – not much of it anyway.

Now you see your inner head will understand my dilemma. But I am afraid I can do nothing about the outer one, which is bound by convention and discretion. There are so many secrets inside you that I'm always trying to imagine what each one is. Do you lie there on the couch with any memory of what happened to you yesterday? Do you know why you fell down and writhed on the floor in a fit? Do we have this effect on one another?

Do you care for me too, Jakob? Or do you have a secret wife who gives you secret children in return for the respectability you give her? Do you plan to marry the widow with the mother-of-pearl buttons? Did you know her before? You're wasting your time if that is so. She intends to marry a man with orange hair and numerous children. I'm almost certain of this, unless she is married to him already. I saw them at the market together, after I left you and before I met Katharina.

First you fainted and now you are sleeping. It was an accident that you hit me with your arms and legs as you lay here. Oh what a mixture of melancholy, lust and guilt. Can you hear me at all, my dear? You know I have watched you throughout the night, watched your breathing and your twitching and the fineness of your face in the shadows, and I've had plenty of time to think about us.

Perhaps if I leant down very close to you, so close as to touch, we'd suffocate because I'd hold you very tightly. Oh my dear, don't wake up to disagree with me or warn me against my own banality. I know all of this is better not described, ridiculed or denied, which is why I destroy all my letters to you before they can ever be read. Did you know that Jakob? Well, how could you, since I always destroy them? That way, I can remain yours in my thoughts at least,

— Nannerl
Maria Anna Walburga Ignatia Addlepated Mozart

CADENZA

by Jakob Hofmann

I heard the door to the stove being opened and the sudden whoosh of paper being burnt. It seemed to me that everything I felt before I fell asleep was irrelevant. The feelings I had were still the same, but what was the point of having them? I am a practical man in my scholar's way. I decided if I could not declare my love, I would bury it. I had done so before and I would again

– in a common grave, seven-and-a-half feet deep. Then I opened my eyes and the first thing I saw was the spider, still clinging to my sleeve. I shook it off and watched it scuttle into a crevice at the foot of the couch. Nannerl saw me move.

'Ah, so you are awake at last,' she said calmly. 'I was wondering what would happen if I played very loudly on the clavier. Are you feeling better?' Her face was composed as she sat down in front of me but I thought her eyes might be avoiding mine.

'You can see from where you are,' she was staring straight over the top of my head, 'that you are still in Salzburg.'

'How long have I been here?' She was laughing at me.

'Just the night. You have snored for the greater part of it. The doctor said that we should leave you undisturbed.'

But I remembered no doctor. Only dreams. I could have wept.

'My dear Fräulein. I do believe I can't sit up. My arms don't seem to belong to my back. As for my legs, they're as stiff as two Greek columns and not so useful.'

Nannnerl came towards me, her face concerned.

'They creak!' I moaned, trying to unfold all visible parts but I gave up at the sitting position and fell straight back.

'You are meant to be in Frankfurt, Herr Hofmann. Why must you go to Frankfurt, Jakob?' she whispered near my ear.

I thought of saying that I was running away from her or that I was to meet my future bride, not that there is one, but instead I found myself standing, inventing the most obvious excuse and wishing at the same time I could speak the truth about my feelings.

'There is a meeting I must attend – urgent business that cannot be delayed.' To stop myself from saying more, I made small clearing noises in my throat.

Nannerl listened, hands dangling at her side, slowly losing themselves in the pockets of her dress. Again I was in danger of saying what I felt, so I turned away from that dear, sweet face to hide my distress.

'You will be returning soon?' she asked softly.

'No.'

'I see,' she paused, moving in a circle around me to catch my eyes. 'And does that bother you?'

'Bother? Ah . . . Yes . . . No. Not, I think, exactly. No, no . . . You see, Fräulein, I travel to survive.' Had I been on stage, my audience would have wept. She believed everything I said. Of course she would. The dear girl is incapable of deception, whereas I – I also lie to survive. It's a professional disease. But is it better I feel shame or that I try to prove there's a shred of accuracy in what I say? Somewhere there is a meeting. It will have been arranged, in a manner of speaking, by members of my family – not, I must confess, that anyone specific was waiting for me in Frankfurt and since this was a small deceit on my part, it means that I see myself as only a minor hoaxer.

'Are you well enough to travel, Herr Hofmann?' The tone of voice was vague and the formality of her address had returned as if it had never gone away. She rose from her chair and covered the palms of my hands with her closed, outstretched fingers. How I wished she would call me Jakob, just one more time. I looked down at her mouth, which curved upwards in perfect control, at the whiteness of her skin, which ran down from the top of her forehead to the top of her dress and the thin arms that were inclined towards me with such trust and my throat tightened until I found it impossible to speak. The form of her breasts was framed by the tucks of her collar while her breath, which I felt against my neck, rose quietly from underneath its gauze, then fell and rose again. I kissed her fingertips briefly.

'Herr Hofmann?' She stood there before me. Dear God, I will have to tell her the truth. What truth? Even if I understood what it is, would I recognise it myself? I removed my hands from beneath hers and touched her shoulders briefly so that her hair fell across my knuckles with the movement. I had never felt so bold or so confused.

'Please accept my apologies for any strangeness in my behaviour last night. I can't think what could have caused it, except that clearly I was ill. It is . . . It's never happened to me before. I hope you'll forgive me . . . and of course, Frau Mozart . . . I must thank . . . I must thank you both for all your kindness. Yes, yes, I'm quite well enough to travel.'

Nor had I ever been so cowardly or so circuitous. Why couldn't I just say we are not meant to be husband, wife or lover? I am a Jew and you're a Catholic and since this is an unchangeable circumstance for both of us, let us continue as we were before we played games with each other. You could be free to enjoy your friendship with a hundred Katharinas without my gloomy presence. But of course I said none of these crude, hurtful things. Instead, I bowed and left the house without returning to Salzburg for what would be at least another three years – a time when I would resume my uncontroversial violin lessons with Leopold Mozart, my talks of haberdashery, fresh targets for shooting practice with Frau Mozart and discussions of gavottes, gigues and the art of restrained modulation – or the perils of a running bass with my dear Nannerl. And who knows what subject with the boy Wolfgang? All of this I thought to myself as if I'd been away for a matter of weeks.

But on that morning when I left the apartment at Hannibal Platz, I turned to look back at it from the other side of the square. I could see she was watching me from a window and as I returned her gaze, I felt myself stir and swell hard against the pocket of my hose. I pushed the trolley into a corner to be less conspicuous. While I was trying to hide under my cloak, she waved. A simple, delicate, erotic wave. I ducked in reply because my head was the only part of me that was still free. For several minutes, we both seemed to hover in our different places until Berthe's face appeared behind hers like an unexpected, dull shadow that cast its pall on both of us.

My darling moved away from the window and remained with her back to the square so I had no choice but to walk away, dragging the trolley behind me. My wig had slithered across the top of the box and was hanging over the edge, half on, half off. I examined it with disgust because it still smelt of the market and I decided to leave it there in the hope that it would fall off altogether. I began to plan my return to ease the uncertainty of the journey that lay ahead. By the time I had crossed the bridge to the other side of the Salzach, I had convinced myself once more it was not the detail of this that mattered, but the principle. I looked down at the layers of different paint on my wooden box, each with an ancient history of its own and I saw to my satisfaction that the wig had disappeared. I asked aloud:

'Nannerl. What price have we paid?'

'Too much,' I could hear her say.

'Ah well,' I replied in a more optimistic mood. 'Wait and see. One day I will come back to claim our love in such a way that each of us must reckon with it until one of us is dead.' I explored several versions of this under my breath until I had had enough of theme and variation. My mood was buoyant. The resolve put a spring in my step and the anxieties which made me so miserable in the last few hours were temporarily forgotten. My face must have reflected my delight, because all the people I passed on the way out of the city seemed to smile at the draper who was whistling on his travels. The trees by the side of the road may have been oozing damp out of their bark but I was only aware of the warmth I felt in my bones and the promise of country air, which I thought I could see as a violet haze in the distance when I reached the top of a hill. I took off my cloak, which was threadbare and a disgrace to my profession, and flung it over the handles of the trolley. I might lose that as well I thought, but it hardly mattered.

FUGUE 4

'I don't like carting ghosts,' said Otto in a sullen voice. Otto had been sitting at the back of the coach and was generally the first to start up any conversation when they were on foot. 'It's asking for trouble,' he tried to explain.

'It's not a ghost. It's a body,' protested Heinrich, who'd been a gravedigger for most of his working life.

'Same thing,' replied Otto, lighting a pipe and looking like a ghost himself behind the flame. 'It's not just flesh and bones in there. It's spirit life all round. It's bound to get out sometimes.'

'What are we doing it for then?' asked Franz, who was small and pugnacious and acted as their postillion on this journey because he was the lightest of the four and a deft horseman.

'Money,' answered Karl. 'We're paid twice over for this one. You all knows it and you agreed we'd do it.'

'Sure we're doing it, but that don't make me feel good about it.' Otto had abandoned his pipe and was climbing to the box at the top of the coach. 'The horses aren't willing either. They can smell something I reckon.'

'Let's get on then,' said Karl. 'You all right in there?' He tapped on the window and stared at the strange passenger who remained as silent as the coffin at his feet.

Chapter 7

Karlsbad, 1844

I make another leap in time to emphasise its passing. It is a fact that Hofmann disappeared from Nannerl's early life for several years, although they wrote to each other at length about what they were doing. She surprised herself by the way in which she accepted the inevitable, consoling herself at the beginning of their separation by composing a violin sonata, which more or less obeyed the rules of fashion. By the time she had finished it, any heartache she might have felt at his absence was subdued. If he failed to visit Hannibal Platz or if she could no longer find him at his stall on market days, there was a brief sense of disappointment and then nothing. She had expected he would resume his violin lessons when her father and Wolfie returned from Italy and eventually, this did happen. But by then she had placed a cork on her darker imaginings in order to enjoy her life and any adolescent passion that remained had to be stored in a jar and examined only rarely for the mysterious comfort it might have given her.

She believed what happened between them had been tacitly acknowledged and that was the end of it. The distress of thwarted feelings had to heal like any other wound and in its place, she hoped for a fading memory. Only occasionally, either one would recall their emotions as they once had been, which would feed their misery until sleep swallowed up the memory or they would fling themselves for a while into an exchange of chatty, anodyne letters that passed time and assuaged the pain. And so, in this way, very gradually they drifted apart.

Certain people are afraid of spiders because they stay still for such a long time and just when you least expect it, move sideways only to become still again – rather like a crab, except that people eat crabs and they don't eat spiders, which is fortunate for me. The number of times I have been nearly swiped into my grave since I began this tale – to be worried about whether or not I was going to end up on someone's plate would be too much. I am about to move sideways. At some point I will describe what happened to my Aunt Nannerl when she married the Baron Berchtold zu Sonnenburg and moved to Saint Gilgen. But before I can, there are a few other tit-bits still to be explained.

After the Novellos left Salzburg in the middle of July, 1829, my aunt's room seemed darker and damper than ever. She insisted the shutters remained closed, which meant the smell of urine, the pustulent bumps on the walls and the staleness of her bedding and breath were intolerable. Her health was mortally frail, yet she was determined to speak while she had wind. On a grim afternoon, when she refused to let me turn her in the bed, change her linen or rub oil into her flaking skin, in short, give her the slightest bit of physical comfort, she begged me to read aloud some correspondence between herself and my father. This was the only pleasure she would allow and I already knew by the stubborn pinching of her lips, she was determined I should read them all.

'Franzerl, don't be upset with your old Auntie. If you want to make me happy . . . Those ones . . . In there . . . ' She pointed at an open drawer, filled with rows of neatly parcelled letters. 'My eyes can't see the ink. You will read them for me won't you? They help me to remember the past. You've no idea how difficult it was.'

'What was Auntie?'

'What was what?'

'What was difficult?'

'The past of course.'

She would speak in disconnected phrases and assume I knew what she was talking about – brother, sister, father and daughter – it was usually one or the other. I watched her raise the paralysed arm with her good one, holding it in the air for several seconds, dropping it, lifting it. Such determination, such painstaking effort. I remained watching as she repeated the process many times until I could take it no more.

'Auntie, do you want me to stroke your fingers, your hand, your arm?'

I leant forward until my face was almost touching hers and I held my breath so I wouldn't have to breathe in hers. I thought at first she was going to cry because she was making little mewling noises as she tried to cover herself with a corner of the coverlet.

'At least,' she said in a plaintive voice, 'Jack Pudding was dead soon after you were born.'

Well I like that. Did she mean because my father died when I was five months old that somehow I was spared the agonies of comparison? It's not true. I have to live under his shadow. I always will, I thought miserably as I picked up a sheaf of letters from the top of the pile.

'So now you see, Franz Xaver Mozart, I do not have to unsex myself to prove my worth. I was just born before my time.' She spat it all out with the abrupt devilishness of the old, since this was her angry rationale for a lifetime of tact, sacrifice and silence.

'If it were today, I'd be paid in gold instead of jewelled toothpicks.' I looked away as she added in a louder voice, 'I'm talking about all the concerts your father and I gave. They bought us with knick-knacks and there was little we could do but accept.' The crooked smile widened until her jaw was hanging open on one side of the face more than the other. What a pity there were not many teeth left to pick.

'You must compose a little bit every day Franzel as you don't have any children to distract you and it's more a question of muscle than mind.' Now why does she have to remind me of my childlessness? Is she saying I have no excuse for not quite measuring up, but that she does because there was a son, a daughter and five step-children for her to worry about?

'Unfortunately,' she continued smiling more hideously, 'I never bothered to develop my compositional muscle, unlike Wolfie. You see his was vast. Mine was puny! I practised the keyboard and not much else, so that's all there is to that. Perhaps if I'd kept on writing more songs . . .' I stared down at her hands because with blind people it doesn't matter much where you look. They reminded me of old tubers, brittle, covered in fungus. Was it her music she was hearing inside her head or someone else's I wondered.

'I destroyed most of what I wrote because it wasn't good enough. So please don't be sentimental on my behalf Franzel. And please,' she said quietly and firmly, 'never distress yourself by thinking about all the wonderful compositions I might have written. Just think about your own.'

Great God. I'd stopped thinking about them long ago. I thought I was here because she was my aunt and my father's sister, not because I was indulging in an act of cheap sentimentality. Naturally I was concerned for her welfare since her own son was out of sight. As for her compositions, I have to admit I never thought they were as bad as Hofmann implied. In a way, I think she might have achieved more if she had believed in herself as a revolutionary spirit – but then she doesn't know I heard absolutely everything she ever wrote, while in my spiderly disguise.

Auntie certainly broke more rules of theory than my father but her style, if obvious, was wonderfully passionate. However I knew that Auntie had no serious interest in my opinion, so I sat on the window seat and felt myself disappearing into the shadows behind the lamp. I had recently taken to late afternoon visits after her nap. It meant that Metzger had a break from sitting there for hours and I wanted to show him at least that someone in the family still cared about the old girl. Maybe I am being sentimental after all. Anyway, my presence was an excuse for her to resurrect the past and I saw how elated she became with each successive memory until I almost forgot she was meant to be dying. The last throes I suppose.

'There's no point in self-deception,' she rattled on. 'I make no excuses. People become mythical because we worship their gifts. We worshipped Wolferl because he was the most gifted of us all and because he was a genius. I was left to explore my abilities and pick my nose in secret. Meanwhile half of Salzburg tried to find me a compliant husband, who wouldn't object if I sat at the clavier from two o'clock to five every afternoon. Of course I agreed with my father's final choice of husband because I could see the sense, but in my heart I thought it was like knocking on stone walls.'

She had said more or less the same things yesterday and the day before, so I suppose they must be true, though there is a limit to how much I can guess of what she sees in her inner mirror. Even a spider of the mind has to react to what is outwardly visible. The letters she kept in her desk and which she wanted me to read aloud could be interpreted another way.

Chapter 8

RONDO

I was determined she would hear me clearly and so I made a point of reading each letter like a newly appointed archbishop. Since Auntie is deeply religious, this was not a problem and I suspect from the pleased expression that settled on her face, it was probably a comfort.

> *Mannheim, 4ᵗʰ November, 1777*
>
> A ma très chère soeur:
>
> I want to discuss targets if it's not too late. What I have in mind is a short fair-haired man, doubled over and showing everyone his arse. There's a balloon coming out of his mouth that will say *bon appetit* to a dark haired man wearing boots, a crimson cloak and a fashionable wig. He should be of ordinary height and placed in such a position he could lick the other man's arse. There's also a balloon coming out of his mouth with the words: 'Poof, there's nothing better than this!' Mama sends kisses to you and Papa but she also has a message for Berthe. Please would she air all the quilts in the hall cupboard? Meanwhile I embrace you with all my heart and remain your obedient brother,
>
> — *Wolfgango Amadeo Mozart*

A burst of wheezing from the bed might have been laughter, but I could not bring myself to look up. I was haunted by this dreadful image of a hyena in petticoats and thought the only way to get rid of it was to go on reading.

> *Salzburg, 11ᵗʰ November, 1777*
>
> Mon très, très cher frère,
>
> The bull's eye should be somewhere inside the mouth of the blond man, perhaps on the tip of his tongue. If you and Mama are agreed, I'll save this particular target for your return as you seem to

58

fancy it so much. Please do not forget that the Salzburg post goes on Mondays and Thursdays and it would greatly ease Papa's worries if you would remember to begin your letters by saying, 'I received yours of the—.' It upsets him to think that what we write may never arrive. Last week we had some shooting in our house. Papa provided the target. I shot on Mama's behalf and lost nine kreuzer. Katherl shot for you and won the most. You are rich at last! Farewell from Pimperl. I kiss Mama's hands and embrace my brother, although I am your old grandmother,

— Marianna Mozart.

Auntie was in one of her dazed moments of calm. For a short while we contemplated each other from opposite ends of the room, me with impatience as I was in a hurry to continue and she with satisfaction because she was remembering what she had felt when the letters were first exchanged. At last she signalled for me to continue with a return of that twisted grin and I decided she understood what I was thinking and wanted me to know that it amused her.

Mannheim, 15th November, 1777

Ma chère soeur,

Yes, yes, yes. We have received every single letter, so please don't fret about the post. I've been to the lavatory and now I'm less full of shit. There is ice on the windows in Mannheim and I intend to heed Papa by staying in bed to knit. Mama has produced umpteen skeins of wool which she bought from Herr Hofmann and when we are fed up with clickety clacketing, she and I will play cards or tell our fortunes in such a way we all become disgustingly rich.

I hope you received the first two movements of the sonata safely and you approve of the appoggiaturas. The treble runs are not so tricky after prima vista, although an aquaintance of mine in Mannheim insisted on playing all the downward runs prestissimo with his thumb and first finger. What a mess. I fear he is too deaf to improve, therefore I shall recommend that he takes up knitting instead. I kiss Papa's hands 100,000 times and embrace my sister with all my heart. So does Mama. Our best regards to all our good

friends and especially to Herr Hofmann and Mlle. Gilowska.
— *Wolfgang Amadé Mozart*
Oh and I almost forgot. Mama says to tell you we have to pay twelve
kreuzers for each letter we receive or send – eighteen kreuzers for
a long one. She believes we should write once instead of twice a
week, since we are always having to fork out for laundry, shoes, hair
powder, pomade and other necessary trifles which are very expen-
sive in Mannheim. I am beginning to realise how much we owed
Jakob Hofmann for such very things. Now I am off to the closet once
more so I won't have to shit in my pants. Has Pimperl been snarling
since we left? Do not answer that, because if she hasn't, I will feel
she does not miss us and if she has, I will be sad that she is. What a
clever brother you have.   — *W.A.M.*

I heard my aunt shifting in her bed when I mentioned Jakob Hofmann
three times by name. The eyes were shut as her fingers struggled with some
imaginary notes up and down the coverlet. I found myself trying to understand what mattered most to her – the great love affair or music. Perhaps
each took its turn in waves.

'Go on,' she said quietly, settling herself deeper into the pillows while I
picked up the next set of letters from out of the drawer. They were numbered
for order and were held together with yellowed bits of ribbon that I could
see had been tied and untied many times before now. The ribbon around
this particular sheaf was so tattered it fell apart in my hands when I undid
the knot, slipping through my knees and onto the floor as I began to read
yet another letter written by my aunt, which I realised must have been
returned to her by my mother at some point.

Salzburg, 24th November, 1777
Dearest Brother Mine and Oh My Darling, Gorgeous Mama,
    I am pleased, thank God, that you are both well. We too are as fit
as possible in this dull old place. Thanks for the Andante, which I've
already played through. It requires great concentration and attention to detail but I like it very much. One can see from its style that
you composed it in Mannheim. I especially like the trills, which you
know I do so well. (What a clever sister you have my little piggie-

wiggie). I'm now looking forward to that Rondo you promised. You might be interested to know the wife of Anton Lodron, the Marshal of the court has died. There's no other news I'm afraid.

I hope you'll be able to stay in Mannheim for the whole winter, as it would be too trying for Mama to have to travel in the frost. I kiss Mama's hands lots and embrace you fifty times I think. Pimperl, is quite fine and jolly. She curls herself up at your feet I'm sure, as does Barbara Eberlin, the Hagenauers, Katherl Gilowsky, the Andretters, Bawanzky and all of Salzburg who send their greetings to you both so there.

Kissie-kissies,

— *Maria Anna Bella Mozart*

P.S. The above is my reply to last week's post for we had no word from you today. Perhaps we'll receive one by Friday? Papa says about that German opera, who composed it, who sang in it, what did you think of it? Not one single word. And that other concert you went to last week, who whistled in it, who blew it? Again not a word. And who is this mad friend who plays all the downward runs with his thumb and first finger? Not a word my friend. We might as well whistle. — *N.*

Mannheim, 28ᵗʰ November, 1777
In the evening, nocte temporis,
puncto & most definitely on the stroke of ten:

Mon très cher père,

(I almost dropped into the feminine but I can quite safely)
— à ma très chère soeur,

About that German opera by Holzbauer, called 'Gunther von Schwarzburg'. Well, it's not referring to our worthy Herr Gunther, court barber of Salzburg. I've already seen the score and played bits of it on the clavier, but I won't say anything about it I don't think! That target you had someone paint on my behalf as Master of the Shoot is quite brilliant. So are the verses. *Dum-de-dum-de-dum-de-dum*. Heigh-ho.

Well there's nothing left for me to write about except to hope that you all sleep soundly until I shake you up with this boring smelly letter. Adieu. I kiss Papa's hands a million times and embrace my big sister, our precious blister, with all my heart, until I sting or raise a fart, just a bit or not at all, remaining your most obedient son and brother, hoping you shall not run away from Mama and me, ever.

— *Wolfgang Amadé Mozart*

Knight of the Golden Spur and from the moment I marry, also of the Double Horn, Member of the Grand Academies of Verona, Bologna etc. Aurevoir mes amis s'il vous plâit!

I could hear a strange clicking sound as if the clock on the wall had become a new fangled-metronome. The clicks grew louder, faster and wilder and it took me a while to realise Auntie was the cause of the tick-tick-ticking. Tears rolled from the corners of her eyelids as she laughed. I could even see the occasional tooth inside her mouth through the thinness of her skin. She managed to wave me on with such a reckless, sideways banging of her head that I worried she would hurt herself and that if I laughed with her, she might fall out of bed onto her head and kill herself. I quickly ploughed through the next two letters, praying she'd stop this bizarre percussion, willing her to sit still and listen to her own words.

Salzburg, 22nd December, 1777

My Dearest Mama and Adored Brother,

Since you have now become so famous and your days are so filled that you cannot write to me, you probably won't have time to read this either. I therefore ask your permission to talk to Mama on her own. Besides, I intend it to be entirely women's chat. I hope you're both well and happy. Mama very kindly told me that the coiffures and hats they wear in Mannheim are so much more exciting than in Salzburg. She insisted that the ladies are altogether smarter than here. I can believe it. And if I'm lucky enough to have my darling Mama back here in two months' time, then I should like to ask her to discover how that frisure is made and if she could bring back a toupée cushion with her, that too would be very special. I'd also like a hat in the latest fashion and anything else she may choose of

course. If only I could earn some more money by giving lessons as
I did before, I should really like to have my garnet-red gown made
with a train and trimmed with lawn. (The lawn might be cheaper in
Mannheim don't you think?) But I must try not to think about new
fashions I suppose. We're really pleased that you have a comfortable
room and I sincerely hope that Mama no longer feels the cold. I
must stop writing, or there will be no space for Papa. I wish you both
fine health and I kiss Mama's hand and squeeze my brother.

Your completely adoring daughter (and sister),

— *Nannerl*

'You see, do you see?' Her voice snapped at the air without any more
humour. 'Do you realise what we are coming to?'

'A reunion perhaps,' I said quickly, knowing all the time she wanted me
to be wrong. I felt I was her resident clown who sometimes failed to be
amusing.

'You'll see, you'll see.' She was tugging at her ruined arm and her tongue
kept darting in and out between the remaining teeth which rattled this
time with the rhythm of her tongue. 'Continue. It's my letter next,' she cried
with great passion, withdrawing under the bed sheets into a world of self-
centred unhappiness. Her most acute suffering seemed to come from her
failure to believe her life had been worthwhile.

Salzburg, 9ᵗʰ February, 1778

My dearest Jack Pudding,

I never have enough room to write to Mama or yourself when
papa begins the letter. This time I have stolen all the space. I hope
I am seeing Mama soon and I ask her not to forget her little Anna
Maria when she leaves Mannheim. God speed to Paris with the best
of health to you, my dearest brother and my adored Mama. I do
hope, however, that you won't be too long gone. God knows the day
of your return. We are most keen you become rich, for surely that
means happiness to us all. I kiss Mama's hands, and yours if they are
clean, and I hope you will always remember us as we would wish.
But you must only think like this when you have the time, perhaps,
for ten minutes and fifty seconds or when there are no more lessons

and you have a pause in your composition! I regard you most highly,
— *A.M.M., your very old sister*

Auntie was now lying quietly as I picked up the next one from the pile. It was not a letter but an extract from what looked like a diary.

Salzburg, 4pm, 13ᵗʰ July, 1778

'Mama is dead. So is Voltaire. He the devil, pegged out like a dog but Mama died, shivering in her bed. The Abbé Bullinger has been and gone to tell Papa and me that it's true. My brother wrote to him and asked him to convey the news. There was no black powder, no Pulvis Epilepticus in France, no husband, no daughter to ease her delirium. Baron Grimm, who lives in Paris, sent his personal doctor and Wolfgang, who remained at her side for those last few days, had to shout in her ear because she was deaf at the end.

'Mama, Mama, I want you back. I can see you through a pane of glass. When you laugh, we laugh. When you die, we are devastated. Papa is locked in his room, writing a letter to Jack Pudding. Berthe is hovering in the hall, sniffing very loudly. I'm lying in my bed, vomiting. I'll say a Paternoster for your soul. I cannot touch you on the other side of the glass. It's another world. I've tried to convince myself that this was the will of God, but the pain won't go away and I'm sick all over again.'

When I finished reading the extract there was a loud groaning from the bed and I hurried to the next letter.

Paris, 20th July, 1778

Dearest Sister!

Your name-day has arrived! I know that like me, you do not approve of too many words, and that anyway you know how much I already care for you from the bottom of my heart, everyday and not just today – as faithfully as you would expect from a brother who loves his sister.

I'm most sorry I can't send you a present of music, as I did some time ago. But let's hope a happier future is not too far away when we, so like each other and so close, can exchange our most intimate thoughts and feelings. In the mean time, farewell my dearest Nannerl – and love me as I love you. I hold you close, you know this, with all my heart and soul. I remain forever, your true brother,

— *Wolfie*

I could see her blind eyes were trying to find my face as she struggled to explain.

'At first Wolfie couldn't bring himself to tell the truth about Mama. He wrote to tell us she was gravely ill when all the time she was lying in her coffin in the next room. By the same post, he sent a letter to the Abbé Bullinger, asking him to tell us she was dead. Not dying but dead! What was he thinking? That we would blame him for neglecting her? Of course we never did. How could we? We weren't there. But we wanted to know everything.'

The milk jellies quivered and I worried they would slip from their hollow bowls onto the bed. 'Your father believed this was the kindest way to deliver bad news. That is the simple truth.' I thought she was going to fall asleep because the eyes closed, but then she started up again. 'What does he mean we don't like too many words? Hmm? We loved them. He ate them. It's a family disease. Why, you're the same my dear boy. I listen to your voice and I swear I can hear Wolfie again.'

This was the second time she had referred to our relationship in the space of one afternoon. It seemed she needed either anger or distress to summon up her awareness of others. There were other, calmer times when I felt she'd forgotten who I was or why I was there. Her head and her wretched teeth would start wobbling from side to side like a puppet or the twisted mouth would slowly curve upwards as if she were smiling at a stranger who has just wandered into her room and is pleading to be told everything about her past. At such moments, I'd hold her hands in mine and allow her to think I was this stranger who'd come to pay her homage. It was the least I could do to restore her belief in her own worth. I knew she felt bitter because her life and talent had been overlooked in the cause of my father's genius but I also knew that she basked in his reflected fame.

'Do you want me to go on reading, Auntie?' I asked. But there was no way I was going to stop reading now and she knew it and I knew it and I didn't even bother to wait for her reply as I unfolded one of her letters to my father.

Salzburg, 23rd July, 1778

Dearest Brother,

Did you receive the black powders, which Papa sent with his last letter? He's very worried you will get sick like Mama – you avoided all mention of her in your letter to me. Of course I understand you did not want to upset me so near to my name-day, but please, my dearest brother, I beg you not to bury this particular pain under the bedclothes. Besides, if you talk about it, we will learn to accept her death. Papa is desperate to know every single detail about the manner of her dying. Try and understand that because we were not there, we need to grieve in a different way – perhaps even publicly. Everyone we know in Salzburg keeps telling us how much she will be missed. There. I have said it without crying all over the page. As regards your gift of a composition, I look forward to it one day, but not tomorrow. Papa insists I accompany him on the clavier in the evenings and we end up playing a mish-mash of symphonies, arias, masses and vespers with lots of figured basses and complicated fugues. My extemporising improves by the minute! Come home soon.

Your loving sister,

— M.A.Mozart.

The next letter to follow was from my father to my grandfather – I could guess by the length and weight as much as the handwriting. I unfolded each page with great delicacy and took a long, whistling breath to calm myself before beginning. My aunt was unusually still but because of her silence, it seemed obvious she knew what was coming.

Paris, 31st July, 1778

My Dear Papa,

I kiss you for the powders; I'm sure you'll be glad to know I don't need them! Sad as your letter made me, it brought relief to know

that my father and sister have understood what it's been like . . .
You know I have never seen anyone die before, though I used to wish
I had. How cruel then that my first experience should be the death
of my own mother. I feel quite calm now, for I know I have nothing
now to fear from the two people who are the most precious to me
in all the world. That you can imagine the extremity of my torment,
gives me strength.

 . . . You would like to have the details of her illness and of all
that happened? You shall have them, but I beg you to understand
why I am brief. I'll stick to the main facts since everything about the
manner of her dying is in the past and none of it can be changed.
(I also need space to write about other matters, which relate to our
present circumstances and I beg you to hug my dearest sister on her
birthday).

First, I must tell you that my dear, departed Mama was bound to
die. There is no doctor in the world who could have saved her this
time round. It was clearly the will of God and her time had arrived
so he took her . . . I can't say exactly how much blood was let, for it's
measured in these parts by the plate and not by the ounce; they took
slightly less than two platefuls in the end. For a few days she seemed
to recover and then the diarrhoea began. No one paid much heed, as
foreigners who drink a lot of water in Paris will find it acts as a laxa-
tive. I had it myself at the beginning of our stay, but since I started
adding a little wine and ice to my glass, I've been free of it.

She complained of headaches, then shivers, then a fever and so
I gave her an antispasmodic powder. I got a terrible fright when
suddenly she lost her hearing, but she refused to let me get her a
French doctor and when I finally found an old German one of about
seventy, he gave her a rhubarb powder made up as wine, which
I can't make sense of at all as wine is supposed to be heating and
anyway my poor mama was thirsting for a glass of plain water. You
can imagine my feelings when on the 26th June, the doctor told me
she may not last the night if she's taken with pains again and I should
therefore arrange for her last confession.

I immediately ran out into the night and made arrangements
for a German priest to visit us next day, telling my mother that I'd

bumped into him in the street and that the priest wanted to hear me play. This seemed to satisfy her and I even thought she seemed a little better, although I admit I'm no doctor. Our old friend Grimm was most distressed when he heard my news and arranged for his own doctor to visit her as well . . .

I see now that it's impossible for me to describe a thing briefly. You know I like to write about everything in detail, but the rest will have to wait for my next letter. I have sorted out all of my beloved mother's possessions – her clothes, linen, jewels, in fact everything she owned, will be sent to Salzburg as soon as possible. After saying I would discuss other personal matters in this letter, I now find I am unable to say any thing about them just now. For your peace of mind, know that nothing will change your circumstances for better or worse. Trust me. When we are all happily together again, which is my dearest wish, then we can talk fully and everything will depend on how you respond . . . Meanwhile, I'll continue to try and earn enough money by teaching, although I can't wait to get away, because unless you take on a hoard of pupils, which I won't, you can't make much money.

This is not laziness. It goes against my genius and my way of life when I can't soak up music all day long, plan my works, study and consider. It is a fact that the few free hours I have at my disposal I need for rest . . . I must, if I am to succeed here, write a grand opera. I wouldn't get so much money for a little one and besides, it is work I would take delight in doing. True, the devil must have invented the slithery language of these people, but I'm still not put off. I must find a commission somehow and show them how to respect and fear the Germans. For me, the most difficult part of all this business would be the singers, but as I don't care to wrestle with dwarfs, I'll avoid a duel!

How my heart and spirits lift when I think of being with you both again. Adieu. I kiss your hands 10,000 times, embrace my sister with such brotherly love and send greetings to the whole of Salzburg, especially our good friend, Bullinger.

I am your most obedient son always,

— *Wolfgang Amadé Mozart*

My aunt struggled to raise herself up the minute I said my father's name but her poor head fell back onto the pillows and she spoke with her face turned to the ceiling. Her lips moved but the rest of her body looked like a corpse. She was that still.

'Such a letter was bound to make me jealous as well as miserable,' she explained. 'How I would've liked to inform pupils that my genius and my whole manner of living were threatened by the business of teaching them. But I never did. I found the best way to cope with these feelings was to enjoy my position as his sister and so I threw my energies into more teaching, more practice and more devotions to both the church and my father. It's easy for people to forget that Papa was so lonely after Mama died.'

The lamp above her bed threw its light on her white face making it whiter. What she said sounded unexpectedly gentle, considering what she had to say was so full of grieving bitterness.

'With everyone thinking about my marriage or theirs, I began to think about it too,' she whispered. 'Oh I was sorely tempted, especially as Jack Pudding was almost married to your mother. Papa had not yet been told about Constanze, but I encouraged the match at first because I knew she was more than a ball of fluff with half tangerines above her corset and two little black eyes.'

She hesitated as if struggling in her dying gasps to be fair to my mother. 'I admit,' she said at last, though still whispering, 'your mother had an ear for a fine fugue. Her sister, Aloysia, had the better voice however.'

'Do you think so?' I was polite but irritated by the qualified slur. At the same time I believed what my aunt said was probably accurate. I know my father thought the same. I let it pass.

'To some your mother's voice was powerful and to others it was weak. Both statements are true. Her held notes were very loud and her grace notes very soft. There was too much discrepancy between the two.' Without a pause to let me know Auntie was changing the subject, she suddenly snapped, 'Dear God, help me. They're back again. The flutters. I want to pluck them out. They disgust me. I'm too old. I can see his face by the window . . .'

Whose face Auntie? My father's?

'I sometimes see his hat or his coat on the trolley.'

An unmistakable, sulphurous odour rose up from the bed and smothered us both.

69

'Auntie, you farted.'

'I know. Join me. Then it will be twice as bad, but fair.' She winked with her jelly eye as the insane clicking noise began again. 'Bar for nothing. Three, four. Now.' Her good hand rose to conduct us in unison but I was so bound up with prudery, I couldn't give a puff.

'It's no good Auntie. I can't do it to order.'

'I can.' Her hand disappeared under a sea of linen as the clicks grew louder. She was in danger of swallowing her remaining teeth because she was laughing so much. 'I think I wet my bed,' she persisted. 'Am I wet now Franzel?

Looking down at her thin, little old lady's body, I told her that it didn't matter if she had. Her head turned towards the family portrait on the wall above and I had a feeling that somehow she was stepping in and out of the frame as I read to her. I too play this game when I dangle from my web and the idea of her moving through time in her thoughts seemed to me as natural an event as benign sorcery. It's also a fact that the best magician will not have to explain his tricks.

'Don't fret now my dear. Perhaps I should leave you for a short while to give you some peace.' I turned to go as she tugged at my coattails with all the force of her unparalysed hand. The voice was shrill as a beggar.

'Katherl Gilowska. Do you remember?' I nodded wearily, finding it diffi-cult to hold onto an image of the old girl's fragility while I detached her clawing fingers one by one, from the cloth.

'Katharina was once rejected by someone she loved very much. I have forgotten who it was now and it's not important anymore, but I do remem-ber she made a descriptive list of every Salzburg bachelor to distract herself and me. This one was shorter than the Baron Von Molk, that one was better at sleigh drives, this one nifty at cards, someone else a fine dancer with an excellent leg. Franz d'Yppold was a fine partner in a shooting match and even better, an old friend. Wolfgang would welcome him as a brother-in-law and a much needed accountant within the family. So and so was devout, if a little dull. Baron X was a kind man with a considerable fortune and Herr Z played the organ badly, the violin more so but the flute tolerably well.'

'Good God,' I sighed, aware that I had to say something in admiring tones. She hardly noticed my pathetic contribution and it was then I expe-rienced an overpowering urge to run away and hide between the cracks of the floorboards, an infinitesimal speck of transformed, venomous matter. But I remained in my chair as a dutiful nephew, which of course I was and dirty with my own curiosity, I urged Auntie to continue.

'Can you imagine, my dear Franzel? I felt such heaviness of spirit when I thought about each name on the list. I became quite ill with worry. Jack Pudding had set his heart on my marrying d'Yppold because he heard from Katherl's brother that we were interested in one another. I confess my letters encouraged this opinion. If I took a husband, he, Wolferl, might take a wife. But me and d'Yppold? Never.

'For a start, he had tufts of hair growing out of his ears. What's more, I'm not sure Papa admired his temperament for he was quite tight with money, which is probably why he was such a good accountant – moral but not particularly desirable. A man is not interesting to me unless I can believe in his equality or superiority about most things. Now my dear, read me the next letter and we will stop there.'

Just like that? I hurried on, hoping she would change her mind.

Vienna, 19ᵗʰ September, 1781

Ma très chère soeur!

Our father writes that you are ill, which makes me anxious on your behalf. It seems you have been taking waters for at least a fortnight, which must mean you have been ill for some time and yet you told me nothing of this. Well, I'm going to be blunt with you about these persistent illnesses of yours. They wouldn't happen if you had a husband! Believe me my dear sister, this is a practical solution. Have one even if it is only for the sake of your good health.

In your last letter, you got quite cross with me, which is what I deserved, but my excuse is that I began an answer to your letter before last and never finished it. I destroyed it because I couldn't give you any of the news you wanted at the time. I still can't, but I promise I will as soon as I can. In the meantime, listen to some of my more inspired ideas.

I have several reasons to believe my opera will be a success here. If this proves true, I'll be as popular in composition as I am in performance on the clavier. I will know better when the winter is over but I am optimistic. This will work well for us as a family.

Now to the matter of d'Yppold and yourself. Can't he manage to work as an accountant in Vienna? Let's face it. Neither of you has much chance of making money in Salzburg. Is he completely penniless? Ask him old girl. Find out what he thinks about settling here. Tell him I'll do my utmost to help you both become established. You, my dear sister, could earn a handsome living as a teacher or by giving private concerts. You'd be in such demand I promise you. Papa could come and join us here and it would be quite like old times. Even before I got whiff of you and d'Yppold, I had this idea simmering away. Our dear father was the only obstacle in all this as I wanted to be sure he could move here and enjoy all the comforts he deserves in his old age. Discuss matters with d'Yppold frankly and let me know what's what and how.

Adieu my sister and I hope to have better news of your health in Papa's next letter, preferably in your own hand as soon as you feel like it. My greetings to Katherl and old d'Yppold of course. Be sure to send your letters to me: Auf dem Peter, im Auges Gottes; 2nd floor. My address is so famous at the post office that even a letter bearing my name and nothing more will find me! I embrace you most profoundly, my old piglet,

— W.A.Mozart

Auntie was agitated throughout my reading of this last letter. I had been asked to repeat a good deal of it either because my throat was hoarse, my voice tired and inaudible, or because she wanted to torture herself by going over every painful detail a second time. Her live claw had crept out from underneath the bed linen and was picking at imaginary, loose threads on the coverlet. Somewhere between the beginning and end of my father's letter, I had lost the urge to continue reading. I managed to rescue and tie up all the torn bits of ribbon, taking pains to ensure the bows were in their original positions.

I returned each bundle to the bottom drawer and murmured something about an appointment at my mother's house. She pretended not to hear, turning away from me instead. The mewling noises stopped when she buried her face in the pillow. Her mouth gaped and her eyes were closed. Dust swirled in the light above her face before settling on her nose and chin. I thought to myself quite coldly and for the second time – yes, that is how she will look as a corpse. I kissed her lightly on the cheek, turned out the lamp and slipped out the door, expecting her to call me back. If she did, it was much later when I was hurrying away from the square. It's your turn now dear Metzger. Your turn to watch over her and listen to her and talk to her. I swallowed up the outside air and stopped on the bridge to calm myself. I decided to climb to the top of Nonnberg to clear my head before returning to my mother's house.

FUGUE 5

'We could take the whole thing out and drop it in that ditch over there.'

Otto wanted to leave the coffin by the roadside and was wondering how to persuade his companions that this is what they should do. Even Karl had agreed that it was a bad thing to carry a body in the dead of night from Vienna to Salzburg and that nothing good would come of it.

'And what about him that's sitting in there, guarding it?' asked Heinrich. 'What are we meant to do about him then? Just say, sorry mein Herr, but this is as far as we're going and it's up to you to stick with the body.'

The other men laughed uneasily while Otto pulled at his lower lip and thought about the colossus inside the coach. It was not that he had forgotten him. It was just that he had not yet found a solution for that one.

Chapter 9

THEME

My aunt waited long enough for marriage, being thirty-three years of age herself and without independent wealth. It has to be the most damning characteristic of women that they waste so much time seeking someone more interesting than themselves. Foolish virgins, yet perhaps this is a natural rite of summer. In Nannerl's case, Baron Johann Baptist Berchtold zu Sonnenburg would reward her patience with five thousand gulden after their wedding night. (Morgengabe seu in praemium virginitatis.) It was the custom, neither more nor less. My father, being already wed and revelling in his experience, sent her his congratulations in the usual way.

Vienna, 18th August 1784

Ma Plus Chère Soeur!

Pop goes the weasel! I'd better hurry up and write this letter if it's to arrive while you are still a vestal virgin! A day or so from now, you'll lose it! My wife, Constanze and I, your devoted brother, congratulate you on what will SOON be your TRANSFORMED state.

It is our great regret that we cannot embrace you on your wedding day and call you Baroness von Sonnenburg but we will do so next Spring when we come to Salzburg. Our only other regret is that our dear father who has been a slave to that wretched Kapellhaus and its Archbishop for so many years, cannot go to him and say how he has lost a child to marriage and could he, our father, not retire to live his last years with his daughter in domestic bliss or else be free to go to Vienna and live with his only son and his family? Do your best to persuade him that he must swallow his pride and ask for his dues. I have written to our father today to say much the same thing. But back to the happy subject of your wedding day. I send you a thousand kisses and wish that you will know the same pleasure in marriage as we do. Now you can enjoy my significant thoughts on the matter!

Marriage brings a flawed bliss
and in the mysteries of this,
the arts of Eve
That gave her Cain
Will bring such joy
As mewling girl or puking boy.
Yet nothing is pure harmony —
The counterpoint we surely know
Is there to stop the sickly flow.
Rejoice when ere your husband says
He's out of sorts!
Just think sister, this is man's sports,
And say, why then, your will by day
And mine by night I sorely pray.

From your brother, the poet with his tender kisses! Keep well my blister, stretch your arse to your mouth, shit in your bed with a fortissimo crash to awake the gentle heavens. It's already one minute past the hour and now it is time for you to make your own rhymes. Addio.

— W.A.M.

Leopold Mozart had also encouraged the match in the beginning because he was afraid there would be no one to look after my aunt when he was dead. Shortly after her marriage to the widower with five children, he began to develop serious doubts. He complained he was no longer made welcome at his daughter's house, while Sonnenburg insisted the journey from Salzburg to their home in Saint Gilgen was too tiring for an old man.

'What? Too tiring to see my beloved daughter? A puny six or seven hours by coach? I'd walk on one leg.' Leopold tossed angrily in his bed at nights or raged to anybody who cared to listen. His wife was in heaven, his son was with a ball of fluff and his daughter with a nincompoop. He wallowed in his bitterness while Nannerl, caught between her husband and father, denied anything was amiss except in her thoughts.

The story has moved out of Salzburg by eleven kilometres and up some hills and down again. Think of a town tucked into the edge of a lake at the foot of small mountains. There is one church and graveyard, a town hall, an inn, several shops, hunting lodges and the ordinary homes of the people who live there all the year round. It's small enough to be pretty and not big enough to escape the feeling of being suffocated by everyone's intimate knowledge of each other.

At the end of ——— Strasse, if you walk a few metres down a road past the town hall and an expanse of wild primroses, you come to the lake itself. The water is as calm as a duck's pond but wide enough for the mountains on the other side to seem like another world. On your left is a solid, rectangular house whose walls are almost the same yellow as the flowers in the grass. The back of the house looks across the water to the mountains, while its front door faces life in a town called Saint Gilgen. This was the house where her mother was born and it comforts Nannerl to think about the connection while lying on the bed and wondering how to please her husband and five stepchildren.

There's enough space for a family of ten or more. The main rooms, upstairs and down, open onto a corridor that divides the house into four parts. Each is similar in design, if not in function, for the salon, dining room and bedrooms are defined on one side by windows that are framed with blue curtains. These faded draperies are threadbare, bald in patches, tied with tassels that have once been gold. There are several oval mirrors with pastoral scenes of shepherds and shepherdesses guiding sheep across the gilded wood at the top of the amalgam. Their glass is badly foxed by damp, not neglect, and it is only visitors who attempt to discover their reflection in such mottled gloom. The furniture is neither ornate nor plain, being serviceable and yet modestly carved around the corners. Each sprawling curve smells of polish and gleams more brilliantly than any nearby glass. At least two, sometimes three melancholy portraits hang on the interior walls and since each painting appears to be by a different artist, there's scant resemblance between any of the subjects. Just blotches of deadness hanging on the walls.

Nannerl is resting on a large four poster bed with her hand on the side of her face and her elbow dug deep into her pillow. The early swelling of her stomach is visible from the open door where her father stands, uncertain if he should enter.

'My darling Nannerl,' he announces to the cat, which is lying at her feet and staring back at him with cold curiosity. She lifts her chin to survey her father. They haven't seen one another for a while and he's taken pains to look his best.

His dress is old style, with a starched cravat and a frilled shirt under a coat of vivid red cloth. To the best of my wit and memory, there was much fuss about buying its gold enamelled buttons from the market in Salzburg. His hat, stick and white kid gloves have been placed artfully on a side table. The apricot hair has been curled and powdered to a dull cream. You can see at a glance that he's a fine old dandy.

'Good heavens upon my soul, after being cooped up inside a coach for half a day, I thought I'd stretch my bones and stand right here until you were awake.'

The cat stretched and leapt from the bed, landing on Leopold's hat as he leant for support against the frame of the door. His body was too heavy for spindly legs, criss-crossed with alabaster veins, visible through the weave of his stockings. The eyes belonged to a lizard – viscous and liquid under the lids – eyes that swept across his daughter on the bed. There was nothing erotic or incestuous in the glance, unless to look upon someone with love is to be a speck away from lust. Nannerl stifled a yawn in that sly, guilty manner, as if she were making an effort to stay awake.

'You must sit down Papa. Johannes is still with Father Eiberle. They're discussing town affairs I think. Now look at you – quite unable to stand without support. Do sit down my dear. The bed will be much more comfortable than a seat in a coach.'

She dragged a pile of slithering blanket to one side and made a space, promptly taken by the cat but not before Leopold had collapsed on top of it. The animal retrieved its tail from underneath the old man as his groans brought five children running into the room to find out if they'd missed out on something interesting.

'Cat's dead,' said the smallest child, still with baby fat.

'Good,' replied Leopold, shifting his coattails to check there were no bits of animal underneath.

'No Karl. The cat's not dead. It's under the bed,' said the eldest and only female child who had a sweet, disappointed face with a slight swelling around the base of her neck that suggested goitre. Everything else about her was thin. Like her stepmother, her name was Maria Anna and confusingly, she was called Anna Maria, Nannerl for short, or Marianna.

Another, smaller brother grabbed the animal around the stomach. It hissed, spat and scratched his face so deeply that small drops of blood fell into his eyes as it fled to a dark, windowless corner.

'It's just a scratch, Andra. Just a small cut above your eye. Nothing serious now.' Nannerl wiped his face with a corner of her sleeve, uncertain how to console the child. She knew she was being studied and worried that she had failed an important test. 'Just a scratch,' she repeated hopelessly. 'Just a scratch.'

'But he hurt me in the same place yesterday. And I'm blind already.' The sobbing boy was battering his fists against his stepmother as if her words meant nothing to him.

'It's strange the way you hurt yourself in the same place where you've already been hurt,' remarked Leopold calmly. 'So what's this in my right hand?' He withdrew an apple from his coat pocket, holding it in the air as a prize while the boy clambered onto his lap to reach the fruit. 'You must say what it is before I give it to you.'

'An apple.'

'It's yours.' Leopold laughed, tossing it into the air where it fell to the floor. His authority was at his daughter's expense but he saw no point in modesty.

Nannerl began to panic, overwhelmed by a self-preserving desire to clear the room of all children.

'Maria Anna, take your brothers outside and tell Liserl to put some lint on Andra's cut.'

She despaired of ever being what others called a natural mother. What is natural? She would cry into her pillow when she thought her husband was asleep. Is it this lump that's growing down there? And then she would touch it to believe in it and to reassure herself the swelling was not a hideous blunder of nature before she allowed her hand to rest on its curve. 'I am not comfortable with them and they are not comfortable with me,' she repeated as distracted with these thoughts, she would rise from her bed to walk up and down the room until anxiety made her so tired she would almost fall asleep standing on her feet.

'So. You're not ill my dear? Exhausted perhaps?' They were alone in the room and Leopold patted the figure under the blankets and Nannerl relaxed under his caress.

'It's been a considerable shock to acquire a large family all at once,' she replied, intending to be humorous although her father missed the ironic tone. She thought sadly that the only things that made him laugh these days were his personal victories and the occasional, covert obscenity.

'Does the noise bother you?'

'Sometimes.' She imagined this was the way large families always were – chaotic and dissonant and everyone wanting the same thing at the same time. Her problem was that she didn't enjoy their games any more. She was bored by the constant urge to play and hadn't yet worked out how to ration the amount of time they spent in energetic frolics and quiet studies with their books. Her father would of course know exactly what to do in her place and even Wolfie, she suspected, would have both the energy and the inclination to climb trees with them or play cards and generally have fun. She recognised she was being boring, inadequate and far too serious. She had been like this she realised, ever since her mother died.

'It's like teaching.'

'Is it?'

'You have to keep control.'

'I try to Papa.'

'Do you have time to practise?'

'What time?'

'You must make time.'

'Can I add three more hours to the clock? I have no spare time. I'm always doing something else.' There. She hoped he would note that her life was mapped out to the minute.

'Tell your husband you need a personal maid. This maid, Liserl, is clearly not enough. I'll tell him that you need another, my dear.'

'Papa, you mustn't. I've no need.'

'Then have Berthe. I give you Berthe.'

'Do you want to get rid of her Papa?'

'You're trying to change the subject. Hmm?'

'But I'm not sure what the subject is. My practice or my domestic affairs?'

'Both of course. Shall I tell you what your brother does all day?'

Nannerl toyed with the tassels on her shawl, submitting from a sense of duty to the barrage which followed and which she had heard before, reflecting on the delicacy of tie between father and daughter. She loved him. She loved him not. Leopold chose to ignore her discomfort.

'Your brother's hair is always dressed by six o'clock in the morning and by seven he's fully dressed. He composes until ten. From ten to one he gives lessons. He then lunches at home or elsewhere and he can never work at his composition until five or six in the evening. Even then, he's often prevented from doing so because of a concert. Otherwise he composes until nine and if he still has the energy after a concert, he might compose until one in the morning. Then bed. Then up again before six. And so on.'

Her tongue was scouring the front of her teeth in an attempt to control her anger. 'Are you telling me to do the same?' She thought of denying everything, declaring her brother's industry as a sham, except she knew that his devotion to work was a symptom of his talent and a reminder that she had made other choices. She thought of defending her name against accusations that had not even been made, but instead, allowed herself to be pointlessly absorbed by the taste of blood in her mouth.

'No my dear. Your life and his . . . It's impossible. Besides, your brother has a wife.'

'Does my brother's wife have one maid or two?'

'Ah. She has no need for more than one.'

'And I do, Papa?'

'You can't compare yourself with your brother's wife.'

'But you are comparing my life with my brother's.'

'Of course,' he almost said but stopped himself in time. Instead he waved both hands in the air and kissed her on the cheek. For what seemed a long time, all they could hear was the sound of each other's breathing.

'I shall play you the fugue Jack Pudding sent me,' she whispered. 'What do you say?'

At this point, Sonnenburg entered the room and the painful intimacy that existed between father and daughter slipped away. There was something in the way the husband planted his feet securely on the floor and stood with his hands behind his back that suggested this was another man who wished to be obeyed. It was a look of order, efficiency and command. You couldn't fault it and yet there was an impression given that he had smothered his instincts to the point where you weren't sure that he had any left.

'I hope you are not too tired after your journey, sir.' He was fair wigged, straight-backed and not obviously middle aged. He exuded respectability and believed in his own authority.

'I can't complain,' replied my grandfather, who then did. He had been obliged to wait three hours in the cold without food, while the driver arranged fresh horses for the coach. He hoped his bed was ready if that were not too much trouble. He hoped on second thoughts, that his son-in-law was in better health than he, and that the municipal affairs of Saint Gilgen were in good order as a result of his magistracy.

Sonnenburg bowed in polite acknowledgement, opening the door that led them through to the salon of faded blue draperies and Nannerl's newly acquired fortepiano in one corner. Within minutes, Leopold had dashed up a rondo not a fugue, very fast in the Turkish manner, which I suppose is the right of a father, but I hate it when someone marches up to the clavier in my house and plays unasked. In fairness to Leopold, any unresolved difficulties between himself and his children, were usually exaggerated or presumed by those absent from their squabbles. The assumption that it was his right to begin playing without formal invitation was here a proof of the hierarchical intimacy that plagues most families.

'Bravo, bravo,' Sonnenburg clapped as Leopold tugged at his cuffs and looked set to play some more.

'The fugue, Papa. Play Jack Pudding's new fugue.'

Nannerl was sitting on one of the overstuffed chairs at the other end of the room and fanning herself briskly. She had dressed in an elaborate lace costume, full of tucks and scollops and numerous silk fringes that rustled whenever she breathed. Her hair hung loose as far as the tops of her ears and the rest of it was tucked into a silk net.

Leopold played the opening line so slowly that each note had a pause between it. At about the sixteenth bar, he stumbled and stopped clumsily where the sound should have been smooth. 'It's no good,' he grumbled. 'I must practise this or the result will be a dirge by a dead organist. Fetch me my fiddle and we'll play together my dear.'

'Allow me, sir.' The low, solicitous tones of his voice and the speed with which Sonnenburg left the room were aimed to please. The son-in-law was behaving impeccably but Leopold could only find fault.

'I'm afraid, my dear, Maria Anna. He and I . . . We are just like . . . '

'Please don't say what you think Papa. I am his wife.'

'My child, how can I forget?' Leopold's eyes were fixed on an amorous shepherd and shepherdess. They lay entwined across the top of a mirror with their crooks perfectly crossed at the bottom. 'We are ... Yes, I'll say it. We are two boars sniffing at one another and not liking what we smell.' He turned his face away from the lovers and blew theatrically into his lace handkerchief. Nannerl said nothing because she was afraid it was the truth.

'I remember when I first became aware of the baron,' he continued mercilessly, nose still buried in the cloth, 'just after the death of your mother. Your Sonnenburg, my dear, drew me aside at one of Hagenauer's gatherings and said it was a sad time for all of us. I thought at first he was talking about you, me and Wolfgang, not the entire parish of St Gilgen. But of course, he is their magistrate and it was your mother's birthplace.'

Leopold deserted the fortepiano to pace up and down one length of the carpet before returning. Absorbed by the memory of what he said, he forgot the aching stiffness in his bones.

'I thought, what a pleasant, reverent person. How sympathetic and not at all a pompous, quasi-ecclesiastical prick. He was married to someone else at the time, so I could hardly imagine him being my future son-in-law. Soon after that, your husband's second wife unfortunately died.'

Nannerl tapped her foot angrily against the wooden floor. 'But Johannes is a kind and reverent person, Papa. You are being unfair.' Her emotions were invisible in her face as she smoothed the silk leaves on her bodice with her fan, combing them so they fell uniformly across her breast.

Leopold attacked the keyboard as if he had never left his seat. Extraordinary that he should ever have approved of a penny-pinching pipsqueak with one foot in the grave for his only beloved daughter.

'He has not changed ... It is your expectations which are different, Papa. We may be living at some distance from each other, but we are still able to visit ... Johannes understands the importance of that. You will see. He is,' and she hesitated briefly, 'most considerate of our needs.'

Her words appeared conventional enough, but the way she spoke, lacked raw feeling. Leopold explored a simple, repetitive tune and sealed his lips.

'Ah, Mozart, I believe,' said Sonnenburg as he entered the room holding a violin case.

'It's one of Papa's new compositions.'

'Why, yes, yes, my dear. Without doubt by Leopold and not Wolfgang Amadeus.' The more he tried to ingratiate himself, the more my grandfather mistrusted him and behaved abominably. Sonnenburg in turn, was irritated by the other's unbearable smugness and his irritation crept into his voice. 'I hear you're planning a trip to Vienna.'

'You hear but you don't hear. Hmmm?'

Nannerl slowly closed her fan with the tip of one finger. 'Johannes knows Papa, that you are going to Vienna because of Wolfie's concerts.'

'Yes indeed. Don't worry about being stuck with me for more than a day. I have to be there in time for Lent.' He tuned each string of his instrument, lavishing special care on the E string which kept slipping, before launching into an account of how his son would at last be earning large sums of money with a series of six subscription concerts. He waved his violin at Sonnenburg to see if the man was impressed. Did they understand that all Wolfgang had to pay each time for the hire of the concert hall was half a gold sovereign? Did they realise how each person in the audience would then have to pay a gold sovereign for the series? Do the mathematics. This would be straightforward profit.

'You must know your brother has sold six string quartets for a hundred ducats. Altogether, he's a public success! Even the Emperor has taken to calling out 'Bravo Mozart,' when he comes onto the platform. My son is an embellishment to the court.'

Bull's eye. The talk of court life was an exaggeration and a case of wishful thinking on Leopold's part, since that was Salieri's domain, but the reference to the Emperor was perfect. Sonnenburg clapped his hands by fluttering the tips of his fingers together, not very noisily, but clapping. Nannerl smiled at her father, which meant he promptly forgot he had ever been out of sorts in the first place.

'Are you going to accompany me on the fortepiano my darling girl? It won't be too much for the – too uncomfortable or something? Hmm?' Leopold stabbed the air with his bow and was surprised at how well he suddenly felt.

Nannerl lowered her fan, spreading it over her waist to conceal any thickening.

'I'm not an invalid yet, Papa. Of course I will play.'

Sonnenburg yawned after the opening bar. He was bored and this was the first time since entering the room that he'd allowed himself to sustain a genuine emotion for more than a minute. He knew he could at least relax for the duration of the sonata as his wife and father-in-law were reliably engrossed in playing molto espressivo. He observed with distaste that Nannerl was no longer youthful, that she was not particularly pretty and any show of handsomeness depended on her mood, her face resembling a horse when she was serious. He should have waited a little longer instead of rushing into things like a panicky widower with five children on his hands. But who knows what may happen? He'd had such bad luck in the past with the loss of two wives. One could hardly be certain of anything.

'What do you say Johannes? Will it catch on in St Gilgen?' Nannerl turned to her husband in a reproving way because he had failed to applaud.

'Shall we play it again for you my dear, so you can give it your full attention?'

Neither his wife, nor his father-in-law, would ever know with certainty what he thought. His marriage required a diplomatic deceit for it to be tolerable and as he pulled up another chair to sit beside her, he realised that he saw the birth of their child as a reflection of a husband's duty and little more. He resisted an overwhelming desire to retire to the bedroom and relieve himself, instead, crossing his legs with great care so as not to snag his stockings with the buckles of his shoes. How strange that this time he found himself enjoying the sensation of listening. The theme, which kept returning in different disguises, first on the violin and then on the forte-piano, absorbed him unexpectedly.

'Bravo,' he cried when they stopped. 'Bravo Mozart.' Just like the Emperor.

'That was the introduction, my dear.' Nannerl launched into a repeat of the first variation while Sonnenburg appeared momentarily embarrassed. Leopold was caught up in his own dream, curling his hand around the neck of his violin and allowing his third finger to vibrate gently back and forth, releasing such exquisite sounds that I, in my window seat, stopped spinning. Like Sonnenberg, I became spellbound for the entire set of variations and by the time they had finished, I knew by the way his shoulders were thrust forwards and his head thrown back that he had passed through some sort of ecstasy. This cold fish of a fellow. This master of magisterial control was transported! Now that is the power of my father's music.'

Leopold placed his violin on top of the fortepiano and took out his lace handkerchief to wipe his forehead. 'God forgive me if I'm not going to be emaciated by the time I leave here. I could eat a lump of stale bread or the backside of an elephant and I wouldn't mind a bit.'

Sonnenburg appealed to Nannerl who was putting the music away.

'My dear?'

Brushing his hand lightly across the back of her neck, his wife made no connection between this unusual show of affection and the music she had just performed. How could she be so unaware, so remote from whatever it was that he was feeling? Musical sensibility is not exclusive to musicians, he thought with a fierce bitterness, fidgeting with his thumbs, impatient for her reply.

'I suggest we eat some elephant immediately.' Nannerl accepted Sonnenburg's extended arm and swaying as a picture book wife, left the room with her upright husband and her aging father.

I watched the different motions of the two men, the older one with a raucous splash of red and the beginning of arthritic steps and the middle-aged one in shades of mud brown, with smooth, dovetailed strides. The spell was over. Sonnenburg behaved like a cleric at a funeral executing some automatic ceremony, while my aunt held her ground between her husband and father and felt the child inside her move for the first time.

They sat down at a table fit for thirteen although they were only three. Two candelabra with seven candles apiece lit the meal, which was laid out at one end on so many green-rimmed plates, the edges connected with one another like a giant caterpillar. The glasses were dull from careless washing but everything was plentiful and Leopold drank too much at dinner, which inflamed his gout. It was a storm of talk. Talk for talk's sake. At the best of times, he needed little encouragement.

'Science dislikes beauty because beauty has no consistency or order. The peahen hardly notices the peacock's colour and the nightingale sings best when the courting is over and the eggs are laid.' Leopold winked at Nannerl and helped himself to another glass of wine.

'I daresay this is a matter of effect being the cause as well as cause having effect.' Sonnenburg's thoughts were of the maid in the kitchen, whose appeal had increased considerably since the beginning of his wife's pregnancy, and of the satisfaction this had given him on more than one occasion.

'Which is the greater cause, the bird's desire at the beginning or its reward at the end?' Leopold may have been muddled with wine, but his passion for argument was intact.

'Perhaps you should talk of instinct, rather than desire.' Nannerl's great fear was that somehow, like her husband, she had none left.

'Yes, yes, yes! But everyone's instinct for what is beauty can be different. What we choose to call beautiful is truth as we see it.'

Leopold spread his legs under the table, pleased with his own sense of urbanity. Sonnenburg was remembering the music he had heard an hour before. One minute it was beyond him and he was bored – in the next, revelatory. Was that his fault, theirs or Mozart's? He considered this while returning the cork to the bottle.

'Tell me.' Leopold surveyed his half empty glass and wondered if he would be offered any more. 'Are three people ever moved by art in the same way?' He became louder and more excitable with each successive tangent that popped into his lonely mind. His voice was the human drone of the hurdy-gurdy.

'In music my dear friend, unlike a painting, the performance will be different each time. Everything depends upon the execution and the listening. How often is a miserable scribble made bearable by a good performance? And what about the best composition played so badly the composer can't recognise his own work. How about that?

Sonnenburg remained silent, subdued by private, pessimistic answers and aware that if he offered them, they would be ignored.

'Of course a person who values a bird for its feathers or a deer for its antlers will also judge a violin by its polish and the colour of its varnish.'

Nannerl despaired that conversation might last a further hour and longed for sleep.

'How do money, pomp and curly wigs induce a man to become a scientist or a counsellor? For a sad piece of music, do we have to believe in our own sadness to arouse sadness in those who listen? I ask you, if I drink too many glasses of wine at supper, am I drunk for a night or am I a drunkard?'

'A little tipsy Papa.'

Nannerl saw a quiver in the folds of her dress, which snaked across her stomach until it was still again. With unexpected tenderness, she leant forward to pat my grandfather's hand and remove the glass from the side of his plate. It had not occurred to her she was mothering her own father. It had to Sonnenburg as he wrinkled his eyebrows and watched this curdling display of family affection. He liked to believe he was a reasonable man and for that reason, he would allow his wife to return to Salzburg for the birth of their child when it was due. Poor man, he was not pleased in his heart.

FUGUE 6

Stones sprang upwards and outwards in all directions. It was a miracle the sleek, lacquered frame did not fall to bits or the horses were not lame. When they reached a sharp corner at the bottom of a hill, instead of slowing down, the postillion cracked his whip on the lead horse. The animal plunged forward until his head was parallel to the ground, dragging the other horses with him in an insane gallop. The left door of the coach swung open and banged back and forth on its hinges. You could see that one end of the coffin had been buried under hay while the arms and chin of the passenger were thrust above its lid like parts of a giant squid.

Chapter 10

'I've found a new maid!' Leopold entered his apartment in Hannibal Platz with a great flurry of cloak and self-importance. Young and attractive maids who were efficient in their work were essential to his happiness. Nannerl was holding a baby no larger than a doll and standing by one of those windows, which overlooked the square. She shrugged her shoulders and began rocking the child as people do when they have one in their arms.

'I have met the perfect servant at the convent this morning and the nuns cannot praise her enough. She was gravely ill when she came into their care and since her recovery, she's worked for them in all sorts of ways – as cook, seamstress, even wet nurse to a tribe of orphans. In short, she has the qualities of a saint.'

'A saint Papa? I'm not sure I can live with a saint.'

'My dear Nannerl,' Leopold flung up his arms in impatience. 'Hear me out. Her own children are recently dead but the nuns insist she's particularly fond of the orphans in their care. She teaches the older ones to read and spell and they tell me this charming woman is like a mother to each one. A born nursemaid. Even Berthe approves. 'Just what the Baroness needs,' Berthe said. 'Another mother, since her own dear one is dead.' So you see my dear, there is no need to ask any more questions about her worthiness.'

'And is this paragon to be with me while I am in Salzburg or is she coming with us to St Gilgen as well?' She disliked to be reminded of the day the Abbé Bullinger had announced her mother's death. If she stopped to dwell on it, she would smell the vomit on her bed and the pain from losing her would return as strongly as before. Nannerl pushed her knuckles hard against her lips to try and forget. Her milk was hardening into small, aching bumps behind the flesh and she wished her father would disappear or pick up his violin or just talk about something else, but then he seemed so pleased with himself and so willing to persist.

'This charming woman,' he argued emphatically, 'is ready to start work now and if you decide to return to St Gilgen she's free to go with you. It's as simple as that.'

'Simple? I'm sure it can't be simple. What's her name Papa?'

'Frau Heller, although they call her Nandl. You see my dear? Even the name is perfect. Think of the sound – Nandl – Nannerl. How they go together. And did I make clear that she is no ordinary maid? Her education is undoubtedly superior to the good Sisters themselves. She plays the clarinet, though how well she plays it is another matter. As far as the Sisters are concerned, she's a prodigy on the chalumeau.'

'No doubt you're planning to teach her the violin as well Papa.'

'Why does everyone swear they know a prodigy? And why is it when I hear them, they sound like dogs with their ears cut off? Can you tell me why? Hmm?'

'Perhaps everyone is deaf except you Papa.'

'Perhaps.' Leopold stared unhappily at a speck of rust on the cuff of one sleeve.

Nannerl stopped rocking her son, who was crying because of the awkwardness in the way he was swaddled. She stared down at his wrinkled, little old man's face, roaring, bright red with indignation and pulled back the folds around his head as if to check that he were really hers. She bent down to smell his warmth and to feel the stirring of his body through the linen. She thought about how much she wanted to love him and how she was still waiting for some powerful emotion to swallow up her senses.

Without thinking twice about her father's presence, she undid her bodice eagerly and pressed the child next to her skin, enjoying the way his wetness slipped against hers. With each tug on her nipple, she could feel her stomach contract in small, discreet shivers but it was nothing wild, nothing extraordinary that could either make her forget herself or prove the strength of any maternal feelings. Leopold turned, glimpsing her boldness, enthralled by a Madonna with cherub, his daughter with his grandson.

'My dear . . . ' he said at last. 'Yes, yes, yes of course you must approve of Frau Heller. I wouldn't dream of asking her to come and live with us if I thought it would make you unhappy. But trust me. I have an eye for a good servant.'

She laughed at the ridiculousness of his statement and because she realised he was incapable of letting go, despite her marriage to a man who was almost as old as himself. The baby was having trouble staying attached and milk spurted in small, wave-like gusts, which bubbled round his face. You could see him gulping alternately at the air or nipple as she threw her head back until her hair became tangled in the scroll of the chair. The mother was laughing properly for the first time in months. She thought her father was being sentimental and sheepish – with his unbridled lust for any half pretty maid. It was, she decided, the same for her brother, her husband and all men. It was grotesque. It was, however, like a redeeming smidgen of common wear and tear. And all the time, I, Franz Xaver Mozart, disguised as common spider, could have sworn Nannerl was already examining the pesky little old man in her arms for early signs of wanderlust.

'Very well,' sighed Leopold. 'I know what you're thinking. Yes, the woman is quite handsome as it happens, but this has nothing to do with why I find her suitable.' He bent over my aunt, lowering his head onto her shoulder and stroking his grandson tenderly.

'There is another possibility my darling girl. You could leave young Leopold with me if you wish.'

Nannerl pressed the child closer to her breast and sat there, quite rigid except for the milk, silently repeating her father's words and trying to make sense of them as she did.

'Not forever, my dear. Just for a short while. It would give you some . . . time for your husband. Time to adjust . . . to prepare yourself for little Leopold.' He removed his head from her shoulder and eyed the damp stains on her dress. Although the look was not in any way lascivious, there was perhaps an ounce of envy in it as he observed what was beyond him. 'And someone for me to love,' he added quietly as he closed his eyes. She wondered if he had actually said it or if she had thought he said it.

'You cannot be serious Papa.' When Nannerl spoke she was surprised to hear her own voice in the room. The baby's head drooped and lolled while he slept in her arms. A wet bubble clung to the end of his nose as she cuddled and stroked his wrapped up, trembling body. 'You cannot be serious,' she said again but she knew when she looked up at her father and saw his expression of profound forlornness that he was.

'Only a very short while, Schätzl.'

He was pleading, bargaining, wheedling. If she pleased him by agreeing, she would lose her child. If she disagreed, she would disappoint her father.

He looked lonely and old as he moved closer to her. A faint, brief drum roll disturbed her imagination. This man, her father, loved her, loved her son. It was quite clear to her, but until now, she hadn't understood. 'Not yet Papa, not yet,' she thought to herself. 'I am not ready to let him go just yet.'

Chapter 11

VARIATION 2

'Allow me to introduce Frau Nandl Heller. Frau Heller, this is my daughter, Freyfrau Sonnenburg. I will leave you to talk to each other about my proposal.' Leopold waved his protegée into the room and left in a hurry before Nannerl could make excuses. The woman was dressed as a widow and appeared to be about thirty-five years old, although she could have been forty-five, such was her fine figure. Nannerl seemed startled.

'I believe – yes I'm certain we've met before. Do you remember?'

'No, Baroness.'

'Well, I think I do. I even recognise your voice.'

'I'm sorry. I have never been here before today.' Frau Heller's eyes addressed the floorboards. 'I rarely leave the convent walls.' She was clearly one of those fantastical creatures who lived her fantasies as fact.

'I could be mistaken.' Nannerl knew that she was not. She could tell from the furtive way Frau Heller's hand crept up to cover a row of mother-of-pearl buttons gleaming at the base of her collar, that these delicate fragments were a painful reminder of ancient feelings for both of them, and that Frau Heller was lying. She gestured to the widow to sit opposite her.

'Well then. You have been highly recommended as a wet nurse for my son – but I must warn you, I am still uncertain of our need for such a service. Perhaps you will tell me a little about yourself.'

This was a cold beginning. Frau Heller tugged at the buttons one after another as if to check that each was secure. She was regretting that she had no other dress to wear that day, or had agreed to come with Herr Mozart to meet his daughter. She was, thought Nannerl, very beautiful and quite agitated.

As with many fantasists, who seek to subdue time for themselves, or to play around with reality and deal in gothic symbols of death, the invitation to tell the story of her life proved irresistible. What followed was a melodramatic drifting between fantasy and reality.

Time was immaterial to her gist, since Frau Heller had no desire to subdue its effects or deal with notions of accuracy. She had the actor's authority to believe her own myths and her conviction gave a type of truth to what she said.

'I had a husband and three children until a plague came into our home. They all died in front of me. One by one, in my arms. I could do nothing except pray I would get sick and die quickly so that I could be with them.'

Neither woman spoke for what seemed a long time. Nannerl was struggling with mediaeval images of putrefying corpses. The widow's face in the window light resembled a magnificent gargoyle, the mouth open and the words, seeming to come from somewhere else around her.

'All I have left is a lock of their hair.' She clasped her hands together and placed them deep into her lap so they were no longer visible.

'Half the people in our town died from this plague. I left the high walls and the gates that were locked at night. I moved between villages and towns without knowing where I was. I accepted the kindness of strangers and after several weeks or perhaps months, I came to Salzburg to look for work. Anything I could find, you understand, after what I had left behind.'

My aunt knew nothing of ghettos and ramparts and restrictions on where people could live or not live. She had no understanding of a world where Jews were obliged to pay a fee for existing within a town, where they were forbidden to carry walking sticks, where there was a limit on the number of weddings that could take place or on the number of families that could be contained in an already unsanitary, overcrowded compound. Not many people did. It was not their problem.

'For the first few days, I washed and mended clothes for different families but when I became ill, no one wanted me to do any more work for them. I was feverish as I walked away from the city and prayed again for death. I was found, lying on the side of the road by a gentleman. I don't remember very much of what happened – you see I've forgotten a lot of things – but I was told he took me in a coach to a convent nearby. I've been living on the charity of nuns ever since. For some reason – I don't know why – my milk still flows, though my babies have all died.'

It was an extraordinary story to absorb and accept. Nannerl bent low over her child's cot, nuzzling her cheeks against his in a burst of genuine feeling for the child that puzzled her with its strength. She could imagine

Frau Heller suckling a child all the way to her own grave and the thought, though it appalled, also fascinated her. What Frau Heller could not possibly know was that Nannerl, when she placed the child in the widow's arms, was relieved to be handing him over to someone else and what the baroness failed to realise was that Frau Heller, accepted him as her due.

Out of curiosity, I swung myself down a thread to land on the widow's shoulders. Very lightly and carefully, I slipped forward for a closer study of the buttons and saw a glint of orange hairs, tightly woven into fine plaits and wrapped around each narrow stem of mother-of-pearl. If Nannerl saw these lovelocks, she gave no sign. I thought my aunt could have at least asked Frau Heller why she had been wearing widow's weeds in Hofmann's market at a time when her husband and her children were visibly alive. It was not for me to probe an apparition or discover loopholes in a fairy story, and although I can scuttle in and out of time to check up on such matters at will, I'm reluctant to inhabit the same past more than once in case it disturbs the order of events I have remembered. I rely on my aunt to notice any inconsistency, which I suspect she has already because she is biting her lips in that characteristic, contemplative way.

'Our meeting was so brief... so many years ago.' Nannerl was about to say, 'I had such pity for you,' but stopped herself in time, transformed by an unexpected epiphany that helped her understand the roundabout of life and death from the widow's point of view. It occurred to her that Frau Heller was able to see the deaths of her family before they happened. Hence her beseeching, 'I have thirty-seven kreuzer,' and so on. It had been a remarkable premonition, a morbid vision – as strange as the flow of milk, but just as real.

It was this strangeness that made sense of the events and when I looked again at my aunt, her face momentarily handsome with enlightenment, it made sense to me as well. We are a fanciful family with our eyes looking inward. Without a word between us, we shared an understanding that the widow was witch, prophet or seer. That she was a genuine wet nurse was no longer in question with the child, tucked into the woman's opened bodice and sucking noisily and hard as if it had always been so. To Nannerl, it seemed she was witnessing a prize milch cow with her son as calf.

'I'm expendable after all,' she reflected grimly to herself, reaching out to touch the widow's sleeve, and having fingered its rough, tough, black woven cloth, letting it go, satisfied the woman was real and her child was safe in her arms.

'How long have you been in mourning?'

'For as long as I remember, I've worn nothing but black. There has never been any colour in my life apart from my husband's and my children's wonderful hair.'

Frau Heller removed some crust from the eyes of the child as he thrust his thin rooster legs from underneath his wraps and kicked the air in triumph, so that his world widened accordingly. He made delighted noises and dribbled and mewed as babies do when they are content.

'Do you often forget things?' persisted Nannerl.

'Only those that make me unhappy.' Frau Heller clucked at the baby, absently wiping the dribble on the folds of her dress with her cuff. There was something cruel in the way the baroness questioned her. It was, she decided, as if her future mistress already knew the answers. This would change soon enough and she was consoled by the thought, pressing the child even closer, enjoying the naturalness of the feeling, aware that Nannerl was studying her with a small shaft of envy.

The baby whimpered softly because he was wet. The two women came together and talked sensibly for the brief while it took to change the child's clothes. They spoke as if they had begun to understand one another and because it was expedient. I realised that if my aunt still had some unresolved concerns about the widow, she had chosen to bury them, like the pearl buttons. By the time they turned to leave the young Leopold in his cot, it was agreed that Frau Heller would become his wet nurse at a salary of — schillings for the next six months. It was at this point that my grandfather came back into the room, rubbing his hands with glee and saying 'Well? Well?' over and over again. As if he didn't know.

Chapter 12

VARIATION 3

The bells of Saint Sebastian were tolling like a Christian conscience.

'Since God has brought you safely through the dangers of childbirth, we give Him thanks.'

'Amen.'

'We thank Him for his protection from the pains of hell and for the deaths that have passed us by.'

'Amen.'

The Abbé Bullinger and his small congregation bowed their heads as the ritual of churching took place some weeks after the birth of Leopold Alois Pantaleon Berchtold zu Sonnenburg. It was a signal for my aunt's return to daily life and her husband's bed, except, as I have already explained, she lived with my grandfather for most of this delicate period of adjustment while her husband remained with his five step-children in Saint Gilgen and my aunt wrote to them dutifully every day. The letters were brief, bland and detached. They showed nothing so profound as passion or as amusing as gossip and not a hint of the black thoughts which had been swirling around inside her mind on and off since the birth of her child. Only Leopold seemed to notice anything was amiss and even he was at a loss how to soothe his sad, clever daughter.

Nannerl's daily keyboard practice had become so dull and automatic that when she accompanied him on the violin it was without any pleasure. He could not decide what provoked or pleased her. There were times when she appeared content with her lot, if not exactly animated. She would sit silently in her chair, fanning herself and stroking her child as if he were a dog. Leopold would say something to her and she'd pay no attention and then three minutes later when he had given up, she'd suddenly cry out 'What? What? What?' very loudly as if she'd only just caught up with whatever was being discussed. There was no predictability to her moods or rather no one had yet worked out the why or the when of either.

Salzburg, 29th August, 1785

Dear Husband,

It's uncommonly hot in Salzburg. We've had a stream of visitors all morning and despite the windows being open, my room is stuffy. There's a heaviness in the air wherever I move and now Leopoldl has a rash of white spots inside his mouth that make him uncomfortable when I give suck. Papa has concocted some foul tasting purple stuff which he keeps painting onto the sores. When he cries, which is often, I look into his throat to see if the spots have spread elsewhere. Papa is certain the medicine will work but I'm not yet convinced. Please give my greetings to all the children and say they may see their new brother the minute he's recovered.

Your devoted wife,

— *Maria Anna*

My aunt hurried home to Saint Gilgen the day after writing this letter, leaving Leopoldl behind with my grandfather, Frau Heller and another maid called Monica. The desertion of the child by the mother was not without precedent. Women did this, often because they were unable to nurse their newborn child or because they chose not to. In Nannerl's case, it was the latter. Sometimes when I'm crawling round inside her head, I think I hear her saying over and over again – 'It's a present for Papa' – and of course it was – the greatest present she could give an old man who has been left on his own and wants a reason for continuing to live. Then my aunt talks about plants and gardens and I realise that she thinks of Leopoldl as a plant. She says her father is going to cultivate him like some sort of prize rose. A second Wolferl for the world. Userper, I almost cry aloud and then think better of it.

Salzburg, 15th September, 1785

My dear Herr Son,

You must know how deeply I love the boy and today, I was overjoyed to see he's much livelier than yesterday. His eyes are clear and the worst of the fever seems to have passed. He slept quietly for the first time through the night and I do believe the fungus in his mouth is at last responding to the medicines I've given him. Thanks be to God.

Now I've a proposal, which I hope you will listen to most seriously. I naturally discussed it with Nannerl before she left Salzburg and was delighted she seemed to think it was not such a bad idea. In case you've not heard already because of some delicacy on her part, it is this. I ask you to leave your son with his grandfather for the first nine months. You know how often I have studied children and young people, not only in matters of music. You know me well. You also understand and agree with my theories on education I believe.

It seems to me quite wrong to let six children live so much in each other's pockets, especially when one of them is a six weeks' old child. Then there is Karl, who's at an age when you have to watch that he doesn't get a hole in his head or break every bone in his body and it's not fair to put all the responsibility for minding the younger children upon your eldest, Marianna. I daresay what I am saying is that your house has, if you'll forgive me, enough children already. Think on it Herr Son and let me know your opinion on the matter, good or bad. I also am thinking of my darling girl. It will help Nannerl to recover her health more rapidly if she has less to worry about.

Your old father-in-law, in his ancient wisdom,

— *Leopold*

P.S. Friends in Vienna tell me your brother-in-law has dedicated his quartets to Herr Joseph Haydn with an Italian dedication that shows great respect and affection for his dear friend. I am pleased but could do with a line from my son on the subject. — *L.M.*

Salzburg, 21ˢᵗ September, 1785

Dear Nannerl and Herr Son,

I am devastated. Little Leopold is unwell again. Prepare yourselves for God's will my dears. Yesterday, Nandl Heller was convinced the thrush was on its way out but now it's decided to reappear with a vengeance. I cannot describe the fear of all of us as we await His decision. Do not think matters are worse than I've stated. No. There's always the compassion of hope. Birth is halfway to death and I ask you to have patience and to pray for his quick recovery.

Do not put yourselves out with travel at this uncertain moment.
   Your loving father,

— Leopold

Salzburg, 28ᵗʰ September, 1785

My darling daughter and Herr Son,
   God be praised, Leopoldl is healthy and his grandfather is
delighted he'll be staying here for quite some time. You'll also be
pleased to know my dear Nannerl that I am sending Berthe's cousin
Monica back to Saint Gilgen to help you with young Karl and all the
other children. Nandl Heller and I are perfectly able to cope with
any problems here. She is not only diligent, but healthy, always well
presented and appears to love the child. Our lives revolve around
young Leopold and I have to say he reminds me of your brother at
the same age. You should see his bright little eyes try to follow me
about when I play the spoons! I have not yet tried the violin.

— Your loving Papa

P.S. I hope my dear daughter is feeling better. I recommend
regular walks around the lake and twenty arpeggios daily after
lunch. It reduces bile and prevents rheumatics in the finger joints.
Assolutamente si. One million kisses.

— Leopold, the Terrible.

Nannerl, unwell since the birth of her child and unreliable in her emotions,
resented the letter's tone. She chose to believe her father was rubbing her
nose in her maternal failings by praising Frau Heller. She sighed and pulled
a black hair from a mole on her chin to punish herself for her jealousy and
crumpled the letter in her hand. She had been carrying it in her reticule all
day and couldn't be bothered showing its contents to her husband. He had
never once, she argued, shown any sign that he was missing his newborn
son.

   Sonnenburg was preparing for a game of écarté beneath the ancestral
portraits and my aunt had agreed to the game only in the sense that she
failed to say she had no desire to play. Not another living soul was in the
room apart from one spider and a sleeping cat. It was a rare moment of

quiet. For Nannerl, the cat and myself, it was also a time of apathy and indifference as Sonnenburg began picking out the unwanted cards from the pack.

He studied the Queens that looked like homely housewives with their bunches of stiffened flowers and checked that they were all there. He sifted through the knaves and kings with their drooping moustaches and strange Indian turbans, which reminded me of stories from the Arabian Nights. The drawings were childishly simple and yet the detail was not. My grandfather had hand-painted each one in delicate oriental colours and given them to the baron as a wedding gift. It was clear by the fastidious way in which Sonnenburg dealt the cards that whatever bitter feelings he might have towards his father-in-law, he nevertheless treasured this present from him. The moment he saw his trump was a king, he gave a pleased snort and neatly recorded his point before proposing an exchange of cards with the stock. Nannerl's face was expressionless, which should have been to her advantage as she silently discarded and added to her hand. When Sonnenburg finally suggested they go ahead and play, he won five tricks in a row and without seeming to try, won trick after trick with an embarrassment of voles. Throughout each game, his wife only said 'I'll play,' or 'I'll exchange,' in a faint voice that was without any connection to her surroundings. She looked at her husband as if he were a stranger in a coach.

'I touch his stickiness with my hand. It dries like egg against my skin. I'd like to talk but there's no one to listen. Is there no tenderness afterwards? No peace? No intimacy? I'm not sure I know what that is. But desire. Oh yes. Lust happens when I am least expecting it. He rubs his face against me and I am trapped until I look at him and see myself in his reflection and feel nothing. I shut my eyes and lie perfectly still so he can climb above and push himself inside. I lose my sense of self and think I'm somewhere else. Sometimes he slips out by mistake. I shiver and draw his hardness back again. He pretends not to notice. It is ownership, not possession. The indifference follows and here I am, with my husband at my side with a pack of cards between us. God knows I've waited so many years for all of this and now there's not much time left. The doctor says Leopoldl is too weak to travel and Frau Heller, no, Frau Cow will have to help Papa look after him when she has wiped his arse and feathered her own bed. It's not so strange a circumstance. Papa loves Leopoldl as if he were Wolferl all over again.

Papa even says he cries just like Wolfie and he longs to place his dear hand on a keyboard. He told me so. He also believes I'm not yet strong enough. By looking after Leopoldl, Papa says he's looking after me. So many reasons then.'

'What is wrong my dear? Are you feeling ill?' Sonnenburg, an ace in hand, could barely conceal his irritation. He was reluctant to have whatever victories spoilt because her head ached. She always seemed tired these days and rarely without a pain in her head since the birth of their child. He decided she looked not the way she was meant to look.

'Am I ill?' she asked vacantly.

'I am asking you,' he replied irritably, 'since it is most unusual for me to win at cards.'

Nannerl felt the bile rise into her mouth. She lurched dangerously to one side in her chair, which shut him up immediately.

'Marianna!' he cried as loudly as he dared to his eldest child. He had no desire to introduce a servant into what was a private family crisis. 'Marianna,' he called again more desperately, watching a trickle of bile spill from the corners of his wife's mouth. But Marianna was either unable to hear or chose not to come.

My aunt refused to speak. She just sat there with no attempt to catch her own vomit, still leaning at a sideways angle but remaining in it like a dead person, completely rigid. Sonnenburg felt the sweat from his hands run onto the cards and he pushed them away violently, spilling them all onto the floor.

'My dear – stay there. I'll fetch Marianna and bring you a glass of water,' he muttered not to his wife but to the door, as he stumbled from the room and heard his own heart thumping loudly. 'Wretched creature,' he said to himself. 'She is doing this deliberately to frighten me.' In his heart he thought otherwise and he was only saying it because he was already afraid.

My aunt had neither wit nor spirit for anything so energetic as revenge. She looked pathetic because she was so obviously ill in her mind and if I were not a prisoner, trapped in my own web of time, I would have dropped down from the ceiling and in some protean guise, helped her. What I would have done, I've no idea but it was quite clear to me as I studied her sad, mad face that she was not going to help herself. The look of withdrawal reminded me of how she had taken to her bed for a month when Hofmann criticised her composition. Well, maybe there was more to it than that. Whatever the reason for her apathy at this moment, it was as real as it had been then. Sonnenburg was in for a shock. I think my aunt was definitely disturbed by the birth of her son and being pulled unnaturally between father and husband made matters worse. She chose to retreat into this private, deranged world with no one but herself living in it. I could see her alternation between high spirits and melancholy as a pattern that had always been there and would remain the same to the end. I am now certain that Leopold knew this too and that in offering to take responsibility for her child, he was doing more than just staving off his own loneliness or trying to create another Mozart. He was helping his beloved Nannerl. Yes I think so. That is a more sympathetic way of looking at it.

'Mama?' whispered Marianna. 'Come with me,' and the fourteen-year-old child took her stepmother's hand to lead her gently from the room and down a corridor and up some stairs into another, much smaller room which contained a bed, cupboard, a wash basin and little else. It would have been Frau Heller's room if she had not stayed in Salzburg and because it was unused, the children claimed it as their own private play area.

Marianna undressed and bathed my aunt in silence, wiped the vomit from her hair and still without any words between them, dressed her in a nightgown from the cupboard. Somehow this solemn, dignified child persuaded her stepmother to lie down on the narrow bed which was so narrow that if you turned over in the night you'd be in danger of falling off it. Sonnenburg poked his head round the door and saw that his daughter was in control and that his wife was lying quietly staring at the wall.

'Goodnight my dear,' he said to Nannerl. 'I will come and see how you are in the morning. You may go to your room now, Marianna.'

'I'd like to stay,' said his daughter timidly.

'If you wish.' Sonnenburg entered his own room and observed his wife's shawl on the floor with distaste. Very methodically, he removed each piece of clothing that was his, placing it in a folded pile on a chair. He picked up her shawl and held it as far from his body as he could with one hand, opening the cupboard door with the other, dropping it inside. A completely cold gesture. This was, he argued, his third marriage and he was genuinely tired of it. Uncomfortable with his thoughts, and stretching himself out on his half of the marital bed, he was longing for sleep, being one of those who believe that when he wakes up the next day, everything will be all right with the world.

'Your wife has been bled without success and I can see the valerian I prescribed has failed as well . . . I therefore recommend a visit to the spa,' apologised the doctor, dipping his hands in and out of a small bowl of water being held for him by Marianna. 'It doesn't matter which spa. They're all the same. It's the company and the routine that counts, not the waters.' He smiled at the serious child before him and cast a professional eye over her body. Too thin and still, a sign of goitre round the neck. He turned to his patient, who had not stopped staring at the wall throughout his examination. He was foxed and boxed by her stillness. She reminded him of a grieving horse whose foal had been removed too soon. Enormous dull eyes in a pasty face. What a pity. Too much blood lost, considering her pallor. Too late to undo the damage. At least he was sure she was not yet dying.

Sonnenburg bowed. 'Whatever you suggest.' He assumed someone like Katharina Gilowska would have to accompany his wife to Gastein, that the journey would involve a great deal of expense and that it carried no promise of a cure. He waved his daughter from the room impatiently and felt cross with himself for asking the doctor to come in the first place. Naturally all doctors recommended these ridiculous watering holes. He should have known it suited the doctor to send troublesome patients somewhere else. But then a wife, no matter what her musical pedigree, was certainly no good to him shut up in the maid's room, incapable of maintaining either a house or the simplest conversation. How he longed to sit down and absorb himself in his papers, to be undisturbed. That's why he had married her. For the peace and the order it would bring to his life and his children's.

But oh those spas! There had been a visit some years before with his second wife, or was it his first? He remembered long dark corridors that were not overclean and dressing rooms that were full of steam, resembling dungeons. The memory of their smell was still in his nostrils. At least the baths were in the open air, even if the men and women walked up and down beside the springs in bathing suits. Whichever wife it was, wore a little tray around her waist, containing her handkerchief, snuffbox and puff-box. If he closed his eyes he could picture the absurd parcels floating out in front of the ladies like a flotilla of toy ships. The majority, he recalled, would retire to drink the waters in a large assembly room, obliged to listen to fashionable dance music and share their gossip with the other bathers. Or his wife had. Oh yes, yes, yes, he knew exactly what to expect and the expectation made him grimmer.

'What counts is the delight of meeting others.' The doctor spoke as though he could read the contempt in Sonnenburg's mind. 'Think of the ladies shopping and riding and going to church and parading up and down in their finery, attending balls in the evenings or playing cards or going to the theatre. My dear Baron, your wife is melancholy. Her spirits must be revived. The spa my dear fellow, the spa is your answer – and your wife's.' He patted the end of her bed kindly but if she heard him, the enormous dull eyes that had bothered him throughout, revealed nothing.

Chapter 13

Katharina Gilowska arrived in Saint Gilgen on the hottest day of the year. The horses were dribbling a stream of foam and the coachmen were in a pink sweat. She came with a dozen hat-boxes and an assortment of trunks and it looked as if she had come to stay for six months instead of six weeks. Nannerl was asleep when her friend crept into the maid's room and opened the shutters. She remained sleeping as Katharina sat on a chair by the foot of her bed and studied the room disapprovingly.

'It's quite obvious to me you won't get better here,' she declared.

'What, what, what?' Nannerl kept her head to the wall. This was the first time she had spoken to anyone in several days.

'I said you'll never get better lying in this stuffy little room.' Her friend adjusted her hat-pin as she removed her hat.

Very slowly, Nannerl rolled her head to one side until her eyes were level with her friend's knees. 'I prefer being on my own,' she whispered so that Katharina had to bend down low over her face to hear her.

'Your breath smells, Maria Anna. You need to be washed and your hair needs brushing.' Katharina was able to ignore Nannerl's rudeness by matching it with her own variety.

'It is a fact. You can always go away, and whatever I am like will be a matter of indifference.'

'I can't go away. I've just come.'

Katharina was already opening the cupboard drawers in search of a brush, and when she found one, swooped on her friend with a triumphant, terrifying wave of the handle.

'What a disgusting bird's nest. You're lucky a magpie hasn't laid any eggs in it.'

'I'm glad you came,' and miraculously, my aunt smiled.

Katharina lifted her friend's head above the pillow and began brushing the matted hair with surprisingly gentle strokes.

'Of course I came,' she soothed, 'as soon as Johannes wrote to say you were ill, I caught the very next coach.'

Nannerl observed her friend in her first show of genuine interest, knowing that Katharina could never make any journey without considerable time being lavished on the preparations.

'You seem cheerful enough to me, Anna Maria,' insisted Katharina in a mocking voice. 'You're allowing me to pull at your dreadful hair and here was I expecting you to be in tears at least.'

'If I could be bothered to feel anything I would.' Nannerl was returning to her morose mood. 'I can't feel anything. I don't even mind your pulling at my hair and I don't mind if I go on lying here forever. I don't really care.'

Katharina understood her friend well enough to accept that this might be true so she changed her strategy. 'Very well,' she said brusquely, releasing her hold on Nannerl's neck and restoring the brush to the cupboard drawer. 'I'll go home then.'

Nannerl was silent and when Katharina turned round she saw the corners of her friend's eyes were wet. She sat down beside her again, kissing her on her clammy forehead, catching the small, fluttering hands like moths' wings and pressing them both against her cheek, holding them there for several seconds before carefully rearranging them on the bed, pinning them down with her own hands so they were forced to be still.

'But I'm forgetting that I can't leave right now because I've let the coach go already and besides, I promised the children I'd go for a walk by the lake with them. So my dear Nannerl, you are obliged to have me here a little while longer.'

'I'm sorry,' Nannerl removed her hands from underneath Katharina's, rubbing her eyes with the backs of her wrists.

'Well then, that's that then.' Katharina sounded pleased. 'When I come back from the walk, you will have recovered from the shock of my arrival – it was a shock, wasn't it my darling?' Nannerl nodded as Katharina picked up her thread again. 'I asked Johannes to say nothing at all to anyone about my coming because I knew if I gave you half a chance to think about it, you would have said no. I'm right about that too aren't I my sweet?'

'No,' said Nannerl, wondering why, if the purpose of her friend's visit was to cheer her up, she suddenly felt gloomy again. 'I don't know if I would have said anything at all. I have been asleep most of the time.'

'I'm not surprised you'd want to sleep all day if you had to stay in this room. Why you don't sleep in your own room my dear, I cannot imagine. This is ridiculous purgatory.'

Nannerl turned back to the wall to avoid the smell of musk that clung to her friend. Katharina bent down to kiss the back of her hair, leaving the room in a peal of talk.

'I'll be back my darling – with fresh trout from the mountain, which Andra will catch with his bare hands. Marianna will instruct Monica how it is to be cooked and I will show you the latest fichu I have bought with silk trimmings – and my darling, if you like it, it is yours. There! You are warned.' She left without closing the door and Nannerl could hear her laughter as she hurried down the corridor mixed in with the sounds of excited children calling out 'Katharina' and 'Fräulein Gilowska'.

'Hurry up!' 'We're waiting for you.' The sounds drifted away and Nannerl felt the loneliness of her room once more in the silence that followed.

'I wish I were dead, I want Mama,' she said aloud just as her stepdaughter slipped into the room and placed some flowers in a vase on top of the cupboard. The scent of poppies drowned any smell of human sweat and lingering musk. Marianna was unnaturally angelic and it seemed the more she was ignored by Nannerl, the more she tried to please her stepmother.

'I don't remember my first Mama, just the second one,' she remarked. There was nothing cloying or sentimental about the way she said it – just the matter-of-fact sound of a child trying to interest an adult.

'If you would like me to feel ashamed of myself, you're succeeding Marianna.'

Marianna covered her swollen throat with her whole hand. She seemed nervous and anxious as she sat down beside the bed, tucking her feet neatly under her skirt. Nannerl knew she had come to sit with her just as she had done every other day since she had first slept in the room. The child was undoubtedly a saint. What do you say to a saint? Go away because you make me feel inadequate? Or Liebling, go and play with the other children and let me be sick in peace? She suddenly opened her arms out to the child and hugged her for what seemed a long time.

'Can you help me to get dressed, Marianna?' She detached herself gently and placed both feet on the cold floorboards. 'I must be out of this room before Katharina starts scolding me again.'

The child arranged her stepmother's hair so that it fell against the light from the unshuttered window, waving in a mote of dust. She wanted her new mama to be well again. She wanted this more than her father, more than the maid skulking in the kitchen, more than her brothers, more than Katharina, more than anyone because above all she longed for straightforward peace and a sense of continuity in their lives.

Leaning heavily against Marianna, Nannerl walked down a path to some trees that stood like giant umbrellas at the end of the garden. She felt the rasp of cloth against the side of her breasts as the material of her dress stretched and sagged when she walked. A trickle of milk ran down the inside of her dress and she thought about the child she had given away to her own father. As mother and daughter, they sat in the black shade of the branches on a mound of pebbles and stared out across the lake. They were quite content saying nothing to each other and listening to the occasional sound of fish popping on the surface of the water or the waves coming into the shore. They were waiting for the return of Katharina and the other children. Neither was in a hurry to have them back.

———————

Her friend stayed for three whole weeks, not six, and Sonnenburg was pleased when Fräulein Gilowska and his wife announced they would not go to Gastein for the waters. Katharina had gone home with a chorus of 'Don't go's' and 'Come back soon's' following the wheels of her coach for at least three minutes. But if his wife and children were sorry to see her go, he was relieved. Her high spirits and easy intimacy with Nannerl had begun to grate. It was not that he was jealous of the friendship or the easy intimacy but he found the constancy of both was noisy and wearing. His relief was greatest, when one ordinary summer's day, his wife resumed her household duties and her daily practice at the clavier, which he took as a sign that she was properly recovered. In a sense he was right and I was reminded of my grandmother's similar reaction to her daughter's illness while the family was living at Hannibal Platz.

As the milk dried inside her, the balance of Nannerl's nature seemed to have been restored. She made an effort to play with the children and read them stories. Marianna became her pupil at the keyboard and was showing signs of talent, which made Sonnenburg feel more secure about his own musical provenance. He even noticed that his wife's vacant stare had disappeared when she was in company, although he did not realise it sometimes returned when she was alone with enough time for introspection.

As she began to make an effort with the children, so she did with him. In the course of one of their musical evenings or after a civilized game of cards, she would make a great fuss about seeking his opinion on everything. Had she played the adagio of her sonata too fast or too loud? Was she wise in her strategy, given the hand she had been dealt in their last game of cards? Was there a want of feeling in the way she had tackled the rondo? Would he prefer his supper to be brought to him in his study when he was absorbed by affairs of the parish? And as she fussed over him and listened seriously to what he had to say about the worthy burghers of Saint Gilgen, he found himself liking her so much better than before. Her thoughts were more logically presented and her suggestions for how to settle the squabbles of the town were really quite sensible.

He noticed too that she was taking more trouble with her appearance, something he regretted she had not bothered to do since the first months of their marriage. This was, he decided, one of the better influences of Katharina Gilowska and because of this, he encouraged her fondness for pretty things by giving her some of the jewellery that belonged to his former wives. She displayed the more extravagant of these baubles at the soirées where visitors who came all the way from Salzburg were unlikely to have seen her in such finery before. His satisfaction was complete when the Abbé Bullinger had taken him aside to tell him confidentially that marriage had improved her looks.

As Nannerl controlled her desire to look inside herself, she became more cheerful and less judgmental. She no longer flinched when her husband repeated the last words of someone's sentence and she smiled when he cleared his throat before converting a thought into a speech. On the nights when he approached her in her bed, instead of removing herself to the other side, she stirred his interest further by curling her body like a spoon around his. He was surprised how often he found himself desiring her when only a few months before he had not only regretted the marriage but prayed to God in his darkest moments that she would die in childbirth.

FUGUE 7

'Whoah, ease up there, whoah now!' cried Karl who was feeling each jerk of the coach in his ribs and was pulling hard on the reins, cursing the postillion at the same time. A final lurch before the coach stopped short of a tree and everyone climbed out. Karl closed the wayward door and noticed that one of the back wheels was broken. He kicked at the loose spokes to make the point to the other drivers.

'It's no surprise,' said Otto. 'What do you expect when you cart bodies all over the country by night time then?'

'Sun's up Otto. If you ask me, it's just bad luck – and don't start blaming me neither,' said Franz, the postillion, looking defiantly at Karl. 'I didn't see the bend for all them trees.'

'Well, we haven't got a spare wheel,' continued Otto. 'Do we sit here and wait for another coach to come by?'

'No,' said the passenger, startling the coachmen with his vehemence as he climbed over the coffin to get out.

'But what to do?' asked Franz who was staring up at this strange giant with the awe of someone who feels permanently dwarfed. 'We can't move without a new wheel,' he added. His eyes swivelled across the length of the man's coat, silently reckoning there would be enough material to make two for himself.

'Mend it,' replied the passenger, climbing back into the coach and drawing the leather curtains that were hung on either side of the windows until he could no longer be seen.

'You heard him,' said Karl. 'We can bind the broken parts in front of the wheel with a bit of wood from those trees over there. Then it won't run away.'

And they set to work and did it all, chopping and sawing like a team of cartwrights, despite Otto's gloomy predictions that it wouldn't hold.

Chapter 14

PASSE-PIED

'I'm a haughty, wicked rascal, though not ruined by venereal disease as luck would have it, but a man who affects severity of manners and at the same time keeps a mistress. I refer to Nandl Heller, the maid. I admire her legerdemain, her worth. She stitches linen, she washes it, she gives suck, she cooks, she sits down at table and makes easy, cheerful conversation to this very rascal. When she rises, the table is cleared, the dishes are cleaned, order is restored without obvious huffing and puffing and it is then she returns to be with me, to play the clarinet comme une ange or to sing one of my son's arias in a voice as sweet as honey. In all this, she gives pleasure. Only a juggler could achieve as much, or my dearest wife who did the same and more, but is dead.'

Leopold opened his eyes without shifting so much as a hair from where he lay and watched the face next to him. Nandl Heller appeared to be asleep and he could feel her breath on his cheeks and see the stirring of dark hairs inside her nostrils. An arm was flung at right angles to her body and except for her face, was all that remained visible. Leopold smiled at the ceiling like a starved man after a feast and patted his stomach. He savoured the fantasy that he was young again and that the child sleeping at the other end of the room belonged to them both. Yes, there was his grandson to be considered. Even catching the child's waste in a pint-pot was a joy to the old man and since his curiosity about everything was limitless, he never failed in the most quotidian tasks.

'Nandl,' he whispered into her ear. 'It is time.' He wanted to wake her up and watch her feed Leopoldl from those swollen melon breasts but as she yawned and unbuttoned the top of her nightdress, he buried his long nose between them in a sudden fit of geriatric lust. His mouth trembled with greed and longing to swallow the hard brown tip of a nipple that was tickling his hair. As if she understood what he was thinking, this paragon of his invention turned very slightly so that the mound rocked tantalisingly against his lips. 'Oh my dear,' he sighed and found himself moaning as he sucked convulsively across every inch of her exposed flesh. He wished he were not so old and rheumatic or that he could find the strength to lie with her again and again and again to prolong the ecstasy that always took him by surprise. Instead, he was overcome by another more feasible urge to murmur somewhere just below her throat:

> 'Here I am at last
> Riding on my own sweet whore
> In common game
> Despite my shame
> I wonder why
> It took so long
> To start this hanky-panky?'

Nandl Heller sprang from the bed, grabbed Leopoldl from his cot and held him tightly in front of her with folded arms as she ran to the other end of the room and back again. 'Vile, revolting and vomitous,' she railed in false fury. There was no way Leopold could hobble up close to her without squashing the child in the process. The baby twisted, wept and kicked, eyes blinking, uncertain where to focus. There was so much jigging and shaking going on above and around him, his pink, slippery legs shot out from underneath his blanket and pumped the air. It was becoming his regular exercise.

'What have I done wrong?' demanded Leopold, looking foolish and disingenuous.

'You offended me,' but she was laughing as she struggled to quieten the child.

'How? With my rough verse or my prick?'

'So you call it verse, you feeble old man. I call it disgusting nonsense and I daresay you think you can get away with it because this is how you treat your maids.' It was an odd remark as Frau Heller no longer saw herself as one.

'Do I have a harem then? Hmmm? Do you really believe I'm in the habit of bedding all the servants who come and go in this apartment? Do you suppose I am familiar with Berthe, eh? I suppose you do. Well then, good grief! You are wrong. Why you underestimate your effect on an old man.

I care for none other.' A faint inkling of remorse and fear had crept into his voice as he knelt before her, despite his arthritis, missing the smile that crept around the corners of her mouth. 'I'm sorry Liebling. Truly sorry,' he wept. 'I know I'm a wicked old rascal but I have never … never thought such a thing.' His voice had become hoarse and he was unable to continue, realising he was afraid of losing her, unable to bear the thought. Disturbed sleep. Recurrent nightmares of inconsolable loneliness. Not much point to hanging on. He hauled himself back onto the edge of the bed because that was the easiest way to get there, lowered his head into his hands and sobbed. Frau Heller, baby tucked over one shoulder, bent down until her face was almost level with his, removing his hands with her free one, very gently covering his wet cheeks with tiny butterfly kisses. She had no illusions about her place in his scheme of things. While she was not exactly cunning in a venal, unforgivable way, whatever she did was calculated for its effect and her survival, as it was now.

There was also the matter of her magpie's eye, which I had observed a number of times even if Leopold had not. It was more straightforward cupidity than venality where she was attracted to pretty things like pearl buttons or that occasionally this attraction made her light-fingered. She would, whenever she could, go straight to a box of jewels on a chest of drawers beside Leopold's bed. These were the baubles of the late Frau Mozart, which she knew he intended for Nannerl. The widow liked to take them out of their box and try them on when no one else was around. There was one particular garnet ring that caught her eye and she was pleased it fitted the middle finger of her right hand as if it had been made for her. It was this ring, above all the others in the box, which conveyed to her what she had never had.

'You are forgiven,' she said coquettishly to Leopold, slowly drawing a pattern of circles in the palms of his hands with her fingernail. 'I don't believe you, not at all, not one bit, but you are forgiven.' Out of the blue she added, and how he wished it had been irrelevantly, 'Jakob Hofmann admires you very much.'

Leopold studied the woman crouching next to him. 'How well do you know Jakob, my dear?' The stains from his tears had dried in streaks against his powdered cheeks and he looked both vulnerable and old.

Nandl Heller tried hard to remember the degree to which she might have lied or avoided the truth about her other life. She herself did not seem to know how much was the result of fact or invention. After a brief silence, she shrugged her shoulders, jolting the baby who was promptly sick across her shoulder.

'I'm not as close a friend as you are to him, because you are his teacher,' she answered, wiping away the clots of milk from the back of her neck as if this were a daily occurrence. 'We meet from time to time. It would seem we have much in common.' She looked so pleasant and unconcerned as she turned away to smooth young Leopold's back with her neat, rhythmical strokes.

'I expect there are many people in Salzburg who know Hofmann.' My grandfather sniffed the scent of his mistress on his palms, his eyes following her around the room. He could not remember if Nandl had been at home when the draper came for a violin lesson the day before yesterday. In the depth of his brittle bones he was not sure he believed her, and in his mind, he pictured his mistress being fondled by Jakob Hofmann in some attic room on the outskirts of the city. He was not quite sure why he had put them there, except that he saw both as rootless travellers, a desolate and unfathomable pair, walking back and forth, back and forth together. The image in his mind was so vivid it caused him pain. He would not share her with anyone, as he would not and could not his son and daughter with the trivial or boring, unexceptional people they had married. The more he imagined her in Hofmann's presence, the more he suffered irrepressible jealousy. She and little Leopold, they both belonged with him did they not? He had been so lonely after Nannerl had left. And now . . . His lower lip would not stop trembling. To calm himself he leant his face very close to hers and kissed her on the end of her nose as a fish spits out a stone. Such thoughts were in and out of his soul when she lowered the child into his cot. 'Of course, I have no proof.'

Leopold was no different from his daughter. They were each fanciful or pessimistic in matters of the heart. They were also fond of imagining what had not been proved. Thus Nandl Heller was in a position of enigmatic power and Jakob Hofmann would continue to behave when they met as if nothing was amiss. I had my own ideas on all these matters because I saw what was going on from my secret hiding place. It is fair to say that Frau Heller did remain a mistress to my grandfather for quite some time and that out of fear of losing her, he asked no questions about her past. Nor was he ever aware that she wrote a letter to Jakob Hofmann when he was in Prague, in which she said:

Dear Friend,

Let me tell you what your teacher does when I am busy as I know it will interest you. He gets up at nine, puts on a sumptuous dressing gown, plays determinedly like a child himself with Leopoldl until ten, then idly with the dog until ten thirty, practises his violin until twelve, providing Leopoldl and I are out of the apartment, then dresses to spend several hours at the card table of Hagenauer or Doctor Barisani, who's here from Vienna. He may sleep at one of their houses until suppertime, after which he frequently strikes bargains on behalf of his son-in-law with either the sale of the baron's jewellery or perhaps one of his own musical instruments. When he is filled with fine wine and venison with currant jelly, he is carried on a chair back to home and bed. Sleep well and I look forward to your next violin lesson and discussions of important matters in music with Herr Mozart,

These thoughts from your newly acquired cousin,

— *Nandl Heller.*

P.S. I have been vexed by some ideas of philosophy. You once said to Herr Mozart that all black souls are redeemable. You might have added that not all souls are redeemed. I am of course grateful to you for what you have done for me since I came into your life. I cannot thank you enough for the arrangements you made on my behalf with the help of Herr Metzger. Now you must claim something back from me in return. You must choose what it will be. That way, I can surely find redemption, which would be a good thing since I am such a sinner. — *N.H.*

The truth is out. Frau Heller and Herr Hofmann, as well as looking quite like each other, are indeed distant cousins, a fact they discovered when they met at an extended family gathering in Frankfurt. Forget the improbability, think of the pain of these two people who by birth and soon by events in later life, were obliged to shift from town to town, scrabbling for a living and hiding from their past for most of their days because they had a wanderlust. I can see why Nandl Heller was drawn to thoughts of black souls and Christian concepts of salvation. I do not mean she was referring to any lies she may have peddled to survive outside the ghetto walls or that she was hoping for forgiveness if she led a pious life according to the New Testament. I happen to believe she had an insatiable appetite for ideas and dreams and found stimulus in philosophical discussion with Hofmann. She was no ordinary maid. Nor was she a straightforward, calculating whore who sold her body for a dubious security. Her affair with Leopold Mozart is best explained by saying they were in mutual need of consolation at the same time. How often that is the way. Both of them, lonely, available and clever. The arrangement hurt no one.

Though Nannerl recovered from her illness, she either failed to notice or refused to admit the affair between Frau Cow and her father, while her husband, Baron Sonnenburg, said nothing on the subject because he was uncertain there was a relationship to be observed. He was touchingly grateful that their child was being groomed to become a prodigy and regularly in a way he had never done before, sent greetings and small gifts of pomade or wine to his father-in-law. Throughout all this eventful time, Leopold sustained his passion for his grandson and made a point of recording each stage of his development.

Salzburg, 11th November, 1785

My darling girl,

I look at the child's fingers and I am moved without fail. The most gifted pianist cannot place his hand so beautifully on the keyboard as Leopoldl holds his by custom. Often he doesn't move the fingers. Often, when asleep in particular, they are placed in the playing position.

The hands lie in such a way as if the fingers were touching the keys. Imagine the most natural relaxation and curve of those fingers. In short, one could not see anything more beautiful. When I admire him through my tears, I wish he were three years old tomorrow, so that he would be ready to play.

— *Your loving Papa.*

Salzburg, 29ᵗʰ December, 1785

My dearest Nannerl,

Leopoldl is full of joy and mischief, in his LOOK, his EARS, his FINGERS and in his cherub's ASS. He shits and pisses with some accuracy while sitting on a decorated chamber pot . . . I love him completely and without reservation.

— *Your devoted and grateful Papa*

27th to 28th January, 1786

Dear daughter,

Thank you for the shirts and linen, which you sent for Leopoldl. They suit him admirably . . . Now I have some interesting news. I haven't yet introduced him to a VIOLIN but I performed a careful test with a BRASS CANDLESTICK, where I played PIANISSIMO one minute and FORTE the next. I accomplished this with the beat of a small key on the RIM and all the time was singing with it. At the sounds he became so still and attentive that he could not draw his eyes from me; his feet, his hands, his fingers would normally be in constant movement but at these times they were motionless . . . People could try to interrupt but it had no effect in distracting him from his fascination. In short, he never moved while looking at the candlestick and his grandfather.

— *Your loving Papa*

Sometime between February and March, 1786

Dear Daughter and Herr Son,

In confidence, for I would prefer your brother and his wife not to know of my ideas just yet, I write the following and this I say to you: I shall keep little Leopold at my side, long after I have taught him his alphabet and how to read his letters. (It is true that he already knows the difference between his 'A' and 'B!')

I wish him to remain here for as long as I live. This was my intention from his birth and so my plan persists in all its original resoluteness. When it is summer, I will bring him to you with Nandl for a short time but then he shall return with me . . . I pray that Leopold will stay here for as long as I am patch-worthy and able to maintain him. God sees into my best reasons and the fate of all of us lies in His hands . . .

— Your Devoted Father

Six months or so after this letter, Wolfgang heard that Nannerl's son was being brought up by Leopold in Salzburg while Nannerl remained in Saint Gilgen. I think – no I am sure – he felt badly about this. Here was his sister's child for his own father to love and educate simultaneously. But what about HIS children? Why not love them, teach them, choose the books they should read, determine their precise pleasures, turn them into prodigies and give them iron-black powders when they had sore throats? My father's solution was direct. He would ask my grandfather to take care of his two sons while he and my mother travelled through Europe. But my grandfather refused point blank and wrote the following crusty, adamantine letter to my aunt, not knowing that as he wrote it, the baby who had been named after him and was a Mozart by name, had died two days before.

Salzburg, 17th November, 1786

Dear Daughter,

I have had to reply to a letter from your brother, and as this took me an unexpected time, I will now be brief. I also am off to the play today, as I have a free pass, and have only this minute completed that letter to Vienna. You can imagine how determinedly I had to express my opinions when I tell you that your brother and Constanze have asked me to take charge of their two children. All this has come about because he is planning a journey through Germany to England in the next carnival. It would seem he has heard from Herr Müller, the silhouette maker that I am looking after Leopoldl. I had never said so much as a peep about it. But the good Herr Müller was praising my pedagogical brilliance to my son – as if he needs reminding – and this gave either him or his wife, the brilliant idea that I might do the same for his offspring. Pah! The circumstances are very different indeed. But I wrote in some detail why this was not possible and added that I would send him the rest of my letter in the next post. Can you imagine it? As if Nandl and I are not busy enough. They could disappear for months or decide to remain in England and I would be expected to send Leopoldl back to you and follow them abroad with the children. As for the payment which he offers to cover my possible expenses in all this, well, basta!

Before this uncomfortable conflict of interest with his children's children and ever since his summer visit to Saint Gilgen, Nandl Heller noticed Leopold had become quite frail. There is nothing like a mixture of guilt and disappointment to make one ill. He complained of humming noises in his head which made violin playing a sticky business, and while he had always been something of a windy old tomcat, she realised his digestive problems were becoming serious. At about the time when he was regularly complaining that Wolfgang Mozart, (never 'my son'), had not sent him a single letter of the alphabet, Nandl consulted Doctor Barisani. Blockage of the spleen was diagnosed and despite the lavish attentions of his mistress, a new maid called Lisel and the late arrival of his beloved daughter to show daughterly love, it became obvious that he was slowly dying. In consolation, he dreamt about his grandson the way he had once dreamt about his son.

'Again I say, I will return Leopoldl to you only when he can take my hand and lead me to your door and play the fiddle to your clavier and then I will sit and listen to such music that would make your brother weep in recollection. I am blessed with a child who is always obedient, if only he hears my voice or name . . . '

Nannerl was pleased that Leopoldl gave her father the will to live, but despite even this incentive, my grandfather proved he was not immortal by dying on the 28th May 1787 at the age of sixty-seven. Berthe retired to the convent while Nandl Heller was instructed to bring Leopoldl back home to Saint Gilgen. Instead of becoming a wunderkind, my aunt's son – my cousin, became a lieutenant in the army, and after that a customs officer in Austria and Bavaria!

Now I reflect on it, I'm glad my grandfather was spared the knowledge that my relative was a perfectly ordinary child, and that he did not become the second Mozart, making my current position untenable. I'm sorry Auntie, but it does not say much for the hothouse hypothesis, although, to be fair to Leopoldl, he was only about three years old when grandpa died. Not enough time perhaps to shape another genius in the family.

And in the aftermath of death, in that gloomy vacuum left by the absent figure, there came the murky letters of a brother to a sister on contemplating their inheritance:

Vienna, 2nd June, 1787

Dearest Sister!

Believe me, I feel the loss of our father as profoundly as you. The pain that I experienced when I learnt of his sudden death was insupportable. Unfortunately I cannot leave Vienna at the moment, though how I wish we could embrace. As my presence is unnecessary for the overseeing of our late father's estate, I share your opinion that it is wise to have a public auction. However, before it happens, I would appreciate the chance to see the official inventory of his effects that I may choose a few mementoes.

For this purpose, I enclose a letter for our dear friend, Herr d'Yppold, that he may represent me in these matters where there is a need.

Farewell Dearest Sister,

— *W.A. Mozart*

Saint Gilgen, 7th June, 1787

Dearest brother!

We both wish to share our grief in each other's presence, but I understand that you cannot leave Vienna. It was the other way around when Mama died. You were on your own with her and far away from us, just as this time, I was here with Papa and far away from you. It's always difficult to grieve at a distance.

I'm glad we agree that a public auction of our father's estate is practical under the circumstances and I'm also certain any inventory of his effects would show there is nothing to interest you there. Papa had already sold most of the snuffboxes, fine clocks, jewelled toothpicks etc. from our travels. As for Mama's jewellery, I must say he gave it all to me a short while before he died.

I have delivered your letter to Herr d'Yppold as requested. I remain your loving sister in great haste, because I want you to receive these words by the next post.   — *A-M.*

Vienna, 16th June, 1787

My Dear Sister,

I understand why you did not write to me sooner to tell me of my father's death. May God protect our father's dear departed soul so that he may rest in peace. Be assured my good sister that I wish to protect you at all times and if you were in need I would wish to leave you everything with the greatest pleasure. But you are not and my little family is at this moment as I write. Since the property would be of no use to you but would be greatly so to me, I regard it as my duty to put my wife and child first.

— *Your devoted brother, W.A.*

Saint Gilgen, 23rd June, 1787

Dearest, most beloved brother!

It is quite natural you should consider the needs of your wife and child and therefore, my dear brother, I am anxious you should know that I also am considering them. My husband has suggested you might accept a fair percentage of the monies that accrue from the auction in lieu of a few personal effects, such as my mother's jewel box etc., which are of no great financial value and which would come to me . . . When I die, these may be divided equally between your children and mine. Please do not forget to send me your latest compositions for clavier as I am running out of new music to play at soirées in Saint Gilgen!

Your most affectionate sister,

— *A-M Sonnenburg*

Vienna, 1st August, 1787

Dearest, most beloved sister!

For the moment I am writing practically nothing at all as I am so busy. It is not just my brother-in-law but I also, who am anxious to

settle these affairs as quickly as possible. I accept his offer for that
reason. However, I expect to be paid the agreed thousand gulden
in Viennese currency and not in Imperial. I would also like it to
be a bill of exchange. In the next post I will send your husband the
draft of a contract between us and after that, two original copies of
agreement, one signed by me, the other which he will sign. When
I have a minute to do so, I will send you some new compositions I
have written for clavier. Please do not forget to send me my scores as
requested. A thousand farewells from my wife and son Karl are sent
to you and your husband. I remain your sincerely loving brother,

— *W.A. Mozart*

Vienna, 29th September, 1787

My Dear Berthold,

Forgive my haste. I am most pleased by our arrangement and
would ask you to address the bill of exchange to Herr Michael
Puchberg, care of Count Walsegg in the High Market. This is
because I will be in Prague as from this coming Monday. Please kiss
my beloved sister a thousand times on behalf of my family and be
assured I remain your devoted brother-in-law.

— *W.A. Mozart*

Saint Gilgen, 10th December, 1787

My dear Wolfgang,

Perhaps your maid is pocketing the money you gave her to
post your letters! The Barisanis, d'Yppold, the Gilowskas and your
beloved sister are all complaining that you have not written to them.
Not a word. I implore you to write as soon as you can to your old
horse face and your friends in Salzburg. Greetings to your wife and
to my nephew Karl . . .

Your ever devoted sister,

— *A.M. von Sonnenburg*

Vienna, 19th December, 1787

Dearest Sister,

I do beg your forgiveness for having not written sooner.

Don Giovanni was a great success in Prague but I gather that you may have heard this already. What you may not have heard is that the Emperor has given me a position with an income that surpasses my colleagues I think.

Will you please send me the box of scores I have asked for at your earliest convenience?

As for recent clavier music, I would ask you to write down a list of names for those pieces you already have so that I do not send you double copies. This will be of advantage to us both.

Well I must stop writing and say farewell my dear Nannerl. Write to me often and if I don't answer straightaway, please understand that it is not indifference but the distractions of work that are the cause. I embrace you many times and send much affection to your family from my wife, who is about to be confined at any moment.

Yours most affectionately,

— *W. A. Mozart*

My own sister, Theresia Mozart, was duly born eight days after the above letter had been written on the 27th December, 1787. To my parents' great distress, she only lived another six months. When I have wanted to torture myself, which is not such a rare occurrence, I have imagined that this was the child who would have inherited my father's talent as well as his likeness and that God took pity on me and organised her death so I could live without the shadow of a genius both in front of me and from behind. The world has lost out on this one I'm afraid. I remain Franz Xaver Mozart's younger and surviving son.

I should point out that I was born some three and a half years after the death of Theresia and around five months before my father's death. Some slanderous, cowardly souls have hinted that my real father was Mozart's pupil, Süssmayr. How do they know? This is the Franz Xaver Süssmayr who would complete my father's Requiem on my mother's instructions. This is the same Süssmayr who imitated my father's hand so well that even she could not tell the difference. It was he who kept my mother company on a cure in Baden when she was awaiting my birth. This had been, she explained, an act of great kindness and practicality. Out of gratitude, she and father called me after him. That is all there is to that. Of course I am the true son of Amadeus.

Nannerl had shrugged her shoulders at the offhand reference to Constanze's confinement. 'How did we come to this? We were once so close. I will send him his old box of scores and I will write to him, but in my heart, I fear he won't bother to reply.' She was nearly reconciled to the coldness of her brother's words and to their cause, which she took to be a mixture of Constanze's influence plus a certain resentment on her brother's part about the disbursal of their late father's estate.

She was right about the pattern of their correspondence. He made the odd reply to her dutiful notelets and after a while, they both stopped bothering to enquire about each other at least in letters. Their grief about their father was played out in different ways except in one respect. They both found consolation in composition. For Mozart, there was a great deal of guilt, but there was also some relief that he was no longer answerable to his father's demands, some regret that he had not been with him at the end and natural grief that his father had died at all. What was interesting was the way he threw himself into an unstoppable whirr of work to heal the wounds, which was not just because he wanted to earn money.

Looking back on it, I am convinced the spirit of Leopold badgered my father like Hamlet's ghost. Nannerl had less to feel guilty about and was not haunted in any way as she also picked up her pen to compose. The difference was that her music was being hidden in the bottom drawer or burnt in the stove while her brother's was being constantly performed and increasingly admired. She never expected it to be otherwise. Nor had Leopold, and that was the pus in the pimple. She beavered away at her songs, privately gripped by the music and the words, a better Hausfrau in fact because she was happy.

Nandl Heller returned to the convent, which had also given shelter to the elderly Berthe Salz. In return for food and lodgings, this time she taught the novitiates how to read music. Although she had been reluctant to say goodbye to the child, Leopoldl, she weaned him without fuss and he hardly noticed her absence from his life. His half-sister Marianna played with him and made him laugh and wiped his knees when he fell over and kissed him when she put him to bed and soon he was toddling round the heels of his older brothers in perfect contentment. It was quite the opposite for Nandl Heller who missed both her Leopolds and had imaginary conversations with each one after prayers at Vespers. She would talk to them and make up their replies as she admired the garnet ring on her middle finger in the privacy of her room. The act of Christian worship never seriously bothered her conscience. She found its rituals brought comfort and she was too practical to sacrifice the sense of peace it gave her for a principle.

Throughout this time, Nannerl wrote regularly to inform her of Leopoldl's progress in everything except music, (since there was none). On the anniversary of her father's death she unpicked her share of the mother-of-pearl buttons that had been stitched quite impractically onto the edge of a pillowcase. She now stitched them again onto a piece of card and sent it as a gift to Frau Heller. Receipt was slow to be acknowledged, but when the bread and butter note eventually arrived, expressed in grateful tones, Nannerl believed that a barrier between them had been removed.

As for Sonnenburg, he was relieved that his wife's vapours seemed to have completely disappeared and for the next two years there was peace at Saint Gilgen until one icy March morning in 1789, Nannerl gave birth to a second child, Johanna Maria Anne Elisabeth Berchtold zu Sonnenburg or Jeanette for short. Nandl Heller was summoned to Saint Gilgen once more.

Fugue 8

Dear Hofmann,

Since birth I have been deformed and trapped by another's pity or contempt, and for that matter, by my own dislike. But of all men under a German sky, at least on this night I am the proudest man alive. Lying on the floor of this coach right next to him has helped. The hardness of the floor keeps my thoughts alert and I am, to my amazement, composing this letter on the surface of his coffin. For my paper to literally rest upon it and receive something of his spirit from within has done me much good. I have curled myself into a position which under normal circumstances would give severe cramp to a person of my size, but these are not normal circumstances. I feel joy that I am the one who is bringing him back to Salzburg and for that dear Hofmann, I must thank you with all my heart.

It has been violent travel for much of the journey and now one of the wheels of the coach is being repaired by the drivers as I write. We were tumbling down a hill and about to turn a sharp corner in the road when we got caught in a deep hole and the horses were unable to pull the wagon out. The wheel is badly damaged and the men have been lashing the broken parts of it together with some sapling they lopped from the side of the road. It's fair to say they are a rough lot but not altogether bad, I think. They know they are transporting a dead man but not who he is, which is the way I intend to keep it. I will write to you at your address in Vienna and let you know the details of delivery and other relevant facts when the journey is completed.

I remain your good friend,

— Joseph Metzger

Chapter 15

FANTAISIE

Nandl Heller's milk had dried soon after the weaning of Leopold and no amount of sucking by the new baby would alter this state. Although Nannerl herself produced vast quantities of milk, the problem was that her nipples refused to be drawn out. The child became weaker for being robbed of its due until finally an alternative wet nurse was found who succeeded. To the relief of everyone involved, the baby thrived and slept but Nandl Heller was mortified because she thought she had failed.

As for Nannerl, within a week of giving birth to her daughter, she became a remote creature who avoided being in the same room as her child. There would be the feigned tiredness when everyone else around her was clamouring to rock the baby in the cot and at the same time she was reluctant to hold her in her arms because it made her breasts ache. It is true they were engorged and full of lumps and that one particular night when the pain was unbearable she kept on screaming until Nandl Heller came running. Sonnenburg had just enough time to light the candlesticks when the widow knocked on their bedroom door.

'Herr Baron, I think I can help.' Sonnenburg stepped aside and waved her in.

'You will stay with my wife then?' he asked nervously.

He was privately ashamed of the sad creature thrashing in his bed and was afraid the misery and the pain were somehow his fault. He bowed self-consciously to Nandl Heller and accidentally touched her arm with his as he left the room. He remembered that the widow had been his father-in-law's whore and he shook so violently at the memory that the candles in his hand went out. Alone in the corridor, he leant against the wall and listened to the sounds of his wife's gibberish above the low murmerings of Frau Heller.

'There my dear. There. It's all right now. I promise.'

'Big andez andandlight . . . '

'God help us,' said Sonnenburg to no one but himself in the darkness.

He entered the room where his sons were sleeping, climbed into bed along-side Karl Franz and Andra Averlinus and while they slept, prayed fitfully through the night until morning. He'd never felt so hopeless or disturbed.

'I'll rub the pain away,' whispered Nandl Heller. She said it over and over again as if the repetition into Nannerl's ears would soothe away the pain. Pressing, massaging, pummelling, stroking the swollen lumps that were hardened with clotted milk. 'Rub, rub, rub it away,' she crooned like one of the witches in Macbeth.

'Rub, rub, rub the pain away,' she said more softly than before, and bent down low to kiss my aunt in the hollow of her throat. Nannerl lay still for a moment as if the kiss had caught her by surprise and then the awful thrashing began again. Her eyes were fluttering like someone in the middle of a fit. There were no words, just a stream of nonsense syllables and occasionally a wail that curled up and down as I imagine a wolf bays at the moon. Sonnenburg could hear it from his room. Marianna heard it and covered her head with her pillow to drown out the sound. The wet-nurse heard it in her sleep and thought it was a wild boar. The boys heard nothing because it was more comfortable that way.

'Milk fever,' murmered Nandl Heller as she sprinkled water from a jug onto Nannerl's forehead. Nonsense I thought. It's my aunt's way of behaving whenever she's distressed.

'I'll rub until the lumps have softened,' the widow sang, pounding and squeezing the flesh with her thumbs and fingers and expecting Nannerl to understand what she was saying. 'There my darling. You see? It's coming. The milk is coming. A drop or two. Yes, definitely on its way. Rub – rub – rub the pain away.' I saw with amazement that Nandl Heller's breasts underneath her nightgown were wet and that my aunt's were dry, dry, dry and looking as if they would swell until they burst there was so much milk locked up inside them.

They remained as marble for two or three agonising days. Throughout this time, Nandl Heller behaved more like a servant than she had ever been before. The way she spoke, the rhyming litany, the endearments, the bossiness and the impulsive intimacy were the paraphanalia of a nurse who seemed devoted to her mistress. There was something sensual in the way she tended to my aunt, almost as if she were exploiting the illness because it legitimised the intimacy. For a brief while I almost forgot that Frau Heller had been Leopold's last doxie, that she had a magpie's eye for a garnet ring and pearl buttons, that she had once caught the admiring attention of Jakob Hofmann as well as the nuns in the convent, that she was a widow who had allegedly given birth to two or three children, (supposedly long dead, although no one knew this for certain apart from Frau Heller herself), and that she played the clarinet like an angel. I still don't know if she really plays her instrument like a dog since it is always locked in a brown leather case in her room and at no point did I hear her playing in the presence of Leopold or anyone else at any time.

'Rub a dub dub, three souls in a tub and who do you think they were? The servant, the draper, the unknown composer. So that's who they were.'

Exhausted by pain or maternal dementia, my aunt had at last fallen asleep and Nandl Heller was rocking back and forth on an old, creaking nursing chair next to the bed. I could see her smiling through the shadows of candlelight as she slipped her hands inside the slit of her nightgown, pressing and kneading her own breasts and revelling in every fresh rivulet which seeped through the linen. I knew then that as soon as morning came, the new wet-nurse would be dismissed and Frau Heller would take Jeanette to her bosom.

There was a pattern to the nature of my aunt's illnesses. It seemed predictable that Nannerl would recover both her spirits and her sanity when the fever passed and her milk was finished or when any other physical reminder of childbirth had disappeared apart from the child. Although Sonnenburg did not forget he had been worried about his wife's health, he stopped thinking about it most of the time, or if he did, he chose to believe her low spirits were caused by grief at the loss of her father. Frau Heller continued with her supernatural suckling of Jeanette while Leopoldl became one of the crowd of older Sonnenburg children, who climbed trees or the more scaleable bits of mountains, fished in the lake, avoided grown-ups or sometimes hid with his brothers from his older sister in the surrounding woods.

At the same time as Nannerl revived her daily music practice, her feelings for her daughter grew and she looked forward to the child's cot being placed in the room when she practised her 'galanteries' or extemporised in an unselfconscious manner to no one else apart from the sleeping child. Frau Heller understood this, encouraging the ritual for the benefit of them all while Sonnenburg increasingly admired the widow for smoothing out their lives. He could not help noticing the outline of her figure was sensual without being fat and that as she walked anywhere she would arch her back and tilt her head as if crossing a stage in front of an audience. He found himself staring at the faint shadow of hair on her upper lip when she sat across the table from him at cards. There was also the endearing way she would raise both hands to flatten the loose strands of hair on either side of her oval face. He could not stop thinking about her when he was lying in bed and had taken to lingering in the hall outside her room in the hope he might see her when she was least expecting him. The idea that she was putting his child to her breast gave him pleasure, and when he was alone in his own room it was Nandl Heller, not his wife, who filled his thoughts.

Nannerl was already expecting their third child and he showed his indifference to her by leaving her alone as much as possible. At the back of his mind was the thought that if he ignored her, perhaps she would keep her sanity this time round. Whether he was right or wrong, at least he stopped distracting himself with images of her premature death whenever he felt bitter about the marriage. In his own peculiar way, he probably loved her enough to have developed a few qualms about that.

NANNERL'S LETTER TO JAKOB HOFMANN

Saint Gilgen, 29ᵗʰ July, 1790

Dear Jakob,

It was not pride which prevented me from writing to you before now and returning thanks for your dear kind letter after the death of our beloved second daughter, Maria Barbara. Believe me, it was a type of prudence because I had nothing to say these past few weeks and I hoped that by waiting a little longer, I could give you more cheerful news of myself, Johannus and the children.

Nothing to say? That's not quite true. I could have said that it was unbelievably cruel that I had to lose my child after only five months. I felt bound to her in a way that I was not with Leopoldl or Jeanette, being too ill when they were born.

Marianna has been an angel, playing with Leopoldl and taking all the children out for long walks every day. Nandl Heller has also been most helpful. I think she expected me to collapse with distress as I have in the past, for she has been anticipating the needs of everyone in this house, long before they even know what they want, just so there will be peace. She insists I have time to practise in the mornings as well as in the afternoons while she herself plays cards with Johannes every night after supper. 'You must rest dear Baroness,' she says to me as the table is cleared by a maid who comes every day but does not live with us. 'You must not make yourself anxious or excited,' she insists and Johannes, who has shown an interest in her of late, agrees with her. He seems to be at home more often than he used to be.

I sit and watch them play écarté for an hour and then I excuse myself so that I may read stories to the children before they go to sleep. The arrangement works and I have no complaints, my friend. You, among all those who know me well, understand my solemn turn of mind. Perhaps you admire me for it but I warn you that confessional letters have always been the favourite recourse of gloomy, distracted mortals, of which I am one!

Not all my life is so predictable. Last night we had a ball at Court in Salzburg and today I am in the sweetest spirit, having not slept since we returned home. How strange that want of sleep should produce such an effect. I have a weakness of mind which I readily admit: amidst music and dancing I am as cheerful as if nothing on this earth has ever vexed me and I even carried my cheerfulness home for I was delighted to be with the children and had no desire to practise scales or studies, preferring minuets and jigs. I spent an hour describing the dresses of the people at court to Marianna and Nandl Heller and now I am sitting alone and at peace in my room while Johannes sleeps soundly in his bed. I think we are content with one another but it is rather like two old hats lying side by side in a cupboard and rarely being worn.

As I hope to be truly considered your friend, I wish you to know all the good and bad of my character so you may value the one and correct the other. I suspect that none of my emotions is truly profound for they seem to change with the weather!

Your affectionate friend,

— Nannerl

P.S. Thank you for the length of blue woollen cloth and the lace
pocket-handkerchief. The lace is so intricate and beautifully wrought
I fear for the eyes of anyone who made it but despite this nagging
thought, I am so vain as to use it whenever I can, which is often as I
always sneeze a great deal in July. I enclose what I hope is the value
in coins of both and insist you do not make it a present or I will be
afraid to mention any future requirements. One must be strict even
in little things. Sous le nom d'amitié, — N.

Unusually for my aunt, she did not tear this letter into small pieces or burn
it in the stove but sent it with the next post. Hofmann did not receive it for
several months as he was travelling from Gotha to Leipzig and from Leipzig
to Meissen and across the Elbe into Dresden and then down towards Prague
before coming back to Frankfurt. He read Nannerl's letter as if he were in
a hurry to get to the end or because of his impatience to know everything
all at once and then he sat very still and stared at the wooden knots of
his desk for several minutes. He opened a second letter, which was dated
two months after Nannerl's and only realised that it was from Nandl Heller
when he saw the signature. Where before he had been amused and only
vaguely troubled by what he read, now he frowned and puckered up his lips
in alarm as he discovered what it was the widow had to say.

NANDL HELLER'S LETTER TO JAKOB HOFMANN

Saint Gilgen, 1ˢᵗ October, 1790

My dear Hofmann,

   There are no secrets between us, I think. Did I ever mention that
Nannerl sent me her share of some pearl-shell buttons, which you
gave to both of us as a present on the first day we met? They were
rather pretty and I admired them greatly. At the time I could hardly
bring myself to thank her for sending the rest because I already felt

ashamed of the ease with which I had accepted the original. I did finally convey my thanks.

We are not close, Maria Anna Walburga Ignatia and I. It has always been so. I sometimes wonder what she would think if she knew that you and I were related by blood but I have said nothing at all because you have told me not to and because I can see the sense in certain discretion about our past. No matter how kind people are, we remain as you have often said, alien eyes. Perceived in this way, I sometimes seem to do what others misunderstand.

Now I will tell you that the Baron Sonnenburg and I have become lovers. It is not so strange a thing. We have been so for several months – ever since he came to my room smelling of wine to give him courage and refusing to leave until I had accepted his embrace and listened to him explain the nature of his feelings for me. There you have it. My confession, as confessions do, has given me intense pleasure and I hope not much pain to you. Naturally I understand the strength of your attachment to his wife. Mine is not so great. I cannot bring myself to say, 'Nannerl,' as if it ripples off my tongue without a twinge. We are not intimate. I do not regret my relation-ship to the baron, although it was never planned by me. Sometimes I am afraid that the child Marianna, who seems to know everything, will tell her father what she has observed and then he will be forced to send me away. I dread the idea of returning to the convent for the rest of my life and I cannot return permanently to Frankfurt as I know that would stir up painful memories of my dead husband and my own poor dead children.

I know what I have written will disturb you but dear friend, believe me, the marriage between my mistress and her husband was without passion before I arrived in Saint Gilgen. It is, in effect, no longer a marriage as you or I would understand it. He has told me there have always been great difficulties in this regard and from the beginning of her last confinement, they have not been together as man and wife because he had feared for her health. Extraordinarily, since both the birth and death of her third child Maria Barbara, she has not been the least bit unhinged, nor has she been plagued by fevers. I would say, not just to make myself or you feel better about what has happened, she is strong and well at last. The baron leaves her alone and she is free to practise her music.

Your devoted cousin,

— *Nandl Heller*

———————

Jakob Hofmann shook his head and wiped his forehead with the corner of his sleeve. I watched his long tombstone face and tried to read his thoughts. 'I am not the voice of righteousness crying out against wilful ignorance in the middle of the desert and I am not an arbiter for moral sanctimony, having done my best to escape from it all my conscious life. Nor do I believe in a world with an ordered balance of right and wrong where all you have to choose is which pathway you take.' Hofmann sat down heavily at his modest desk and picked up a quill.

'Dear Cousin.'

He paused, staring helplessly at the empty page in front of him. Several minutes passed without any further movement before he could bring himself to continue.

In your last letter, you mentioned our family's wish for a marriage between us. No doubt they believed that the marriage would bring us both back into the fold. It is surprising not least because the magistrates of Frankfurt say Jews are only allowed twelve marriages a year to limit multiplying our kind. Now it has been a source of great pleasure when you write to me at least as a sister might to a brother, and that we have both derived comfort from this correspondence, but the news of your relationship with the Baron Sonnenburg fills me with concern. I cannot say what you ought or ought not to do, although I will say you are bound to upset the Baroness, despite your belief that their marriage is not such as you would understand. I have no desire to be the voice of righteousness railing against wrong . . .

We already know the substance of that particular outpouring and I was impatient for him to get to the caveat, realising there must be one brewing because of the sighs he gave when his quill became stuck on a loop. I was not prepared for the shock of his melodramatic, hasty proposal slipped in at the end as if it were an afterthought.

> . . . I cannot believe in an ordered world of right and wrong and all you have to do is decide what is right and which is wrong, but I am asking you to leave Saint Gilgen and come to Frankfurt as soon as can be arranged. I am, my dear friend, asking you to fulfil the wishes of our families and become my wife. Please remember in your reply that what you write to me may be read by others.'
> Your cousin,
>   — *Jakob*

In a very different hand from the one he had used before, he wrote the following letter without any corrections and in great haste. It contained what he called a legitimate deceit, though the nub of it lacked certain plausibility.

> My dearest Nannerl,
>   Your words touched me greatly and because I value our friendship, I will write to you with the same directness of thoughts, which you have shown me. You seem able to arrange your affairs with a skill I wish I could bring to my own. I envy the two old hats lying side by side in the cupboard and there is nothing in your nature I would wish to correct, apart from a misplaced desire to pay for what was intended as a gift.
>   I have finally decided to bow to my family's wishes and marry the bride they have chosen for me. It seems she is a distant cousin, who understands my needs to travel and would be content to remain behind. I hear your brother is in Frankfurt right now and I hope to hear some more of his music while he is here. Everyone is talking about what a genius he is; and did I tell you that, in Prague especially, I hear the organ grinders play his tunes and the people in the streets sing snatches of *Don Giovanni* or *The Marriage of Figaro*

more often than not? Now that is the fame of Mozart.

If there are any other bibs and bobs which you require for yourself and the children please let me know. It's so easy for me to obtain them and it gives me pleasure to care for you in this way. How I still miss those violin lessons when you were there to accompany me. Your father's remarkable gloom, which filled the room when I played badly – too often I fear – had the effect of making me go straight home and practise twice as hard. I'm afraid my violin remains in its case these days. Are you writing any more songs? Send me the scores. My address in Frankfurt remains the same and in future it will be my wife and not my landlady who will keep your letters safe until I return from my travels.

I have a longing to sail to Terra Australis or New Holland as it is now called. Six months at sea to get there and another six or seven to come back! Can you imagine the monotony? I spend my evenings making plans for the voyage and suspect my dreams of going there are as important as the act itself. This will be my last great adventure. At any rate my plans provide a source of lively correspondence with Josef Metzger, who begs to be remembered to you. Naturally I would not expect anyone to share such a perilous journey with me and if I undertake it I will travel alone.

Your loving and ever restless friend,

— *Jakob.*

P.S. My future wife is called Hannah and I am told she plays the clarinet better than I play the violin. This, as you must know, would not be difficult. — *J.H.*

Hofmann could hear footsteps on the stairs outside his attic room and realising it was the boy who came regularly to perform errands, he counted out twenty-four kreuzers and instructed him to post the note to his cousin that same day and to keep his letter to Nannerl for the following post-chaise. The trouble was, and I saw it coming even though I was quite sure Hofmann had no idea of it, the boy slipped Nannerl's letter into his pocket thinking that was the one he had to post first while the letter addressed to Frau H. Heller which he put in his bag, remained there for such a long time that eventually the boy forgot about it altogether. Out of such simple accidents, our lives unfold never quite as we expected them to do.

FUGHETTA

> 'Now it wasn't the coughing
> that carried him off
> but the coffin
> they carried him off in,'

sang the Schwager to his mate.

They all laughed at the song and Heinrich, the former grave-digger, who knew the tune better than any nursery rhyme, obliged by singing it several times more as the coach set off with its repaired wheel. He stopped when they changed their horses at the next post or because his voice was hoarse.

Chapter 16

TOCCATA

Have you noticed that each day gets shorter as you get older? It is similar to your body shrinking with the weight of personal history and in my case, I refer unnaturally to two distinct bodies. I have also noticed that the one thing in my life, which seems to get longer is this story, but then there are still a few more facts to be told.

Nandl Heller did not hear from Hofmann for several months because he assumed wrongly that she had received his proposal of marriage and rejected him. He was upset by her initial silence because he was human and she in turn was cross with him for not replying to her letter, in which she considered she had made such a momentous confession. Several months passed before any correspondence was resumed and then it was only because he sent a box of linen to Nannerl with a smaller box enclosed for his cousin, addressed to H. Heller. Both parcels were delivered by Joseph Metzger, who made no mention of any marriage and seemed unaware there was meant to be one in the first place. My aunt never knew that the future bride described by Hofmann in his letter was in fact her child's wet nurse.

Saint Gilgen, 26ᵗʰ February, 1791

My dear, especially good, kind friend,

Forgive me for not having written to you before now. I was of course delighted to learn of your intended marriage and although I pestered Herr Metzger for more news when we met last month, he seems unwilling to say one word. I await your detailed description of the ceremony and the bride in particular. How clever of your relatives to find you a wife who is so accomplished and whose kinship ensures you have much in common.

Thank you, for your generous gift of linen. I have only recently worn the dress, which was made up from the length of blue wool you sent me some time ago. It has been much admired here in Saint

Gilgen. How typical of you to send gifts when it is we who should be sending them to you. Since you are always doing things for other people, I insist you let me do something for you for a change. I have embroidered yours and your wife's initials on half the linen and I am returning this particular half through Herr Metzger, who has agreed to bring it to you on his very next trip to Frankfurt. Please do not be cross with me for this. It makes me feel better to hope you will be pleased with your wedding gift!

I have been writing more and more music for the bottom drawer and yesterday I discovered it had become so full I had to get rid of most of it. There is one piece I could not bring myself to destroy as it reminds me of you. I don't think I ever sent you a copy of that violin piece I wrote so many years ago for you to play. I enclose it with a recent Sarabande for clarinet and beg you not to make any comments about either one until you have heard them played. Instead, I will imagine your reactions and make sure inside my mind that you think both are masterpieces. This is the way I plan to remain confident! I have not sent a copy of either to Wolferl and would appreciate your not telling him about them if and when you run into him on your travels. One day I will let him read both but I'm not ready for his opinion yet.

My husband sends you his best wishes and the children lots of kisses. I am longing for you to see how much Leopoldl and my dear Jeanette have grown. You will hardly recognise them, and as for Marianna, she is no longer a child. Come and see for yourself and bring us your bride that we may admire her.

I remain your faithful friend,

— *Nannerl.*

P.S. The Sarabande is a present to your wife. I wrote it with the guidance of Nandl Heller, who as you know, is my child's wet nurse. She is also something of an expert on the instrument.

Saint Gilgen, 27th February, 1791

Dear Hofmann,

At last two words from you – my name on the cover of the parcel you sent me! I was beginning to wonder if you remembered my existence but then I heard from the baroness that you were getting married very soon to someone she described as a distant cousin and I at last understood the reasons for your silence. I am wondering who this cousin might be. Is it the fat one who is very rich or the thin one who is very clever?

My family has failed to give me any news about anyone since they haven't spoken or written to me in the past year and nor have I to them. As far as they are concerned, I no longer exist as I have denied who I am. I hope you will be very happy and that when you next come to Salzburg, you will consider making that little extra journey to come and visit the baroness and your devoted relative in Saint Gilgen. Perhaps you will consider bringing your bride so we can believe in her existence. I find it most mysterious that Joseph Metzger professes to know nothing of the event!

It has been such a long time since your last visit and the children have grown so much you will have difficulty knowing which one is which. I remain a nurse to the youngest child, Jeanette, but I fear the Baroness will not require my help much longer in this regard! The Baron has talked of arranging another position for me in the village but I think I will return to the convent instead. I'm sure you will understand my reasons without my having to spell them out.

Your loving cousin,

— *Nandl*

P.S. I almost forgot to thank you for the colourful shawl, which you sent through Herr Metzger. It will remind me of you when I wear it. There. I am almost ready to forgo my widow's weeds. — *H.H.*

———————

'I see, I see, said the blind man' and so saying, Jakob Hofmann folded both letters and placed them inside the book he had been reading that morning when the post arrived. I looked for signs of relief or distress in his face, that for want of a letter, he lost a bride, but his expression was impossible to read. He settled deeper into his chair, wiped the dust off his spectacles and hummed to himself for a minute or two. His face was fuller, the eyes smaller under the folds, the flesh around the nostrils remained the same greyish colour, the teeth were longer, his back now curved like a scythe and judging by the hair on his wrists, there was more of it growing on his body than on his head. He picked up the heavier of the two manuscripts that had arrived with Nannerl's letter and turned the pages slowly. Every now and then, he would whistle a phrase, pause, continue to read and then start it up again. He carried on in this way until he came to what I suspected was the coda of auntie's violin sonata. I could hear him trying to roll the double stops of the final bars in an approving way. He turned back to the first page, stared at it for a few minutes before carefully placing the music in order next to the book on the table.

I had such a strong desire to become Franz Xaver Mozart in the presence of this man. At first, I resisted out of common sense and respect but I longed to talk to him about music, my life, my aunt and of course my beloved Josephine, trapped by her marriage to another in Lemburg. I thought if I presented him with a compositional problem, he would unravel it without destroying my delicate esteem, although it's true his opinions once had the reverse effect on my aunt. I wriggled down my web and went as close as I dared without threatening history. If I crawled secretly onto his flesh, I would somehow catch what was going on inside his head. I landed like a breath on a thatch of hair near the back of his neck and was promptly flung to the floor by Hofmann's sneeze.

'Bless you,' said his friend Metzger who had been asleep in the corner of the room until now. 'Are you ill my friend?'

'It's dust,' said Hofmann quickly, more interested in hearing news from Saint Gilgen than discussing his health. 'What are the Sonnenburgs doing these days then?' It was his roundabout way of asking after his beloved Nannerl and although his friend understood this, Metzger was not above a little game of cat and mouse to enliven their relationship.

'They are always busy with town affairs,' he replied.

'And what of those famous soirées? Have you heard her play recently?'

'I heard her practising one afternoon but that's all.'

'And how was it? Were there new works by Mozart? Did she sing at all?'

'I only heard some scales and a study or two and perhaps, yes, a song I'd not heard before.' Metzger was enjoying Hofmann's impatience.

'But tell me about the song. Was it an aria or a simple ballad? Was it her own composition do you think?' Hofmann was hopping backwards and forwards over his friend's mammoth outstretched legs and getting more excited with each leap. I found a crack between the floor boards and decided it was safer to remain there than above.

'It sounded charming. That's all I'm fit to say my friend.'

'Then she's well obviously.' Hofmann was standing still at last and staring at Metzger, though not really seeing him. You could judge the vagueness of the look by the way the eyes refused to blink. They reminded me of my grandfather's and my aunt's, or my father's for that matter, with their poppy-eyed gaze which looks beyond you into the distance and which you know means they might as well be on another planet while it lasts. He must have decided that this was the only news he would extract from Metzger because he turned away from his friend and went back to the table to pick up a parcel of folded white linen. As he buried his nose in its pile and prodded the embroidered 'H' in one corner, I could not help wondering if he felt relief that he was still a bachelor.

'I have been thinking about Van Diemen's Land,' he said to his friend at last. 'The idea of a long voyage . . . perhaps not ever coming back. Are you interested in joining me, my friend?'

Metzger stretched his legs even further and looked startled. 'Why certainly not. I can't bear to cross the Rhine. One ripple makes me sick as a pig and besides, I wouldn't fit in the cabin.'

Hofmann laughed, pulled at Metzger's ears and hugged him hard around the back of his shoulders. 'You old fool. You just don't want to travel anymore isn't that it? Go on. Confess I'm right. You're just an old humdrummical stick-in-the-mud.'

'And you are an uprooted, wandering beggar who gets irritable if you sit in your own room for more than ten minutes. Have you ever stopped anywhere for more than a few days Jakob?' This was the most Joseph Metzger had ever said in a single speech.

FUGUE 9

'If you ask me, it looks like a kite without a tail,' said Heinrich after he had recovered his voice. He enjoyed watching Otto squirm every time he brought up the subject of the coffin. 'Except I wouldn't want to fly it of course . . . Come crashing down on your head.' He scratched himself under one armpit and looked thoughtful. 'And then the body'd be sure to fall out . . . on top of you,' he laughed.

Franz and Karl joined in but Otto turned his back on Heinrich, looked nervously down at his feet, stretched his legs one after the other and grunted, 'I'm off to my station,' which meant he would fall asleep on the bench at the back of the coach. This left Karl and Heinrich to share the reins while Franz, the postillion, was out front on a fresh horse. The moment the wheels began to turn, Joseph Metzger called out from inside the coach and startled them for the second time.

'Can someone give me a hand to lift this coffin?' he asked.

'Whoaah,' came the cry from above as the coach shuddered and stopped before it left the post.

Chapter 17

CANON

In autumn, the spider squirts a fine gossamer when there is a rise of hot air in the surrounding damp. On the sixth of September, 1791, I came with Hofmann to Saint Gilgen when the nights were already drawing in, the days were marked by streaks of last-minute sunlight and thermal winds swirled in invisible spirals around the tops of hills. I hid inside his coat pocket which was dank from the previous day's rain and decided I would spin my thread to pass the time. I remember the date because my father was in Prague for the first performance of his opera, 'La clemenza di Tito.' Technically I was forty-two days old, which is not bad going for a spider but not up to much in human terms.

Hofmann wrote to Nannerl to prepare her for his imminent arrival, as well as to inform her that his marriage would no longer be taking place because his bride had married someone else. No sooner had the letter been sent, he regretted his decision to visit her in Saint Gilgen, though not his lie about his abortive marriage. He worried that she would find him ugly and old. He worried too that he would find her ugly and old. He worried a great deal about what he would say to Frau Heller when they inevitably met. What, he asked, did he owe this woman who had ignored his proposal of marriage and then cunningly pretended she thought he was betrothed to another? Perhaps he should ignore her in turn. The quality of his life was about the unexpected, the accretion of layers through time and the ability to transform his position in society from draper, Jew, to totemic intellectual or holy fool, but he worried that the burghers of Saint Gilgen would see his life as feckless or as fuel for their bigotry. He worried that the baron would receive, not an old family friend, but a travelling draper with a violin as calling card for his wife's soirée. He worried that the baron's children would dislike him as much as he disliked children and he continued to worry about everything that occurred to him en route. He resented paying dues for his temporary exile from Frankfurt. He regretted paying the coachmen for the journey that was already begun. Anticipation, expectation and regrets had merged into a constant state of anxiety and yet, he argued without conviction, it was absurd to see his visit as anything more than the reunion of old friends.

Hofmann listened to the discreet sounds of his own fingernails being gnawed and the insistent rattling of the coach wheels until comforted by their repetitions, he could study the other passengers sitting opposite. These were his sole companions – a wrinkled old woman with pitted face, wrapped in elaborate shawls and taking more than her fair share of the seat next to an elderly gentleman in a wig from another century, who was asleep in the corner. The driver addressed them as 'Herr' and 'Frau Büchner.'

Hofmann turned and stared at the countryside through the window and saw the road fall away in curves that scored the sides of the mountains like mange on a cat. He planned what he would say to Nannerl when they were alone together and tried to imagine her replies:

HOFMANN: About the Sarabande for clarinet . . .

NANNERL: Shshsh . . .

HOFMANN: Or the violin sonata . . . will you let me play it?

NANNERL: If you say nothing about the composer.

HOFMANN: Nothing?

NANNERL: Because we hear the same piece with different ears.

HOFMANN: Then we hear two different pieces.

NANNERL: Words Jakob, words. Not a substitute for music.

She thinks, thought Hofmann, that I like ideas, not people.

NANNERL: So then. Am I to play chords or scales or arpeggios to express what it is I want to say?

She likes me but dislikes my ideas; he continued to torture himself.

NANNERL: Perhaps you could change the strings on your violin, Jakob. Try playing out-of-tune sometimes. Play badly. Play the wrong piece. Then I can blame you and not my composition.

HOFMANN: I'm not talking about your composition.

NANNERL: Then I don't know what you're talking about.

HOFMANN: Imagine.

NANNERL: Someone with dull hair and rough complexion who's stout around the middle.

Hofmann became so absorbed that he forgot he was not alone in the coach.
HOFMANN: My dear Nannerl, let me try to play what's there.
NANNERL: Then we'd better not play.
HOFMANN: Except, – *and he relished the cunning of his thought* – you can't keep on writing music you don't want anyone to hear. You might as well write silence.
NANNERL: Silence? Silence is when the music is finished.

He was in the middle of imagining the rest of her reply when the crone had a coughing fit and he was forced to see that she was observing him from behind her shawls. He ducked his head inside his coat collar.

'Perhaps you are going to Saint Gilgen.'

'I am, Madam.'

'Ah,' she barely breathed, turning her attention from the faded yellow star of his armband to his trunk and the wooden violin case lying on the seat next to him. Hofmann shrank even further into his coat. When it seemed she was tired of examining them, she prodded her companion with her umbrella until he woke with a snort. Neither resentful, nor embarrassed, he had the air of one of those worthy burghers who believes his wife's bad temper may be excused because she is devout.

'We are travelling to Saint Gilgen,' said the husband, either because he was a pleasant fellow, or because he was trying to appear as if he had never been asleep. Hofmann straightened up and stirred his feet in the straw on the floor of the coach. He had resigned himself to a forced conversation for the rest of the journey and short of leaping out of the coach, saw no escape.

'Whoaaah!' shouted the driver, and with that one merciful cry, pulled the horses to a halt and spared him the need to talk further. They were outside an inn, with about half the journey still to go. This was the only stop to rest and feed the horses between Salzburg and Saint Gilgen and Hofmann chose to get out and walk uphill to stretch his legs while the old couple wandered off in search of the innkeeper and something to eat and drink.

'Did you see the Jew's box?' crooned the wife, saliva in the corner of her mouth.

'Shsh my dear. His box?'

'Yes, on the seat next to him.'

'Well, there's no harm in that my love. There's plenty of room and there aren't any more passengers.'

'I'd like to know what's inside.' She was animated by her wishful thinking and stupidity in equal parts. 'I'm told they hide their jewels underneath all the other things they have to sell.'

'It's probably locked.' The husband replied so quickly as to suggest he was thinking the same thing. They were an old weathered couple with plenty of their own secret habits but who could not always see the need for other people to have theirs.

'I'd like to see inside. Why don't you suggest he opens it because we might like to buy something?' The crone was persistent, her bat's eyes glowing with an uncontrollable fit of greed.

'I think you should ask my sweet, since it's your idea.'

When Hofmann returned, he found them both sitting inside the coach, waiting for the return of himself and the driver. The wife was nibbling a slice of black bread with a grotesque chewing of her lips to make up for the absent teeth. The husband looked as if he was dozing again. There was a fresh, dark red wine stain on the front lapel of his coat. Again, his wife prodded him hard with the handle of her umbrella.

'My dear? Mmm.' The old man looked startled and forlorn. 'Yes yes, of course. Your trunk sir. My wife is ... most anxious ... we were having a little discussion amongst ourselves ... wondering, curious really, as to what it contains. Not that we wish any impertinence you understand.'

Hofmann stared first at the wine stain and then at this sad, pecked over husband, his gaze sweeping upwards from the carefully polished shoes to the neat corrugations of his old-fashioned wig. He understood that this was a man enslaved. With great care, he removed his violin case, which had been resting on top of the trunk and placed it carefully on the straw. He took a key from a chain around his waist and unlocked the box, lifting its lid until it was propped precariously against the back wall of the carriage. At this point, the coach lurched and tilted at such a sharp angle that the lid slammed hard onto Hofmann's hand. He turned pale and I thought he was going to be sick as he sat there sideways on the seat with his hand still trapped and his mouth open like a distressed gargoyle. Where had I seen that look before?

'Are you well?' cried the husband.' Do you want me to tell the driver to stop?'

Hofmann shook his head as he lifted the lid.

'Now Friedrich,' began the wife. 'What do you mean, you will stop the coach? What good would that do? Just delay us getting to Saint Gilgen – and it's not as if we can do anything by stopping.'

Hofmann was silently massaging his left hand with his right and wondering if there was no limit to her officiousness or his docility. He wished she would just be quiet or ignore him for the rest of the journey.

'Nothing's broken then,' she cried theatrically, having no intention of remaining quiet. 'All's well, except for the stiffness you will feel tomorrow. You must apply ice to the swelling at regular intervals.' She looked absurdly satisfied, although realising she had lost her chance to discover what was contained in the box.

'Where is he going to get ice just like that, my dear? It's September.' Her husband shifted his wig with an idle finger. 'My nephew will be meeting us in Saint Gilgen. Perhaps he can be of help.'

'Of help?' Hofmann spoke automatically and not because he wanted to have anything more to do with this couple or their relations.

'Baron zu Sonnenburg is the town magistrate and a man of great importance.'

Just so, thought Hofmann, and how typical of my good fortune to share a coach with the baron's relations, one swollen with the taxidermist's art and the other dropping off its perch. 'So I've heard,' he muttered aloud into his box. 'Thank you for your concern, but I expect to have recovered by the time we get there.'

He chose his words carefully, struggling to remember if he had been openly rude to them on the journey, believing in his unreasoning heart, not his mind, that this is a retributive world.

'Oh my dear, dear Nannerl. I should never have come.'

He was, he argued, not fit to speak the most important human words to her in any terms. He locked the box of unseen, domestic heaven intended for his hosts, slumped against the carriage wall and nursing his hand on his lap, fancied he could already see the beginnings of a bruise on his knuckles.

FUGUE 10

'Can someone help me move this coffin?' repeated Metzger.

'Perhaps he means to leave it behind,' whispered Otto hopefully from the back.

Karl climbed down from his box to open the door to the carriage. He was thinking how it was an odd thing about a body, how much heavier it was in death than in life.

'Sideways,' ordered Metzger as Otto, Heinrich and Franz, the postillion joined them reluctantly. The coffin had been cleaned of straw and was wedged across the carriage without more than an inch to spare on either side. Karl could see no obvious advantage in changing the angle but the traveller's arms were draped over the head of the box, making clear that the men were meant to help him move it. Each man heaved, swaying as they lifted, swearing and spitting, except for Metzger, who was exerting the care reserved for a dead king. None of the coachmen was particularly fanciful but afterwards as each returned to his seat, they again wondered who it was that lay within. The traveller crouched on his back beside the coffin and drew up his knees until his body was exactly the same length as the wooden panels. He stared at the ceiling for some time before his head lolled to one side in exhaustion and without realising he was doing it, gave in to sleep.

Karl flicked his whip at the lead horse as the postillion bent down low and whispered something into the animal's ear. They were beginning the last leg of their travels and the spirits of all the drivers rose as they thought about the journey's end.

Chapter 18

ESTAMPIE

'Herr Hofmann, I believe you have already met my husband's uncle and aunt, Herr and Frau Büchner.' Nannerl was walking arm in arm with Katharina Gilowska in front of Hofmann, twisting her head as she spoke, eyeing him sideways as they entered the salon. Herr and Frau Büchner were sitting close by, poised to observe the guests arriving for the concert. Heinrich had a fresh dusting of powder on his wig and his wife, still swathed in shawls, wore so much carmine on her cheeks, the pockmarks looked fresh as she spoke.

'We never miss a soirée if we can help it.'

'Indeed, no.' Katharina's reply was polite while discouraging further conversation. She appeared older and more subdued than Hofmann remembered. A spinsterly air had settled on her features, a compression of the lips with faint lines around the eyes. Separated from Nannerl, she passed Herr and Frau Büchner to sit on one of the new gilt chairs with cabriole legs and blue silk cushions. Hofmann followed. He hoped that unlike the guests who had seemed surprised by his presence, a Gilowska or a Hagenauer would see it as unexceptional in the house of a Mozart. He was drawing up his seat beside her when Nannerl's voice interrupted his thoughts.

'Would you turn the pages for me with your good hand?' The tone was warm and he forgot his swollen knuckles and reluctance to mingle with her guests. Before he could reply, she had moved on to usher her husband's elderly relatives into seats nearer the instruments.

'Jakob Hofmann, I have been waiting for you to say goodnight to the children but you have been hiding from us.' The voice, part serious, part teasing, belonged to Nandl Heller. She was coming towards him, a clarinet in one hand, dressed in her mistress's clothes, made from a blue material, he recognised as from his box. It was, he knew, a common enough practice to supply the servant with cast-offs but its effect further blurred the boundaries that existed in his mind.

'In some years' time, I may be a solid and contented man – but not yet. I must resist those distractions that happen along the way.' It was a thought he kept to himself, not least because he was startled by the transformed appearance of the widow.

'Good evening Frau Heller. I was resting in my room,' and he thrust his bandaged fingers in the air as if this explained his absence. There was no doubt that the Büchners, the Hagenauers, the Gilowskis, the Baron Sonnenburg and everyone else at supper had dined out on his small accident at his expense. He was relieved he had an excuse for his misanthropy.

'Have you travelled all this way to remain in your room cousin? Are you reluctant to be seen in society? I suppose now that I've found you, you will say there's no time left for conversation. That is my loss I see.'

Hofman was a lonely man and susceptible to flattery. From where I lay in the rough lining of his hose pocket, I felt its typical result and pitied him.

'I came for the concert.'

'In that case you will hear me play the clarinet very badly, so why don't you go back to wherever you were hiding until my performance is finished?' She spoke, aware that others in the room could hear her conversation, comfortable with where she stood and laughing at him lightly with her eyes. It was obvious by her manner that she had become more than a servant to the family and as he leaned closer despite himself, he realised that she reminded him of Nannerl in earlier times.

Hofmann was aware throughout that Sonnenburg was observing them. The baron appeared irritated by the intimate way his mistress put out a playful hand to touch the draper's bandaged one, standing so near to each other that the hem of her skirt brushed against his shoes and the smell of musk on her neck invited him to lower his nose into her open collar. Tapping his foot, repeatedly against the floor, Sonnenburg was quite unable to disguise his own jealousy.

It was true that he, his wife, Leopold, the convent nuns and now Hofmann – all in their different ways had succumbed to her charms. The woman never questioned why she had this effect on anyone, instead, using whatever powers she had, thriving on it, defining herself with it, knowing that without it, she was only half alive. Hofmann would recognise the rules of her game she was fairly certain and secretly he thought he could avoid the obvious pitfalls by remaining profoundly cynical about the intentions of all women except one.

'I hope the concert will begin soon.'

Nandl Heller nodded, waiting for him to say more, but in his awkwardness, he backed away so that she was alone in the centre of the room, surprised by his rudeness. Nannerl, who caught the end of this intimate scene, quickly announced the first piece as a song which she had composed before her marriage, but which she had now re-written.

The Sonnenburg party, including the Abbé Eiberle, settled into their seats as Nandl Heller retreated to the wall furthest from the fortepiano and Hofmann, head down, took up his position as page-turner beside the instrument.

'Non voglio amare per non penare . . . I do not want to love because I do not want to suffer.'

Her voice sucked at the notes and swam in and out of the cracks of the keys. A slide of pitches, up and down before settling onto one note in particular. Stretched out, growing, then falling to nothing. Not sweet but rich. Swollen, burst fruit. Her audience of friends and relatives stirred uncomfortably on their chairs. They were not prepared for either unlimited emotion, melodrama or for the fingertip she raised to her lips in reproof when Katharina coughed during the pause before a cadenza.

The concert continued with a fantasia by my father for fortepiano and ended with his trio for clarinet, clavier and viola. I admit I have heard better performances. Marianna had joined my aunt and Frau Heller to play the viola part, which my father had originally written for himself to play, but from the opening double-stop of the Andante, it was obvious that the music was beyond her. Her small fingers when clenching the bow or splayed across the fingerboard were clumsy in slow or fast passages. She tried hard to keep up with the others and Frau Heller, out of kindness, played louder than desirable to drown the child's mistakes. I needed some fresh air. I crawled through a crack in one of the window ledges to spy on a small tan dog, waiting to hang around the heels of departing guests, begging in vain for scraps of food. It reminded me of Miss Pimperl the way it scratched at the ground before hurling itself at a succession of people to become tangled in a sea of legs. All the guests, including Herr and Frau Büchner and Katharina Gilowska had left or were in the process of leaving. All that is, except Hofmann. Nannerl had persuaded him to spend the night in their house and as he undressed in his room, he listened to the chatter outside without hearing its sense. His own thoughts came and went with no particular order but with customary extravagance.

'I had not . . . I could not . . . I never thought it could be quite like this. Is she saying goodnight to the baron? Or the children? The eldest child I think – the girl, Marianna, who stands with a baby in her arms. It suits her better than her instrument. My cousin on the other hand, is not such a bad clarinettist. My family was right on that one. My dear Nannerl. Forgive me. I'm only a tinker peddling thoughts. I too am stout around the middle.'

He threw himself face down on the bed until his chin dug into the mattress and he found it hard to breathe. He wondered if he fell asleep in that position, would they find him dead from suffocation in the morning. He was about to comfort himself by re-reading Leopold's *Treatise on Violin Playing* when he heard footsteps coming towards his room. Light quick steps, padding softly. They stopped outside his door and he raised his head above the coverlet in time to see the door handle turn, stop for a moment and turn again without a sound as the door opened.

Nandl Heller stood at the entrance, holding a candle in one hand. The folds of her nightdress were swept apart and he glimpsed the mat of dark hair that sprawled like a grainy shadow between her legs. He saw nothing else in that moment when she blew out the candle and without waiting for his reply, stepped quietly into the room. Still she said nothing as she climbed into bed beside him, stroking his skin with the tips of her fingers, pressing down gently every now and then on top of him so that he could no longer keep silent, stirring feelings in him that were beyond his control. All the while he thought of Nannerl and the moment he cried out her name, the widow covered his mouth with her hand to stifle the sound, holding it there for several seconds, so that he found it difficult to breathe. She left him curled up, concealed by the night and crept away without anyone but Hofmann knowing she had been there.

Except that Sonnenburg suspected something of the sort. He had gone to look for his mistress and tried to convince himself his failure to find her was not a proof she was with Hofmann. He could hardly spy and linger in the corridor. As for Nannerl, she lay awake remembering how Hofmann had praised her composition. He kept repeating 'It's good, it's good, it's very, very good,' and she smiled and stretched with pleasure until she remembered the private way he and Nandl Heller had been talking to one another before the start of the concert. My poor confused aunt. She heard her husband yawning three times in a row, which meant he desired her and she pretended to be asleep as she always did these days, in case being awake was to give him hope.

———————

Hofmann and Nannerl went for a walk together the following evening when it had been agreed that he would stay in Saint Gilgen for one more night. They were alone because Marianna had decided at the last minute that she would not accompany them. The remaining children were asleep and the baron was happily playing cards with Nandl Heller, the Abbé Eiberle and a visiting cleric.

They began by walking towards the lake, standing at the water's edge, talking at ease with one another and staring at the zigzag of trees like ink blots on the surface of the lake. They pointed at the silhouette of mountains on the other side, admiring the monochrome scene. A moon ball shivered in its reflection on the waves. They wandered further along a path that hugged the side of the lake and felt the sharp needles of rain against their skin. They talked as if they had never been apart and the intimacy was intense although they never touched one another or felt the physical thrill that ran through the other's body when they almost collided in an attempt to avoid the branches of a tree. A wild boar bellowed and the sound rang out, magnified by the circle of hills around them. They stopped and laughed and waited for the sound to come again.

The evening was so far pleasant, she was happy that they had decided to come out, but then he touched her arm and without meaning to, she gave a start that suggested she had something to hide. She was not soothed when he failed to notice her distress and had her wits given her the chance, she would have drawn back to the house with the first excuse. She became very solemn and at last he caught her mood.

'I wish I could stay longer,' he said.

'It would be – so good to have you here for a few more days.' She moved away from him as if studying the condition of the path, which was damp underneath her shoes. Hofmann hesitated and continued walking. Nannerl had an idea he was about to talk about the wife he never married, except that he changed his mind, fearful if he stopped where he was, they would have to turn back. It was not because his face revealed his mood or his reflections; it was because it remained inexpressive that she thought she understood. She was as used to his doubts as he was to her self-recriminations and it was their mutual discontent that made them comfortable again for a brief while.

'It would give me great pleasure to get to know Marianna a little better. As it is, I will have a friendly recollection of her.'

'I have your promise that you will return then? For some other time – in which to be with her and the children – you could stay for as long as you are able. Perhaps I'm not right to speak of that just now; of course you can hardly think of visiting again when you haven't yet gone.' She was rushing to keep up with him as he quickened his pace and memories of their past kept returning to both, in which they talked about everything except their feelings for each other. How long they walked like this, neither could say, except that when the path ended with some rocks that formed the base of a mountain, they turned back and he held her arm firmly, steering her, listening to their footfall as they were now both silent. She felt the violence of his hold, although he did not hurt her and when she stumbled, he tightened his grip and she cried out, despite herself.

'You frighten me,' she said.

'I didn't mean to. I'm sorry. I came with you on this walk so that we could talk to each other and now I am too afraid to say anything.'

They had stopped their incessant pacing and Nannerl felt a sense that was new to her, the feeling of danger.

'Do you remember that day in Hannibal Platz when I fainted and you left me to sleep? I heard every word of your letter, which you read aloud to me – the one you tore into pieces and burned in the stove. I wanted so much to say something then but I was confused and ill and afraid you might be angry or that you would become ill again yourself and so I thought it best to pretend I had been asleep and that I'd heard nothing.'

She wheeled round as if struck. 'Are you mad, Jakob? What letter? I never wrote a letter. You were delirious. You imagined it. The only letter that was written was in your mind.'

'I am quite sane,' he interrupted quickly. 'I understand why you must pretend it never happened. If it causes you distress, we won't speak of it again, but I cannot forget what was real and so important to me.'

She threw her head back as if to look at something passing in the sky. Her face was white in the shadows when she tried to turn away from him and stopped halfway.

'You see?' he persisted. 'You don't know which way to go. Turn to me now, Nannerl. Let us both have a memory that we at least acknowledge. Look at me. I'm yours. I will always be yours. When you have suffered, I have suffered. That is the real reason why I am here. I need to tell you that the greatest step you can ever take is not to do with leaving your husband and family and living in Salzburg again, because we both know that isn't going to happen, but allowing us to at least share the same emotions, just this once, together. Are we never to confess the truth, directly and without shame? Were we born to be afraid of each other? If only you will trust me. It's a large enough world, for no one else to notice or care what is happening to us in this instant. I know that when I leave here tomorrow, I could not live with myself if I had said nothing to you now.'

Nannerl, still with her face upturned, felt herself slipping in his arms as she whispered in an attempt to deny what was happening to her, 'I wrote no letter.' She said it to hear her voice and reassure herself that what was happening to her was real for she found that mixed in with her sense of fear and pain at the hardness of his body against her, that there was a rapture in her emotions which she had never known before. When she could sink no more and there were wet leaves in her hair and she hardly noticed that she had lost a shoe as her stockinged foot shot out from underneath her, he cried into her ear. 'Nannerl, Nannerl.' He repeated her name over and over again until the sound hurt her with its intensity and she had to push him away so that he fell backwards, which was not what she had meant to happen. She struggled to stand and found he was already on his feet, supporting her, as she allowed him, with her arms around his waist, freely to bend his face to hers and kiss her until she agreed at least in thought that she was drowning.

'Please, please go away,' she said as he withdrew.

The moon had disappeared behind a cloud when they walked back to the house and the only movement outside the main door was the small tan dog belonging to Marianna, twitching fitfully in his sleep. Inside, Sonnenburg was dreaming in his chair, not of Nandl Heller but the maid, Monica, who while less handsome and cultivated than the widow, was not at all threatening to his self-esteem. As for Frau Heller's dalliance with Hofmann, it was pushed to the back of both their minds and accepted for what it was – expedient, relatively unembarrassing and deliberately ephemeral. That Hofmann had gone for a walk alone with Nannerl so soon after his meeting with Nandl Heller, was due to another one of those freakish timings that happen in life and over which he believed he had no control. It never occurred to him that the results of one might have fed the other. It was inevitable that for their lives to continue without complication, Nandl Heller, Hofmann and Nannerl would have to bury the memories of their fleeting encounters. As far as I know, when all three eventually wrote to each other, it was because what they had to say, concerned the next crisis in Nannerl's life, the death of my father.

MARS FUNÈBRE

Vienna, 6th December, 1791

It was not a pauper's funeral but the cheapest available at a total cost of eight florins and fifty-six kreuzer. It was arranged by his patron, admirer and friend, the musician Baron Gottfried van Swieten. The cause of his death was registered as severe miliary fever. Or was it? A week after the funeral, a newspaper in Berlin reported that poisoning had been mentioned in some quarters. What quarters? My father had written to my mother in June that year, the month before my birth, to say he suspected he was being poisoned with aqua toffana and that it would be the death of him. There was no autopsy however. I repeat, who knows? And if this were true, who did the poisoning? Salieri, his rival? I think such delusions may have begun at about that time. They would plague him all the way to the lunatic asylum, but there was no substance in it. He was not a murderer. Just sad, jealous and in the end a little mad. It was Salieri after all, who gave me a reference for my first teaching post in Galicia. No. I don't accuse Salieri. But a jealous husband perhaps? It's possible. There were rumours. I have heard talk of a certain Magdalena Hofdemel, a friend of my father and of the composer, Czerny. Her husband killed himself with a razor the day after my father's funeral. He tried to kill her too but failed. Since she was expecting a child, I wonder what became of it and if I have a half-sister or a half-brother somewhere in this world. My mother has nothing to say on the subject. She gets that sharp look in her eye, which I know from experience, tells me that she's not going to say *anything* – certainly not a word about the rumours I have mentioned – suggesting she and Süssmayr were lovers – or, indeed that I might be the son of my father's pupil. Tut, tut!

As for my father's several amorous encounters, they were much talked about behind closed doors – his weakness for his leading ladies, mezzo sopranos in particular. We'll never know. The secret of the poison lies within his body. Perhaps – and this is mere speculation – it was the lead paint that he licked from his glass harmonica. Karl, my older brother said that Mozart would sometimes run his fingers up and down each glass cup, or whirr his fingers around the rims to make them sing. He would repeat the action several times before licking his fingers one after the other in a distracted way. It's possible. It's plausible. He had the family habit of sucking anything to hand when he was concentrating. I've since heard that there is enough lead on a glass harmonica to send a man mad.

I think I will stick with the official verdict of miliary fever.

Papa's grieving friends were obliged to stuff the poor, dropsical limbs into a hessian bag while my mother wept upon his bed. The body was like a man who had been drowned in water and filled with it. Were you to ask me if I were present when all this was happening, I would have to say I do not know since I was five months old at the time and some matters are too painful to recall even in my disembodied state.

Others told me his body was blessed in the open in front of the Crucifix Chapel of Saint Stephen's Cathedral in Vienna. It was the custom with plain funerals that after consecration the dead would be taken through the Stubentor to the Saint Marx cemetery by way of the Landstrasse, to be buried there in a common grave, seven and a half feet deep. The pit had been dug and was ready, but just as the pallbearers placed their load on one side of the hole, the figure of a man, wrapped in a black cloak with his face obscured by a three-cornered hat, approached from the other side and conferred with them briefly. Within minutes my father's body was lifted up out of its grey coffin and was carried in its hessian bag, I cannot resist saying, in deadly secrecy out of the gates of Saint Marx, to be placed as quickly and silently as possible into another coffin which had been lodged inside the waiting coach. And so began that extraordinary journey from Vienna to Salzburg of which you already know.

FUGUE 11

Metzger was standing in a corner of the graveyard behind Saint Peter's when Hofmann stepped out of the shadows and tapped him lightly on the shoulder from behind.

'Ah ... Who's that?' said Metzger with a start. He half-tripped on one foot as he turned to see who it was.

'I had to come,' answered Hofmann, as if this explained why he was standing in these ghostly surroundings and not in Vienna, which was where Metzger had assumed he would still be. 'Where are the others?'

'The gravedigger's gone to meet someone in the catacombs and I came here ... to pay my respects.' Metzger was not sure why he felt embarrassed in front of his friend but was relieved Hofmann could not see his face in the dark. What he also failed to understand is that Hofmann felt just as uncomfortable.

'And the coach?' Hofmann avoided saying 'the coffin,' which is what he really wanted to say. A painful fastidiousness had overcome both men. It was difficult to talk of coffins and tombs in a place full of the dead.

'By the church.' You could see Metzger hesitating before he placed a hand on his friend's shoulder. Hofmann patted it, removed it and together they walked and talked underneath the vast cataract of rock called the Nonnberg. It loomed above their heads like a remote valhalla, stuck there for eternity. Not once did they look up at it as they passed by family vaults on their right and motley gravestones on their left. They walked so close to one another that their clothes touched.

Hofmann continued to talk while Metzger mumbled 'yes' or 'no' whenever there was a pause. They progressed through an arch and came upon the coach with four horses, snorting and kicking irritably at the cobbles in the square. Karl and Franz were throwing blankets over the sweating animals and Otto seemed to have disappeared. There was enough lamp light from within the coach to see the coffin through the open door and as they came close to it, Hofmann leapt inside.

I am not sure if he opened up the lid because his cloak obscured the lower half of the door as he stooped over the coffin. It was several minutes before he came out again, whispered something to Metzger, and with his friend's help manoeuvred it warily until the head of the box was poking halfway out of the coach.

Metzger was about to take its full weight on the humped and flattened side of his shoulders when the missing Otto appeared from round a corner of the square with the rest of the coachmen. They managed to drag and lift it in consort into the air on a count of three by Hofmann, carrying it like a baby in its cot to the graveyard. Heinrich and another, unknown gravedigger were already at the far end of the yard, digging a pit where there was a spare patch of earth. What they removed, they shovelled into a wheelbarrow while Otto held the lamp above the hole so they could see what they were digging. Plain earth. No bones.

Chapter 19

Danse Macabre

It was a while before Auntie learnt of my father's death. My own mother, as well as living in another city, was too wrapped up in misery to be a messenger. Nannerl was distraught. Not with the same baleful pain which left her vomiting on her bed when her mother, my grandmother had died. You only have the strength to feel like that once in your life, said Auntie. But she had wept at the waste and examined her own son in vain for signs of genius.

'I knew I was being absurd. I knew Leopoldl was nothing like Wolfie. I knew I had to let go of him,' she said, extending her good hand to me to show we were sufferers together. 'That is why, in spite of my revulsion, I accepted Jakob Hofmann's last gift.'

What gift Auntie? What revulsion? Why last? Is Hofmann dead? I'm not sure I understand. My web is sometimes imperfect. It looks as though I've dropped a stitch or two. Disturbed. Useless. The angles are wrong. In my distress, I stroked the papery skin of her hand and touched the rock-hard knuckles underneath. If I waited long enough she would explain. If I hurried her, out of perversity, she would say nothing.

'It made me very angry in the beginning. The gift. Frau Heller waited until I returned to Salzburg before announcing what it was. Ten miserable years later! Ten years of not knowing what really happened.' She became silent, chewing her lips until the bubbles of saliva dribbled one after the other from the corner of her mouth. I wiped them away with the tip of a wet sponge and watched as she sucked the moisture out of it all over again. I wondered if it had been like that for my father. The awful dryness of dying. I kept on thinking about it and what my Aunt Sophie, my mother's sister, had said about his last few hours.

'After Mozart became so ill, we made him a night-jacket which he could put on front way round, since his swollen condition made it difficult for him to turn in bed. Then, because we didn't know just how sick he was, we also made him a quilted dressing gown, so that if he wanted to get up he'd have everything he required. We visited him regularly and he was really pleased with the dressing gown in particular . . .

'One Sunday – the day after Mozart had told me he was feeling well enough to visit our mama in time for her name-day, I thought it wouldn't matter very much if I missed a visit and told mama I wasn't going. She said 'Make me a coffee and I'll think about what you should do,' although I knew she was wanting to keep me at home this once as we had no money for the drive and I didn't feel like walking into town in my Sunday finery.

'I went into the kitchen and lit a lamp and made up a fire. I couldn't stop thinking about Mozart through all this. I'd made the coffee and the lamp was still burning away and I thought about how much wax I had burnt and how wasteful I'd been with it when I suddenly found myself staring into the flame and thinking, 'I wish I could know how Mozart is.' While I was staring at the flame it went out as completely as if the lamp had never been lit. I swear that not a spark remained on the wick and yet there had been no draught. A dreadful feeling came over me and I rushed to my mother to tell her what had happened. She said, 'Well then, you must change out of your fine clothes into something plain and hurry into town, then bring me news of him without delay.'

'So I walked as fast as I could and my sister greeted me at the door with a horrified look on her face, though she was trying to remain calm and said: 'Thank God you've come Sophie. He was so ill last night I thought he'd be dead this morning. Stay with me today for I'm afraid he will die tonight. Go and see him and tell me what you think.'

'I tried to calm myself and went into his room and he begged me to stay through the night to see him die. When I tried to make light of his fears he just looked at me and said: 'Why, but I already have the taste of death on my tongue. Don't go dear Sophie. I'm so pleased you're here. Who will look after my poor dear Constanze if you don't stay?'

'Yes yes,' I said, 'but I must go back and tell our mother that you are all right and then I can return straightway.' 'Very well,' he said 'but be sure you hurry back.' You can imagine how upset I was and my poor darling sister followed me to the door and begged me to go to Saint Peter's for a priest. When I got there I spent a long time persuading one of the clerical oafs to come and see him and then I hurried to my mother's and persuaded her to stay the night with my other sister, Josefa Hofer. I ran back as fast as I could to my distraught Constanze and found Mozart's pupil Süssmayr beside him with the unfinished Requiem laid out on the coverlet.

'Mozart was telling him how he wanted it finished after his death, and while he was doing so we were waiting for the arrival of Dr Closset, who was at the theatre. He insisted on remaining there until his wretched play had finished and when at last he came he asked for cold poultices to be laid on Mozart's burning head. The effect was so dramatic that he lost conscious-ness almost immediately and never regained it. His last movement, his last sounds were an attempt to suggest the final drum beats of the Requiem with his mouth and I can still hear them in my head to this day. He died at fifty-five minutes past midnight on the 5th December.

'Herr Müller from the art gallery arrived to take a cast of his poor dead face. It's so hard to describe everything properly. His distracted wife, Constanze, threw herself on her knees and prayed to God for help. She was unable to tear herself away from Mozart no matter how much I pleaded with her to come out of the room. If it was at all possible to increase her misery, it happened the next day when crowds of people came by and wept and moaned aloud for him. In all my life, I never saw Mozart lose his temper – he was truly loved . . . '

I remember being told much later by Aunt Sophie how my dear mother tried cleaning some dust off his death mask and it smashed into a thou-sand pieces. She said, 'Oh well, I'm pleased the horrible old thing is broken.' When I heard this I realised that my mother, for all the love she bore my father when he was alive, was truly pitiless.

December, 1791

My dearest Nannerl,

Grief. Regret. Much love. I cannot write sensibly about such loss. I cannot put a value on someone touched by God.

Since I am obliged to travel for some time, I don't know for how long, I promise I will write often and next time without any mystery. My friend Metzger will keep you informed and I have asked Frau Heller to be of assistance to you in a specific matter. You will know why quite soon but for the moment I must be discreet in case this letter should fall into the wrong hands. My regards to your husband and your children. Please remember me to Katharina Gilowska and her family, the Hagenauers and other friends from Salzburg when you see them.

I remain your devoted friend,

— *Jakob Hofmann*

December, 1791

My Dear Cousin,

Frau Sonnenburg will be requiring your help in a matter of great delicacy and I have therefore made certain arrangements. My partner, Joseph Metzger, will advise you on what to do since I am obliged to leave on yet another long journey and will not be returning for some time. His instructions are to be given to you in person, as it is most important no one else knows what they are.

If my request – when you know it in detail – is at the price of your contempt, I am unrepentant. You might think I am extracting my reward for past events but you would be wrong. If any debt is involved, it would be to Frau Sonnenburg, and certainly not to me. I think in these terms only to anticipate any argument you might have for not agreeing to my plan, which is intended for her benefit. Its successful execution depends on your involvement.

One final thought. It affirms what you once asked me some time ago. I agree that we should remain silent on the subject of our precise relationship to one another. Some things are better left unsaid, even if it is true we no longer have to wear armbands, can enter university and are allowed at last to purchase our freedom. Believe me. The whole truth is not that important. Surviving without comment matters more to those in exile.

Your loving cousin,

— *Jakob Hofmann*

FUGUE 12

A priest arrived as the gravediggers put down their spades. Unseen in the dark, he stood out of the reach of Otto's lamp and began muttering 'Requiem eternam, dona eis Domine et lux perpetua luceat eis . . . '

The men stood listening deferentially to the disembodied voice with its voluptuous, sacramental murmerings. No splutter, no cough, no furtive shift of feet from a single figure until in the silence after the 'Amen', Hofmann announced softly, 'So be it.'

They lowered the coffin into the pit with their ropes and quickly covered it with earth from the wheelbarrow. They smoothed the surface with the backs of their spades and when they had finished, put out the lamp. The priest pronounced a final 'Amen' and waved his hand in an invisible blessing over the flattened mound before he disappeared through the arch, followed by a grateful Otto. The two gravediggers hurried off to the catacombs with their spades and tackle while Hofmann got down on his knees next to some ivy and dug it up from the roots with his hands. Metzger made several holes across the grave's surface with the heel of his boot and together they painstakingly filled in each hole with torn ivy and damp clumps of moss, which Hofmann withdrew from his pockets. Not a word passed between the two men. By morning, the corner of earth would be the same as any other without a stone to mark it. Hofmann had struck a bargain. No one would be allowed to dig it up again. The church was content with its secret prize and the body of Wolfgang Amadeus Mozart was laid to rest.

COURANTE

Salzburg, July, 1829

Auntie's thoughts were intact, though disconnected. The other day she again mentioned the matter of Jakob Hofmann's gift. With no preamble to prepare me for the shock of what it was, she began with typical obscurity.

'Hofmann was a special friend to all of us. That's why he brought the body home. It was a gift.'

I should explain that our previous conversation had been about certain pieces of her mother's jewellery, which she intended to share between my brother Karl and myself. I suppose the link in her mind was the subject: presents. At the time, I was turning her onto her side, rearranging her pillows and generally making her more comfortable. 'Would you cut my nails for me, Schätzl?' she asked, trying to find my face with those sightless eyes of hers by turning her head from side to side.

'Yes Auntie. Of course I will Auntie.' Then quite crossly because I was feeling tired. 'Whose body are you talking about?'

'Your father's,' she whispered.

'My father's?' I felt like Figaro discovering his identity in the nick of time. Perhaps Mama was right. My aunt was senile or at best, she was hallucinating. I felt my hand shaking underneath her good one. Hers had a will of its own, sliding up and down my wrist, trying to play chords. 'Can you hear me?' I shouted into her ear. 'What do you mean? How could Hofmann bring my father's body home?'

'He stole it,' she rasped. 'Such violation. He stole your father's corpse. Without a by-your-leave or a take-your-leave. He just stole it.' Her voice came and went in unpredictable bursts like a deaf person who can't hear the ends of words or the resonance of their own voice. Scratchy. Sepulchral.

'It was revolting. The idea . . . It shocked me. I was so angry.'

And I could barely breathe. 'Hofmann?'

'Yes, yes. Hofmann, and Herr Metzger, with a coach full of gravediggers carrying your father's coffin. But it was Hofmann, who thought up the idea in the first place. I was angry with all of them at first. Can you imagine? She told me this, Frau Nandl Heller, standing right there by the door, their messenger. She said they snatched poor Wolfie before he could be buried in Saint Marx. They mocked the sacredness of common ritual and from that moment on I lost trust in all mundane sacrament. For a long time I could not accept what had happened. I kept remembering Wolfie's birth but then I'd find myself thinking about his death. I thought of Papa and my own darling daughter. Lying side by side in Saint Sebastian's. It spoilt my memories of them too. It almost destroyed me. I had become so dissatisfied with everyone else.' She paused to calm herself. I refrained from asking what is different about her now and held her hands in silence.

'I kept thinking about the way they brought him back to Salzburg. In a grey wooden box without a blessing. In a coach. With those strangers.'

Her eyes rolled back into their lids and I worried in case she fell asleep without telling me anymore.

'I will tell you where he is because Hofmann is dead and you are here.'

Hofmann dead. My lips moved but I said nothing. I could hear my own breathing in the silence.

'Jakob refused to let your father lie with foreign worms, so they dug a grave in St Peter's and buried him in Salzburg. That was his sacred gift to me.'

My father's body, brought by coach to Salzburg and lying somewhere amongst the garden graves of Saint Peter's. Not in an unmarked grave in Vienna, but here in Salzburg! It was both grotesque and unbelievable – and yet – perversely, I wanted to believe that it was so. There was a sense of justice in his secret return. I looked at my aunt who couldn't see me. I thought she had told me everything when she turned her face to the wall. I was startled when she began to speak again. I could just manage to see the end of her tongue as it hung, swollen and grey between her teeth, sometimes getting in the way of her words.

'It was typical of Jakob – that he would have to die a few months after Wolfie. No one told me exactly. But I know he did. Frau Heller sent all his letters to me in one large casket. It was all many years later and there was no explanation for why she would have them in the first place.

'But I remember they arrived the day I had my funny turn in the middle of a lesson. My head was aching more than usual when the wretched parcel arrived. I was tired and I found myself saying 'cat' or 'nightdress' when I meant to say *legato* or *piano*. I was so startled, I picked up a jug of hot water which I found in the hall. I was holding his last letter to me in the same hand and pouring hot water over the other because I – I could feel nothing in those particular fingers. The Barisani child was crying beside me. I heard her as if she were in another room. Could – could hardly see. I kept thinking Frau Heller was afraid to tell me anything to my face. That's why she sent it by post. She knew what it contained. The casket had been opened. It was stiff with rust. As – ath – soon.'

Her tongue was trapped between two bottom teeth and lodged there for a few seconds. It curled over on itself and lolled against the inner wall of her mouth until I was worried she would swallow it. I also worried that if I said anything about Hofmann or Frau Heller, it would hurry her to her grave or at least bring on another stroke. I realised that the idea of any intimacy between the widow and Hofmann was more than my aunt could bear. With extraordinary effort, she turned her tongue around and continued to speak out of the side of her mouth. I knew that whatever sounds were coming out, however strangled they were, however incoherent, I was probably the only person who could interpret what she was saying because I could imagine it.

'After I read all the letters, I forgave him.' She smiled vacantly in my direction, almost peacefully. 'Now Franzel, I want you to make sure I'm buried with Jack Pudding. As close as you can, do you understand? Somewhere in Saint Peter's, my dear boy. Perhaps in a vault?'

Clearly not in the family patch at Saint Sebastien. My snobbish mother had spoiled that particular graveyard without consulting anyone. By adding the foreign bones of her second husband, the count, to those of my grandfather and my sixteen year old cousin, Jeanette Sonnenburg, she had upset Auntie's sense of order. Profoundly. It seemed obvious and natural to me now that my aunt would prefer eternal life in Saint Peter's, especially if that is where my father lies. So be it.

'Whatever you wish Auntie.'

She gave a small sigh of relief that the arrangements for her own burial were settled. It was more of a delayed breath and I thought afterwards that it could have marked the beginning of her dying.

'You'll come to visit me won't you, Franzel? When it's time. In Saint Peter's, with Wolfie.'

'Don't die now.' I said it as lightly as I could and stayed with her for the rest of the afternoon. I watched her sleep, listened to her stertorous breathing, leaving her side only when Joseph Metzger arrived to take up vigil. I could see from the way he studied my face, he knew I knew.

'Look in the bottom drawer next time you come,' he said quietly, his wide apart eyes following me as I went out the door. 'Look underneath her compositions. You will find some papers that will be of interest.'

And of course I found them when I returned the following morning to take the place of Marianna at my aunt's bedside. And of course I began reading them while my aunt lay asleep and I did not stop until I came to the end. I also wondered if Marianna had done the same. Poor, kindly, grown-up Marianna. More devoted to my aunt than my aunt's only son. I rubbed my nose and was certain I could smell her scent on each page. What a shame that Auntie's own two daughters were long dead. Now that was a loss twice over, which as a mother, she could not bear to discuss with me or anyone else. Out of respect, I never questioned her, nor spied upon those terrible events.

Chapter 20

HOFMANN'S FANDANGO

*'For a long time I have not said what I believed, nor do I ever
believe what I say, and if indeed I do sometimes happen to tell the
truth, I hide it away in so many lies that it is hard to find.'*
— *Niccolo Machiavelli*

The Atlantic Ocean, 7ᵗʰ January, 1792

My dear Nannerl,

I know for certain that departure is a time of loneliness, grief or
regret, hope or despair. Perhaps you will never read this letter, but I
like to think you will. I shall write to you anyway because first of all
I made a promise I would, and secondly, (this has the same intensity
as the first), because you matter more to me than anyone I have
known. If you find it difficult to accept my farewell gift, I ask you to
think of all the graves in the world and say to yourself, Mozart's body
could not be left to moulder amongst foreign worms. One day you
will rest with him. But not yet . . .

Joseph Metzger will have told you I am sailing to the other end of
the world. I won't recount all the details of my journey to England
but I'll try to describe life on board 'The Oracle.' It is a perfectly
ordinary ship on an extraordinary voyage. We are one of a fleet of
six bound for Van Diemen's Land, and since I've talked about going
there so many times the reality of my going must seem less surprising to you.

We slipped out to sea quietly at dusk. All through the night,
everything went well. The breeze was strong and a southerly blow
began when we left Portsmouth, which is a small seafaring town on
the coast of England. It was fair wind for our journey and after staring at the ocean for some considerable time, trying to make sense
of my decision to travel to this unknown land, I went below to my

cabin and slept for several days, emerging only when I had need of food and water. I had no desire for any of their company, being still uncertain of those around me.

I was so caught up in Hofmann's tale, I failed to notice the shutters had been drawn in my aunt's room for the first time in weeks. The windows were open and the air coming in from outside was fresh. The room was so bright with light its shabbiness was hidden by the glare. The only sign that time was passing came with the sound of bells from the square every half hour. It must have been Metzger's idea to open the windows but I was so anxious to continue reading, I gave it no more thought.

We are seventeen cabin passengers, twenty intermediate, forty emigrants and ninety-seven convicts with sixty or so others including the captain, a surgeon, a botanist, officers, crew and servants, making in all a total of two hundred and thirty-three souls on board. The boatswain speaks excellent German and he and I enjoy long conversations about all sorts of things during the night-watch. When we are not discussing the history of music, he points out the different stars and planets to me. He calls the crew to work with a whistle, which would be perfect for your father's Toy Symphony – one blast on E flat and shriller than a piccolo.

With the exception of the boatswain and one or two others, the rest of the crew look like hairy pirates. My favourite beard belongs to the second mate, who plaits his hair into small tails tied up with ribbon. These sailors have a way of fixing an eye on you as if to say, give me your gold and all will be well. The trouble is I haven't much gold. They seem entirely free from those rules of decency, which restrain a man on shore. Even the captain, who is generally a well-educated man, has a rough, hectoring manner when he's dealing with the men. I say this, but I also know he rewards his sailors with a glass of gin when they've done well. I continually feel surprised. Nothing in my life could have prepared me for the strangeness of this voyage.

Nothing, I realised, could have prepared me for the idea of Hofmann travelling much further than between upper and lower Silesia. Obviously I know very little about human nature and less about Jakob Hofmann. Hofmann on the high seas? It was so improbable, so ludicrous, indeed, so unbelievable that I laughed aloud. Hofmann on a voyage to Van Dieman's Land? I continued to chuckle in that lonely room for several minutes, which is an odd thing to do for a man who is mostly sad.

> The sheep, pigs, cows, hens and geese make an infernal concert at sunrise. As soon as the honking begins, I hide under my bedcovers and try to imagine what you or your children are doing. I often ask questions which of course you cannot answer and then I find myself talking aloud to you in my cabin. Thank God I have a cabin to myself. Apart from the stray insects hiding in the corners, if I had to share with someone human, that person would surely think me mad.

> *28ᵗʰ February, 1792*
> *The Run between Fernando and the Horn*

> Gone now the steady course, with the wind mostly foul. The ship makes slow progress and I am told a heavy sea took one sailor off the deck at dawn. Our bread's mouldy and maggoty, our beef like oakwood, our water stinking and maggoty and our beans almost gone. With only a few casks of flour we must now eat what the animals on board want, or starve. Dysentery is more a problem than scurvy which we keep at bay with daily doses of lime juice. It frequently occurs as our ship nears the tropics, but in some cases, I fear it will appear again and worse, as we move into the cold, southern latitudes.

> — *Your devoted Jakob*

> Have you my dear, visited the graveyard of Saint Peter's yet?

I tried to imagine what she would have felt, poking amongst the weeds for her brother's bones. It was unthinkable. There was almost a sense of randomness, an eleventh hour perversity to the question, which I found hard to understand. Hofmann was a queer, gothic sort of fellow with his black cloak and his widow, his spade digging friends and his three-cornered hat. And yet I could not read the pages quickly enough.

7ᵗʰ April, 1792

Dear Friend,

We dropped anchor at Rio for three weeks to replenish our supplies. The captain bought more vegetables and fruit and arranged for the cattle to graze on land near the harbour. Imagine market day in Salzburg and magnify the smells and the noise a hundred times. Think of a sun that burns the eyes through the eyelids. That is Rio.

The slave trade thrives in these parts and a clever youth sells for twenty to thirty pounds. We're afraid to venture out at night, what with the dirt, the crowds and more soldiers than exist in an Italian opera. The convicts, poor devils, must remain on board.

After our third week in Rio the cattle were returned to the hold with more goats and sheep and some rabbits. The captain plans to leave some animals behind at various stops on our journey so they can breed as food for future voyages. A bit like Noah's Ark. I sometimes wish we could do the same for the convicts. Set them free I mean. They are always chained as they walk the deck, their bodies half-starved. I'll wager they've not seen the recent hauls of fish when we approached the Horn.

Please convey my best wishes to your family,

— *Jakob*

25ᵗʰ April, 1792

Dear Friend,

Are you well? Are you and your husband and your children all content? Do you find time to practise every day or are the demands of soirées in St Gilgen too great a distraction? Now it is your turn to ask me something. Am I content? Am I fulfilled by my adventure? Do I find time to play the violin every day? The answer is no to each question.

Metzger once told me that a single wave made him seasick. I have been sick for several days and am unable to practise. A fellow passenger told me to gaze unceasingly at the horizon and imagine

I can feel the curve of the world. The trouble is that the horizon stretches above the ship's mast only to sink out of sight again when the boat dips. If I become severely ill, I lie down inside my cabin and hope to die. If I think I can distract myself, I pick up my violin and pluck at it. I wish your father could hear me play on days when it is calm. I have developed a controlled vibrato at last. No more buzzing of a love-sick fly, but just enough movement of fingers to nourish the sound. Unfortunately I keep on bumping my bowing arm against the wall when the ship is in a violent roll.

Your true friend,

— *Jakob Hofmann*

20th May, 1792

My Dear,

We have been battering our way for days through freezing gales. The seas broke across the decks and the rigging went to ice. It is colder than the day I came to see you in Hannibal Platz when you sang one of your songs to me and I found it very difficult to think of the music when I wanted to think about you. I remember the ice on all the window panes and how you ran into the courtyard without a coat because you were so cross with me. Was it because of what I didn't say to you and not what I did that made you angry? Ah my dear, it makes me sad that I will never know your answer.

I do know that in this dreadful cold that is all around us now, the ravages of scurvy play havoc with men's lives. The captain can barely muster a crew for the ordinary duties of the watch and I've taken the precaution of eating more limes.

— *Jakob*

21st June, 1792

Dearest Nannerl,

I wish I could see you once more but it is unlikely to happen.

I pulled a cushion from the end of my aunt's bed and tucked it behind my head. I lay back until I was comfortable, delaying the pleasure of reading.

Miraculously the weather has improved and with it the health of the passengers and crew. I cannnot speak for the other ships. We often lose sight of them and then one or two or all reappear out of the blue like ghostly relations to whom we never speak.

Yesterday we saw an albatross and several penguins which caused us to sound, but we could find no ground despite a line of one hundred and fifty fathoms. One of those birds the sailors call a noddy settled on our rigging and was eventually caught by the ship's cook. Its cry reminded me of the canary you once had, more squawk than song, but looking like a blackbird with webbed feet.

The canary, I remembered, had fallen off her perch and died on the cage floor because Berthe broke all her eggs, cleaning out the cage. It was an uncomplicated, instant grief.

Felix says these noddies never fly far from land. I imagine this one will end up in a pie for the captain's table. Poor bird. Tonight I intend to choose my dreams before I fall asleep. I think I'd like to hear you playing a Bach fugue in the music room at Hannibal Platz. The trouble is that sometimes, without wishing anything at all, I hear arpeggios that go up in a major key only to come down again in the minor. This is more of a nightmare – like last night when I dreamt I picked up my violin and the D string snapped before I even turned the pegs. As I bent down to get a spare from the trunk under my bed, I found I only had packets of needles and an endless supply of lace. When I moved the lace to one side, it fell apart in my hands and when I woke I realised I was holding a tattered length of quilt that had been eaten up by moths, there are so many holes in it.

Goodnight my dear. I will fall asleep remembering our walk together by the lake in Saint Gilgen.

— *Jakob*

Poor Hofmann. I feel truly nothing but pity for him.

Dearest Nannerl,

At last we have met an island! This morning there was dead calm
and a boat from each ship was lowered into the bay where our fleet
was anchored. I went ashore with a group of officers, including our
ship's botanist and several other passengers who wanted to explore
land. The circumference must be at least three to four miles since
we took two hours to walk halfway round it. I found myself in the
company of the botanist who had become very excited by a variety
of plants he'd never seen before. The seaweed looks like cabbage but
its stench is far worse. The sun burns our skin, blinds our eyes and
drives the sailors mad. I sometimes wonder if I should have brought
my box and trolley with me, except I keep forgetting I'm no longer a
draper and that I left any paraphernalia behind in Frankfurt. Thank
God I say . . .

We met some islanders as we were making our way back to the
ship and although we gave them gifts of elephant-fish and bread,
they seemed more interested in the two pigs the first officer had
brought ashore. The tallest one among them carried a stick but
otherwise they had no weapons. I could see their bodies were
painted with red stripes but the effect was more striking than
warlike. I think they had been watching us for some time from
behind the trees and decided that we were harmless, that is, until the
first officer shot his musket into the air to catch a noddy. The islanders ran back into the trees and never came out again.

I tossed the remaining pages of this letter to one side and picked up another.
Its details bothered me with its persistent talk of noddies and natives like
yarns from an old sea-salt. I was overwhelmed by doubts, becoming drunk
on them in a way, slurring my thoughts. Could he, I held my breath at the
audacity, would he have invented all this without so much as sailing in a
ferry-boat on the Rhine, to open our eyes to this strange world where he
could admit his true feelings? I felt a twinge of guilt. I have such a nasty
mind. But I had no intention of stopping reading. It is part of family history
and I am part of her family. Blood-misery I suppose.

31ˢᵗ July, 1792

My dear Nannerl,

Now I am deeply wretched, though not as much as others. A few days ago I saw some convicts with bedraggled hair, their starved faces covered in dirt and I realised when I stared more closely at them that they were women. Chains swung down from their wrists and ankles as they walked backwards and forwards, backwards and forwards, grimly keeping pace with the tacking of the sails. Their eyes hardly moved while they stared at the horizon and although I saw no tears I thought I heard one or two sobbing. It was a dreadful noise, like someone choking when drowning; the unforgettable moaning of a hurricane wind. To me it's the human voice that stamps the character of a gale and if I close my eyes and try to sleep, I know that wail will haunt me through the starry night.

2ⁿᵈ August, 1792

My dearest Nannerl,

I miss you more than I can say, think or write, which is why I cannot continue this poor letter.

Yours,

— *Jakob*

Auntie stirred as I sat with this, the briefest of his letters in my hand, too agitated to resume reading. I was overwhelmed by the despair that leapt off the page and allowed myself to sit there at the foot of her bed, weeping in sympathetic wretchedness. I crossed my legs, holding them together very tightly to prolong the emotion in some way. I was, I can see it now, subsumed by all sorts of desires. I wept incontinently for Josephine, for my aunt, for Hofmann, for myself, for my father. I sat there for what seemed like an hour but must have been only minutes, unable to stop weeping. Somehow, I managed to continue reading and without knowing at what point, the tears dried, along with my own fit of sentimentality.

Right now my dear there is no wind for our sails because the sea is calm again. It makes me think of a vast sheet of lead stretching out as far as the horizon and holding us all prisoners on board. Such merciless monotony. I wonder if we will ever reach the place they call Van Diemen's Land. I asked Felix what he thought at the close of his watch and while he was grappling with ideas of modulation, he looked at me with his gentle, man-in-the-moon face and said, 'Who knows?' There was not a hint of bitterness. I think one of the reasons I am drawn to him is that he reminds me of Joseph Metzger.

I am going to sleep my dear. — *J.H.*

It is a strange thing but I would have liked my Aunt to wake up at that moment. I would have liked to read the last of these letters to her. I would very much have liked that, but she was deeply asleep. I read them aloud anyway. Perhaps she heard me with her eyes closed.

16th August, 1792

Dearest Maria Anna,

1. Van Diemen's Land is nearer than the captain mapped and we are steering a southwest course with a strong breeze coming up behind us. I have glimpsed the greatness of deep water. It is a mountainous sea, making the ship roll and tumble all over the place but I fixed my gaze on the horizon and have found my sea legs at last! We seem to have become separated from the rest of the fleet. This happens from time to time and doesn't worry the captain so I'm told.
2. The sailors acquired a pet, its wing span about six feet and they let it loose upon the deck. The bulwarks balk its flight as it snaps and flounders amongst the rigging. The sailors laugh, showing no fear. It is of course another albatross.
3. I've mastered the astronomical quadrant and a kind of navigation by the stars.
4. Felix says he understands rudimentary counterpoint.
5. Sometimes we see butterflies on deck, competing with the flying fish and the wretched albatross. A wall of moths is a sign of land, according to the botanist. This morning I noticed the quilt on my bed has more holes than cloth.
6. My spirits are improving. I have stopped hearing the cries of prisoners in my sleep.
7. Not a single violin string has snapped, despite the salt sea air.

8. I've been talking to the other passengers and found that we have more in common than any of us first thought. At least three of them are Jews like myself, who have escaped the drudgery of demands from within and without our communities; men of business who were never paid by their German rulers, court Jews who had protection of a sort outside our cities but who preferred to escape. You could not know about such matters my dear. We never did discuss them, you and I. They were our separate worlds. It was better that way.

We will meet in St Gilgen another day perhaps.

I am your devoted,

— *Jakob*

I could have sworn my aunt stirred again. I looked across at her but the eyelids hadn't moved. The wrinkles on her face seemed smoother, the breathing even slower, if possible, than it was before.

15th September, 1792

Nannerl my only love, how long does it take to sail to the other side of the world!

We are sinking and there's not much time left to write. The officers and crew are drenched from bailing out all night. *The Oracle* is two miles from Adventure's Bay off the coast of Van Diemen's Land and it seems our ship will shatter in the surf. Still no sign of the other vessels. I begin to fear the worst as we move so fast towards the land. Pumping useless when she grinds on the bottom with her keel. The planks of the deck shift first one way and then another. Like blows of a mallet on the feet. Now we're caught by the surf. Damn 'Landfall' that it should come like this. Several provision cases have broken loose. The main mast is almost demolished. The convicts not in chains and some of the passengers are jumping overboard as the waves attack and retreat. My dear Felix was killed when he tried to lower one of the small boats into the sea. It smashed against the side of the ship, taking him with it. Tossed like a puppet in his watery grave.

I have decided to stay inside the cabin for as long as it holds. My pen runs like a wild thing across the paper and it is a miracle I can write at all. During all this hell, with screams of men, women, animals – a dissolving ship seems like the dissolving of the world. Too late for help. How many wrecks will follow? What irony in the last instruction of a voyage when the Captain cries: 'Let go.' They say this is the end of a ship's journey and of her toil. For those of us who are still on board, the world will be turning upside down when we are sucked into the deep.

My dearest Nannerl, though we never loved each other openly, that we did so in secret is better than nothing at all. A spider has settled on a corner of the desk while I scribble. I know nothing of its habits, apart from a readiness to spin a web and catch a fly, but as I watch, I am convinced its crumpled face is looking up at me and I resist the urge to brush it away. It wanders across the surface of your father's book, stopping and starting, placing its legs on the paper with the delicacy of a small bird. We are both set for oblivion and yet I find myself thinking unless my death is more real than my life, why hurry up the event? The truth is we have no idea what we are about to face and the spider has started to unravel its thread with miraculous optimism, paying no attention to the chaos all around us. But I must. I am unable to write anymore.

Think of me sometimes,

— Jakob.

Chapter 21

PASSACAILLE

Auntie was snoring, not dying when I folded each one of Hofmann's letters and tucked them away underneath some sheets of music manuscript. Such extraordinary confessions. How strange I had missed seeing them before. Perhaps misery at my continued separation from Josephine had blinded me, so that when I looked in a mirror, there was no reflection, no inkling of something missing in the story. I was about to close the drawer when my aunt spoke up from the bed – and there was I thinking she was at death's door. By the calmness of her voice I felt she understood what I'd been doing for the last few hours and that she approved.

'Tear all my papers into little bits and burn the lot before I die. Now you've read them, there's no reason to keep them anymore. Burn the music too. I am not Mozart.'

'If you are quite certain Auntie. At this rate, you'll outlive me.'

I think she smiled in her lopsided way. I was still puzzling over Hofmann's description of the spider in his cabin. I had no memory of drowning in another life. Perhaps his spider was coincidentally the last of Hofmann's tales – I did not want it to be real.

'Promise me.' She tried to raise her head from her pillows. 'Tear them all up. I want your assurance that you will destroy everything Franzel. Everything that has caused me pain.'

I lit the stove with some wood which Metzger had brought yesterday and pushed the letters through the door of the stove in such a hurry that there would be no time left for second thoughts. Although it was the middle of summer, neither of us could be warm enough. I placed an extra quilt over her bed and shivered with her, listening to the snapping sounds of burning paper and regretting I hadn't enough wit to think of burning something else in its place. She would never see and she had lost half her teeth and hair. It is true she only eats and drinks whatever I, or Metzger happen to give her. When she talks she sometimes forgets who I am. She cannot read, but even if she could, she would not remember the end of a sentence she had begun. What am I doing here, trying officiously to prolong her life or just trying ineffectively to make her comfortable?

'And don't forget the music Franzel.'

So, it's true that she can remember some things.

'When I'm dead,' she wheezed, 'There will be no memories. Nothing to show I walked on this earth. Not a thing. Do you understand?'

Without replying I picked out a violin sonata, a sarabande for clarinet and several songs. All that remained was a scrap of ribbon and some dusty unfinished pages of a requiem mass in a hand I did not recognise.

'Continue.' She mouthed the word with her lips as I rolled the manuscripts into tight cylinders before pushing each one into the stove, two or three at a time on top of the pyre, watching the pages spring back, curl and burn, thinking what a waste but remembering that she had sent copies of the sonata and sarabande to Hofmann as a wedding present. I smiled as I thought of them buried at the bottom of the ocean off the shore of Van Diemen's Land. I smiled at the image and the improbability. They might of course be with Metzger or Frau Heller in Frankfurt. They might even be lying somewhere covered in dust or chewed to shreds by musical rats. I placed more wood on the flames. We are always burning things in my family.

'Where's Joseph Metzger?' My aunt had begun babbling again and despite the shortness of the sentences, she ran words together in her panic. 'I want to say goodbye to him. Bring him to me Franzl.'

I saw a face without eyebrows or eyelashes, with the remaining strands of hair on her skull like veins against the yellow skin. I left the room, worried that if I stood for a few more minutes outside the door, there was a chance she might die while I was out. It was a thought I had every time I paid a visit to my aunt's, but I still wished that Metzger would hurry up. He'd not missed an afternoon since her first stroke five years ago. Good, kind, reliable Metzger. I must go and fetch Marianna. I've written to my aunt's son, Leopold, telling him to hurry home and a month ago I sent a message to my brother, Karl in Milan, saying that there are not many weeks left.

Chapter 22

ÉTUDE

Metzger would have translated Vincent Novello's French into German and my aunt's German into French if his grasp of French were not so flimsy. When we pass him that day on the stairs outside my aunt's rooms he is in such a hurry, he almost knocks Mary Novello down one flight. It is his bad luck that he looks as if he moves with twice the force of others.

'Ah, pardonnez moi Madame, Monsieur. Beaucoup de pardons je vous en prie' he says in a rush. (Exact translation would be a strain so I will adapt only its sense). 'You must be Madame Sonnenburg's English visitors. I am her friend, Josef Metzger, Privatier. I wrote to you on her behalf to say she looked forward to meeting you.'

Novello seems puzzled at first but nods his head to show he understands. His wife breathes hard from her collision, managing to part her lips and smile, showing every one of her small white teeth. When Metzger half uncurls from his bow, all she can see of his face is a pair of hairy eyebrows and a nose as rough as a turnip. He gabbles because he prefers them not to examine his French or begin a conversation without the benefit of a dictionary. He thanks them for visiting my aunt, murmuring good-bye to me in German before disappearing backwards through Auntie's door – a shy, hunchback genie, locked in a succession of bows that make him seem even larger than he is.

Her permanent snores can be heard from behind the closed door and Mary Novello breathes out sharply as people do when they feel the relief of escape. I see her pat the stair walls for support, avoiding the cobwebs dangling in perfect geometry above our heads. Novello is in a trance, unaware that his shoes clatter on the stairs as if to wake the dead.

Instead of resenting what I'd thought was a florid case of hero-worship, I vow to be of help. It is true my mother said they might show an interest in me if I show some in them. I suspect they plan to embalm my father in a manuscript because Novello has asked my mother for a strand of his hair. No doubt he thinks that owning one will help him understand the alchemy. Can a single hair explain so much? But my cunning mother has already extracted every tuft from his hairbrush and I doubt if there is any left. They should perhaps go and commune with a soothsayer. So far none of it explains his genius, although Vincent Novello and I have agreed that my father is the Shakespeare of music.

Oh what nonsense this is. He was Mozart. He was childlike. He was sage. He was funny. He was serious. He liked patterns upside down or back to front and they would still make sense. He took risks. He liked the security of sums. I've heard it all before – the huffing and puffing and the contradictions that occur when you ressurect the dead. It makes me nervous and dismayed. It is so much sentimental nonsense. Especially when my aunt is still alive. Clinging to her miserable existence. Bedridden and overlooked. Poor dear Auntie. I must try for her sake not to be so pernickety and pessimistic. I can always talk to them about my father from her point of view.

'Our family' I begin rather pompously as we turn left out of Kirchgasse, 'owes much to Herr Metzger. But he, dear man, shrinks with genuine feeling from making it apparent. I'll tell you more when we're in the coffee house.'

The sun steals through a window of the Café Tomaselli onto the bald head of an old man drinking coffee, catching him in one of those biblical shafts of light. We smell the scents of cinnamon and coffee but I choose sweet cakes and kirschwasser for my new friends and milk curd for myself. I am their host I remind myself in an expansive moment and I will pay the fare.

'I know you will agree with me if I say my poor aunt is to be pitied,' I announce as we settle. 'Now Josef Metzger feels great pity for her.'

The curd warms my belly and I am more than willing to talk because they listen to everything I have to say.

'Joseph Metzger is an old friend. He talks to her. He shares memories with her. For many months she has been paralysed on one side and so he carries her from the bed to her old clavier and back again, which is why the instrument is placed close by. She can't play any more of course. But he encourages her. He remembers how she was and that is his reward.'

'How very moving.' Novello wipes some cream from his lips with a hand-kerchief and then says what he really wants to say. 'I caught sight of a copy of the Minuet from 'Don Giovanni' on top of Madam Sonnenburg's instrument. We were wondering if she still played, were we not my dear?'

Mary Novello has been watching me from across the table, slowly stirring the spoon in her cup and making small concentric waves at the bottom of it. She is, I am sure, judging me in some way. I like to think she understands my position as my father's son – this impossible position – although yesterday, when we first met at my mother's house I was not convinced either one of them would ever understand.

'Pray continue,' she says quietly, placing her spoon beside the cup.

I like that. I like the simplicity of her order and the idea that she would like to hear more.

'About two days before you arrived, my aunt asked to be carried from her bed and placed next to her instrument. On trying to play, she found although she could finger a few passages with her right hand, her left was without any feeling at all.'

'How very distressing.' Novello exaggerates the syllables to emphasise his pity. His wife twists the fingers of her left hand, also absorbed by thoughts of my poor, paralysed aunt and when our feet accidentally touch, she looks straight ahead, without any awareness of what has happened. I sense their hunger for more facts by the way they edge forward on their seats and I order my second bowl of milk curd with nutmeg, recommending that they try the red berry tart.

'Auntie found it difficult to sleep the night before you came and was afraid you might not call. You see she is blind and feeble and yet appears to suffer no pain. She remains in bed for most days, waiting for the final stroke of death. Several times I have thought . . . but then, she recovers quite miraculously.' Mary Novello pushes her tart to one side, raising a napkin to moist eyes.

A pool of curd is trickling down my leg towards the buckle of my shoe. I leave the table on the pretext that I must clean my hose. This way at least, the interruption would allow our conversation to be resumed on a subject more cheerful than my aunt's inevitable death. I suspect they intend to discuss me in my absence and the idea of it excites me a great deal.

'What a mournful little man.'

'He still feels overshadowed by his father.'

'It's not surprising he feels an affinity with his aunt.'

'There's a despair in his countenance that never quite goes away.'

'His mother is quite charming by comparison.'

'Madame Mozart looks so young, considering her age.'

My mother had made a point of flaunting her youthful appearance in front of the Novellos the day before, lapping up their admiration without any shame. I feel quite sick if I think about her vanity and it only makes me show a greater tenderness towards Auntie.

'How miserable to be convinced of your own mediocrity because you happen to be the son of a genius.' Mary Novello speaks in that clear, melodic voice which I now associate with English ladies.

'I never expected him to be quite so short or stout.'

'And yet his face has the look of his father don't you think my dear? Especially his forehead, which is remarkably wide and his nose, which is long . . .'

'It seems he believes that everything he does is so inferior to what was accomplished by Mozart, that there's no serious desire to compose himself or to publish what he writes.'

'How unfortunate. How most unfortunate,' or words to that effect.

I return to my seat, hoping I appear unfathomable. Vincent Novello rises from his chair and waits for me to sit down with an ease of manner I will emulate if one day I'm in similar circumstances. His wife examines me with eyes that say you are more interesting than I first thought, and she purses her mouth into a small point, which she sustains as people often do when they are whistling, paying attention or implanting a kiss.

'We'd like to hear what happened to your aunt after her husband died and she returned to Salzburg to become a piano teacher.' Novello reveals the shrewdness of a man who either wants to collect material for a biography, or has suddenly divined what would please me in the way of gossip. It is the reason I ask if we should dine, the three of us together, that evening. We agree I should meet them at their inn at eight o'clock, and from there we shall have but a short journey to a tavern where we may dine most comfortably on beef and liver dumplings or whatever else we fancy. Then in our warm, relaxed state I shall try to tell them everything else they would like to know about my aunt, providing I have a mind to it.

Chapter 23

MENUET

I am only a minute early when I arrive at the inn. Under a colonnade on the opposite side of the courtyard there is sufficient standing for carriages with a water trough between two of the columns and I decide to leave the coachman to tend the horses while I go inside.

From the streets beyond the surrounding walls, I can hear the usual hum of the city with at least ten different church bells, all tolling the hour. As the great clanging of Saint Peter's rings louder, deeper and slower than the rest, I imagine all those people buried in its catacombs and I remember the matter of my father's unquiet grave. I find I'm quickening my step deliberately, trying to stifle that memory as I resolve to greet the Novellos in a more animated mood. It's clearly my weakness to look miserable when everyone else is enjoying themselves.

'Do we dine close by?' asks Mary Novello.

'Yes, yes. It's very near.' I am watching her small fingers struggle with the bone buttons of a ruched blue cape. It is cut in the latest style and I wish to describe it accurately to my dear Josephine when I write to her tonight. 'Yes, yes,' I say. 'It is close.'

'Then let us walk.' She transfers her glance from her husband and back to me, turning her head so quickly to one side that the satin bow in the middle of her bonnet doubles over on itself in a charming, lopsided manner. She pushes it back as if regretting the whim that has made her wear it in the first place and when finally she slides her arm around her husband's waist, I am again reminded of my beloved Josephine who is still in Lemburg, thanks to my mother, who has always made it clear she is not welcome in Salzburg.

I dismiss the coach and we begin to walk. We are in high spirits since it is a fine summer evening. Birds of various sorts are flying about on a scavenge after a storm. People are milling between houses and churches as if there has been a fair. Plenty of churches with green onion domes. Plenty of priests. We walk slowly through the cemetery of Saint Sebastian and

I point out my grandfather's frugal grave, a neat rectangle of earth shared with my aunt's daughter, Jeanette and my mother's second husband, the Count Von Nissen.

'Your poor Aunt.' Mary Novello speaks with great feeling after I have explained that sad little story. I resist the impulse to take her soft white hand in mine and squeeze it. Vincent Novello has returned to examine the bust of Saint Sebastian at the entrance to the church and I strive to see the grey stone image, the gilded spears plunged through the heart and the cherubs arranged above the face with the eyes of an Englishman.

'There's so much dying going on,' I remark, 'though no doubt, it's comforting to have a shrine to gore and gloom.' We stroll through the town, pausing every now and then to admire a point of architecture, or, for the Novellos to ask, 'Was your father . . .' 'Did your dear mother . . .' 'When your father and aunt were living together?'

I am too embarrassed by my rumbling stomach to pay much attention, being anxious to reach our inn before all of Salzburg hears it as well.

The Old Trout happens to be one of many yellow or brown plastered buildings, squashed up one against the other on both sides of a narrow street. Not much wider than a coach, the sign above the door has fallen off one of the hinges. It flaps obscurely in the shadows as people come and go. There is nothing to prepare the visitor for what lies within – a confused noise of people eating with the clatter of waiters hurrying between tables. An accordion and a violin are ruining the march from Marriage of Figaro. The walls have been smothered with stag heads and there is a strong smell of beer throughout. I catch Vincent Novello staring at one animal, its fur silkier than the rest, its antlers without a smidgeon of dust. I know venison is out of season and reassure him it is not on the menu tonight, at which point he laughs so delightfully that I put my arms around my new friend, hug him for his sensitive nature and choose a table in the quietest corner under a ring of candles. As I lean back to admire the scene, I decide all we need is the artist to paint the picture and a waiter to serve.

'What has become of Mozart's own fortepiano?' Vincent Novello is leaning back in his chair to digest his roast fowl, sipping the wine in front of him as if in meditation. It sometimes seems that he is permanently adrift with thoughts of my father. No doubt the great book will form itself over the main course.

'My brother had it sent to Milan. Both the fortepiano and my father's slippers have found a permanent home in his house.' My voice has a certain spiteful regret, after all, I am the musician in the family and Karl, my older brother, is a civil servant in the Austrian Kingdom of Lombardo-Venetia. But I keep these thoughts to myself and order some common household bread in preference to the more refined variety on the table.

'My greatest difficulty in writing about your dear father is that I can't seem to find enough papers or witnesses for every part of his life I wish to describe.' Novello studies his knife and fork and spoon with such a forlorn expression, suspecting I am withholding critical bits of a jigsaw and leaving him to the mercy of guesswork. 'Am I?' I ask myself.

'You examine the evidence on both sides of a gap in a puzzle and you presume you know what fits in the gap, but of course you can never be certain you are right. Without precise knowledge, how much can you claim before you are guilty of fiction?'

'Vincent is concerned about the truthfulness of imagination. He wishes to avoid false claims and would prefer Mozart's music to speak for itself.'

Yes, yes, quite, but perhaps truth is inimical to the imagination. I think this but say nothing. For the sake of sentimental fancy, they have pestered me with questions about Nannerl, my mother, my brother, my cousin and my father's fortepiano. What about poor Sonnenburg into the bargain? We have almost forgotten the baron. There is a silence as I soak my bread in the remaining sauce and when I look up from my plate, I see Auntie standing at the foot of her husband's grave in Saint Gilgen's cemetery. (He died of nothing more obscure than old age.) The Novellos have vanished and I seem to be hanging above the newly polished clavier in my aunt's salon, watching a zealous maid wielding a feather duster across the backs of chairs and the surfaces of furniture. I gobble up my thread and scurry inside the instrument to lie on the cool of the strings. Everything has to be spick and span for the guests returning from the baron's funeral. But the strings have turned into corrugated lines on the tablecloth in front of me and I am back again, dining with the Novellos. I brush the sweat from my forehead with the cuff of my sleeve and try another tack.

'You asked what happened to my aunt when the baron died,' I conceal the dampness of my sleeve with my hand. 'Auntie was bereft when they buried Sonnenburg.' The effort of speech is enormous. More sweat is forming above my eyebrows. My tongue keeps getting in the way of my teeth and I can hardly do anything about it after three glasses of Rhenish wine.

'She tried to prepare herself for his death when he complained of pains in his heart but she was not prepared for the loneliness of her bed.' The Novellos look at me with interest.

'He was sixty-four years old and fortunate to have died quickly. Seven children were provided for and there was a small annuity for their old nurse, Nandl Heller.'

The wife smiles approvingly and the husband mutters something like 'Most proper, most proper indeed.'

'Auntie had to leave the house empty for the new magistrate and she returned to live in Salzburg with four of the seven children. The rest of the family was scattered somewhere in the Tyrol, including her son Leopold.'

'She must have been quite young,' observed Mary Novello.

'She was fifty years old when she accepted lodgings with the Barisanis.' Not so young, but not so old. 'She took on a few pupils to keep herself busy. The urge to compose had dried up and she needed to feel useful.'

'Do you have any of her compositions? Are there any left?' Vincent Novello is examining the tablecloth and trying not to sound eager in a professional sort of way.

'None at all,' I lie. 'She burnt every single one.' I make no mention of any possible copies. I am certainly not going to bring up the subject of Herr Hofmann.

'What a pity.' Novello removes a strand of chicken from between his front teeth with a jewelled tooth pick.

'It's quite straightforward really. My aunt thought she would devote herself to her family and teaching. Do you remember? The graves we saw in Saint Sebastian? I discussed the matter indirectly on our walk this afternoon. Her daughter, Jeanette, died from a fever at the age of sixteen. Since she was the spitting image of her step-sister, Marianna, and because at sixteen years of age, Jeanette was not a case of out of the womb and into the tomb, my aunt grieved all the more for her interrupted life. Five months later, one of the step-sons, Joseph Maria died.'

'What a lot of deaths,' murmurs Mary Novello.

I cough into my napkin to hide a smile. 'Auntie,' I hurry on, 'took comfort from her remaining family and the church. Marianna went with her to mass twice a week and they prayed together.'

'And her son? What has become of her only son?' asks Novello.

'Sent to the Tyrol, to become a soldier. No music there I'm afraid. Despite all my grandfather's efforts in the beginning, he's never been interested. And if Auntie once had ambitions for him to become a second Mozart, she dropped them after Leopold, her father died.'

'It's difficult for the parent as well as the child.' Mary Novello says this quietly. 'We have a daughter Clara who wants to sing, but I'm not sure. It's . . . so hard to know what's right.'

'No doubt your daughter will decide for herself,' I reply, unable to resist adding, 'I never wish those I love to earn their living as a musician.'

What would these good people give, I wonder suddenly, to know the true whereabouts of my father's grave. But that is my story, not theirs I'm afraid.

'If you were one of these new-fangled dentists you'd want your children to have good teeth,' says Vincent Novello, unaware of my secret thoughts as he empties the last of the bottle into my glass and ignores my protests.

'Of course, very good teeth and a fine bowing arm.'

The Novellos look quite far away from where I am sitting and I try in vain to see where the table ends or if there is anyone else left in the tavern. The room either sounds empty or my voice is very loud. It occurs to me I might have trouble when I try to stand up.

'When did Frau Sonnenburg stop giving piano lessons?' Mary Novello has a pencil in her hand and is recording what I say in a small leather-bound diary.

I can hear my aunt insisting in that pitiful hiss of hers: 'I want nothing to show I walked on this earth.'

'I am so sorry. Have you said when she stopped teaching?'

And so I continue. 'Auntie had a stroke in the middle of someone's lesson. Very frightening for the child she was teaching. She was already blind in one eye and not at all well.'

The scratching of the pencil suddenly seems louder than my voice. How odd. The woman is tireless and I am very tired.

'Did your mother visit your aunt when she discovered she was ill?'

'Oh they hardly spoke in all the years of living within walking distance.'

I chase a large crumb from the table onto my lap and stare at it without understanding why it is there. 'My mother was re-married to the count and my aunt was surrounded by her step-children. If either of them ever dreamed of a rapprochement, it certainly had no effect.'

'Such family wars are commonplace.'

'The pain of sustaining it was greater than the cause.'

'And your intimacy with your Aunt . . . Has it always been so?'

A double bass is thumping somewhere inside my head.

'We met about three years ago, after a long period in which we saw nothing of each other . . . but Auntie has told me more about my family than anyone else.' The words I utter are becoming slurred and mercifully, Novello proposes a toast to end the meal.

'To Nannerl,' both cry more or less at the same time. 'To Mozart, his widow, Joseph Haydn, to everyone else who mattered to him. God save them all.' We are all forty sheets to the wind when I summon a coach to return the short distance to the inn. Vincent Novello embraces me several times and calls me 'dear fellow' with much emotion, while Mary Novello places her hand on my arm whenever we turn a corner, leaning on it, which is I suppose, a more northern way of showing warmth. We promise to meet the next day at my mother's house.

I admit they have shown tact, not least in their acquaintance with my mother, who has declared many times over to me in the last three days how genuinely she likes them. I think she is speaking with the head of a mother as much as the heart of Mozart's widow. She keeps telling me to show my compositions to the English publisher. When I protest, not from modesty but from a fastidiousness about their worth which would have pleased Hofmann and which no doubt my aunt would have understood, she tells me I am lazy and not at all like my father. I freely admit to this so we can end the subject, but I find if I start thinking I am not myself exactly, I have to ask myself who am I?

After walking with the Novellos and admiring the summer light in the trees, I take them for the last time to my mother's town house. She immediately produces my father's inkstand – the one he used when writing the Requiem and shows them the gold watch he had given her as a bridal present. Looking directly at Vincent Novello, she strokes the circular outline of its face as it lies upwards in her palm, and asks him with the playfulness of a cat: 'Voulez-vous l'avoir?' Fortunately he declines and my mother is not obliged to own that she had already promised it to me.

They leave Salzburg in a coach and four, taking with them a tuft of hair from my father's hairbrush, which my mother miraculously has discovered along with a section of a letter written by my father to my grandfather. No doubt even this show of generosity is sparked by her sense of competition with my aunt. I tell Mama when they are out of hearing that Auntie intends to present them with a print of Mozart and a page of his music when they return from Vienna. 'My God,' says Mama with her fine grasp of reality, 'if she's still alive to give it.'

CHANSON

Salzburg, 29th October, 1829

My dearest Josephine,

Auntie died some time after midnight. It seemed as if she would never let go. She wept in her bed and swallowed cups of water to replace the tears she'd shed. Though unable to see a thing, she mumbled about the clouds on the tops of the Nonnberg, Capuzinerberg and the Devil's Horn. She described that point in the river Salzach where it curves beyond the bridge and where the water runs so fast. I kept waiting for the moment in the process of dying when the suffering is so great that the fear of death dissolves and both the mind and the body stop clinging to life. It happened in the early hours of the morning. The doctor told me that's when most people slip away. 'Wolfie,' she said to me. 'Yes Auntie,' I replied. 'You're still there.' 'I'm still here,' I said. And that was it. She fell deeply asleep and never woke up.

I'll be returning to Lemburg after the funeral, which is being held on Tuesday afternoon at three o'clock. Auntie decided not to be buried in Saint Sebastian's in the end, preferring Saint Peter's. I will explain all when we are together but meanwhile I am busy arranging the singers and orchestra for a performance of papa's Requiem in her memory. A thousand kisses to the only person on this earth I wish to call wife.

— *W.A.M.*

Wolfgang Amadeus Mozart. This is the name I have given myself of late. Auntie said it was a good idea the first time we met, which is one of the few times she and my mother have agreed on something. As well as writing to my dear Josephine, I have also written to the Novellos and told them I shall conduct my father's Requiem for my aunt in Saint Peter's. Where else could it be performed? And her body, where else could it rest? Not as it happens, in that special corner of the cemetery which is still choked with ivy and moss, but next to it, in the first of the arcaded niches that is built against the side of the mountain. She will lie beside Michael Haydn who has been mouldering there for twenty-three years. It is not such a bad thing.

My aunt's stepchildren, all of them middle-aged and worthy have come with their families and are sitting in the first three pews of the church. Marianna is weeping next to her half-brother, Leopold, who sits with his eyes closed, trying to be invisible and almost succeeding. Out of sensitivity to those who would otherwise be behind and might not see over his head, Metzger sits further back than anyone else. He is studying the wreath of white flowers on top of the coffin and I can imagine – I don't have to see – the tears on his misshapen face. The remaining Barisanis, the Hagenauers and the Gilowskis are all there to pay respects. Katharina Gilowska died some years before, along with Berthe, the maid, and so many other people who have been important in my aunt's life. The elderly Abbé Eiberle who has travelled all the way from Saint Gilgen is alone. Not far to the right of him and further back, in the shadows cast by a confessional, is the figure of a man much frailer than the priest. Hooked onto the arm of a widow, his shrunken body has a tremor or more specifically, it shows itself in the way his head is shaking sideways in a continuous shudder. I observe him turn slowly in his familiar black cloak, still gripping the arm of his companion and shuffling down the aisle towards the great doors. From behind, she is stiff, thin, ageless. A walking-stick of a woman. Without having to transform myself into a spider, I know at once who they are.

Da Capo

Karlsbad, 25th July, 1844

Soon I will renounce all I love on earth. There is half a bottle left for me to drink and when that is gone, my pleasures will be turned upside down. I write as a man with a few days left to live and if I repeat myself, it is only because I have enjoyed the wine.

Through an act of will, I cannot explain it in any other way than this, I am able to exist before my birth, like a spider in the corner of the ceiling that has always been there, a witness from beginning to end. This is the story of what happened to my Aunt Nannerl. I have secret knowledge contained in a set of Chinese boxes, stored inside my mind and ready for me to reveal the layers that create the whole. There is not much time left.

Coda

London, 28th May, 2006

'Lot number one hundred and twenty seven: Mozart (Maria Anna, 'Nannerl', Mozart's elder sister) Autograph Letter Signed ('M:A:Gräfin von Berchtold zu Sonnenburg') sent to the publishers Breitkopf and Härtel about Mozart's music, and referring to the editions of Mozart's works being prepared by the publishers in Leipzig.

'Shall we begin bids at one thousand five hundred pounds? I have one thousand five hundred at the back. Two thousand, two thousand five hundred, three thousand. I have three thousand. Do I hear three thousand five hundred? Three thousand six hundred. Three thousand seven hundred. I repeat, three thousand seven hundred. Three thousand eight hundred. Do I hear more? Three thousand eight hundred. Three thousand eight hundred it is.'

A young man and woman leave their seats as the gavel falls. Short, continental, he moves somewhere inside an extra large trench coat. It matches the bleached hair which falls below his collar. His jaw is thrust to the ceiling while the girl, shorter, plump and swathed in shawls, murmurs consolingly in the direction of his ear. I haven't seen either one make a bid. Have they come for the letter?

My neck is burning but I dare not rub away the itch. The auctioneer begins another round of bids: Wolfgang Amadeus Mozart of course. Panic as I watch them disappear through the door. I am certain they long for but have failed to secure the letter – he looks so cross. Perhaps this diminutive Siegfried is writing a book about Nannerl. But he can't. I have. My fingers grip the rolled catalogue in my lap and I count to twenty-five slowly before I too leave the room.

I am walking down New Bond Street in white sunlight, about to cross Conduit Street when I see them again. They are coming towards me from round the corner on the other side. He has his fists jammed in his pockets. She is smiling at him in an adoring way, still wearing her catalogue. They pass me without recognition and I, suddenly wishing to forget them both, head towards Golden Square to buy a flute for my daughter. I can't help wondering who has bought the letter.

Author's Note

The characters of the four coachmen are invented as is Jakob Hofmann. There was no official Jewish population in Catholic Salzburg in the late eighteenth century, although there may have been travel into and out of Salzburg on market days. Frederick the Great of Prussia had a pusillanimous, politician's attitude towards their existence in his territory. Despite a tolerance of all Christian groups and an acceptance of Muslims (not difficult as there would hardly have been many in Prussia at the time), he outlawed Jews as immigrants and levied special taxes from those who were resident. They were banned from most professions, including the civil service, and it is clear that what tolerance was shown was opportunistic.

Joseph II of Austria passed an edict for tolerating Protestants in 1781 and granted a similar one for the Jews in 1782. It was the first law of its kind in Europe and the first time they were allowed to attend university and enter professions. The obligation to wear yellow armbands was abolished and they no longer had to pay special taxes, although they were still not allowed to build synagogues. It would have been unthinkable for Nannerl, who was a devout Catholic, to marry a Jew, and vice-versa. There was considerable family and social pressure on her to make a suitable marriage, yet she delayed any commitment until she was thirty-three. It is presumed her reason for accepting Sonnenburg was because her father worried about her future when he was dead. That Sonnenburg was a minor member of the nobility was not in itself an explanation for her accepting him since there had been similar suitors in the past. Mozart adds to the pressure in a letter urging her to settle down. It has the tactless and sanctimonious taint of Constanze hovering over his shoulder when he suggests that a man in Nannerl's life would be better than taking the waters. But a gifted and educated eighteenth-century female with normal physical and emotional desires, whose brother was a genius and whose father was a remarkable and celebrated violin teacher as well as a composer, would find it hard to find another man who would interest her. Enter the fictional Hofmann. His trip to Van Diemen's Land in 1792 was impossible - there being no official settlement on the island for several years after that date. His character must therefore have lied to Nannerl, as he would have remained in Frankfurt, presumably with the equally fictional Frau Heller.

Joseph Metzger was genuinely a fellow-lodger with Nannerl during her last years in Salzburg. He corresponded with Vincent Novello on her behalf in French and it is thought he looked after her day-to-day needs out of friendship. Katherl Gilowska was Nannerl's closest companion in her early Salzburg days and the names of Nannerl's suitors are also real, as are the names of Lorenz Hagenauer and the Abbé Bullinger, both old friends of Leopold Mozart. Berthe is a fictional maid, as is Nandl Heller, although the names of Nandl, Monica and Liserl are mentioned in the Mozart family letters as names of servants who helped look after Nannerl's children at different times. Berthe is presented as an old crone because Leopold, like Mozart, had a roving eye for pretty servant girls and it is unlikely the prettier ones would have been employed for so long by Frau Mozart. Unless specified, other characters such as the Abbé Eiberle, Herr and Frau Büchner etc. are imaginary.

Despite Mozart's praise of Nannerl's compositions, none has survived. It is unlikely but possible they are lying somewhere, unrecognised. Her musical handwriting may have been similar to her brother's, but if she had written anything as good, it is hard to believe Leopold Mozart would not have acknowledged it. We know from Leopold's correspondence that in his opinion she was the foremost keyboard player in Europe at the age of twelve and while living with her father after her mother's death, showed considerable skill in modulation and keyboard improvisation.

Mozart's death was caused by miliary fever according to official reports at the time. The precise whereabouts of Mozart's grave are still unknown. The body would have been placed in a hessian bag and dropped from its coffin into a communal grave and covered in lime to avoid the spread of disease. It would have been dug over at the end of seven years to make space for more bodies, as was the custom. The Viennese of the time were not sentimental about death and a third-class funeral such as Mozart's was not unusual amongst the middle classes. But speculation about the human remains of the world's most extraordinary composer is natural. It is also a grisly, fascinating fact that only a few years after Mozart's death and two days after Joseph Haydn's funeral in 1809, two Viennese officials illegally and secretly opened up Haydn's grave, removing his skull for examination by phrenologists who were anxious to discover tell-tale signs of genius.

The language of all letters in the novel is by the author. Some are entirely fictional, while others are interpretations of existing letters in the Mozart family's correspondence.

Facts

1719   *14th November* – birth of Johann Leopold Mozart, father of Wolfgang and Nannerl Mozart. Born in Augsburg, the eldest son of a bookbinder, he trained as an organist, violinist and chorister in the Church of the Holy Cross and St. Ulrich. At Salzburg University, he studied philosophy and law before entering the service of the Archbishop as leader of the court orchesta. Among his other duties was composition – his style caught between the old, polyphonic ways of J.S.Bach or Handel and the new 'styl galant' of J.C. Bach with its emphasis on homophony and melody, (e.g. The Toy Symphony). Believed he was put on earth to enshrine his son's genius and did his best to do so until the time of Wolfgang's marriage. In 1756, he wrote 'A Treatise on the Fundamental Principles of Violin Playing' in 1756 – an original, practical and bossy guide to string playing. It is stuffed with esoteric and personal digressions, which make it a joy to read. Although there had been previous manuals by other teachers, his was the most influential for the next half-century. By the year of his death in 1787, it had gone into a third edition. He dreamed of 'cultivating' a second genius when his daughter Nannerl gave birth to a son who was named after him. He also expressed concern for Nannerl's health after the birth in correspondence but is not specific about the nature of her illness. Unfortunately he died two years after his guardianship began.

1720   *25th December* – birth of Anna Maria Mozart, née Pertl, mother of Nannerl and Wolfgang Mozart; born in Schloss Huttenstein near Saint Gilgen and orphaned at an early age. Lusty sense of humour, intelligent and charming but with no intellectual pretensions, a long-suffering wife and mother who died at fifty-eight in the course of mothering Mozart while they were alone in Paris. Seven pregnancies and two live children. Her father had been a magistrate of St Gilgen and several of her family were renowned singers.

1736   *22nd October* – birth of Johann Baptist von Berchtold zu Sonnenburg who marries Nannerl Mozart. She is his third wife.

1747 *21ˢᵗ November* – Anna Maria Pertl marries Leopold Mozart in Salzburg.

1751 *30ᵗʰ / 31ˢᵗ July* – Nannerl born in Salzburg at midnight, christened Maria Anna Walburga Ignatia Mozart.

1756 *27ᵗʰ January* – Wolfgang Amadeus Mozart born in Salzburg – christened Joannes Chrysostomus Wolfgangus Theophilus Mozart.

1762–1766 Mozart family tours Europe.

1763 *6ᵗʰ January* – birth of Constanze Weber in Zell, lower Austria. She had a small but competent soprano voice and sang in Mozart's Mass in C minor, K.427 when it was performed at Salzburg in 1783. Also dark eyed and trim but not considered as pretty or as talented as her older sister, Aloysia who was Mozart's first love and, according to Aloysia, he still loved her when he died. Their mother was volatile, stressful to those around her and fond of a tipple, but Constanze remained loyal to her – a point of her character, which Mozart admired. Nannerl and Leopold Mozart disapproved of Constanze's marriage to Wolfgang and never seriously changed their minds. She disliked them in return. Out of six pregnancies, she bore two sons, Karl Thomas and Franz Xaver Wolfgang, both surviving her. Most of her life was spent in Vienna, Copenhagen and finally Salzburg. Her seeming incompetence as a housewife and businesswoman evaporated after Mozart's death. She drove hard bargains over the sale of his manuscripts, continued to organise her sons' lives when they lived in another country, enjoyed a successful second marriage to the Danish Count Georg von Nissen, published an edited, sanitised version of Nissen's biography of Mozart after Nissen's death and lived to the age of eighty. Reading her own correspondence and those of others, she emerges as a hectoring, manipulative and passionate woman who was not always straight in her business dealings but was direct in her relationships with those she loved.

1769   Johann Baptist von Berchtold zu Sonnenburg is made Pfleger of Saint Gilgen at thirty-three, described as a 'royal and district administrator' by the Mozart Museum, Salzburg.

1770   Leopold and Wolfgang leave for an extended stay in Italy, leaving Nannerl and her mother in Salzburg.

1778   *3rd July* – their mother, Anna Maria Mozart, dies in Paris.

1782   Mozart marries Constanze in Vienna. He is twenty-six and she is twenty.

1784   *23rd August* – Nannerl, aged thirty-three marries Sonnenburg, aged forty-eight and lives in Saint Gilgen with five step-children. At the time of marriage, the children are: Maria Anna, also called Anna Maria and Marianne (1771–1839), who is thirteen years old and eventually became very close to her step-mother. She dies at the age of sixty-eight, surviving her step-mother, Nannerl, by ten years. There seems to be a difference of opinion amongst some scholars about when she died. The dates provided are from the Mozart Museum in Salzburg. Wolfgang Joseph (1774–1787) is ten at the time of marriage and dies three years later, in the same year as Nannerl's father, Leopold. Joseph Maria Cajeton (1777–1806) is seven at the time of marriage and is twenty-nine when he dies, a few months after his half-sister, Jeanette, who dies in 1805. Andra Averlinus (1779–1830) is five at the time of marriage and dies a year after his step-mother at the age of fifty-one. Karl Franz (1782–1855) is two at time of marriage and dies at seventy-three, surviving Nannerl by twenty-six years. All the step-children remained in contact with Nannerl throughout her life.

1784   *21st September* – Karl Thomas, the first son of Mozart was born in Vienna and died at his country estate, north of Milan on 31st October, 1858. He was never rich, but shortly before his death he had a windfall from performance rights for 'The Marriage of Figaro' in Paris. He was also a beneficiary of Nannerl when she waived her rights to proceeds from Mozart's Requiem in favour of her two nephews. Like his younger brother, Franz Xaver, he was unmarried. The story that there was an illegitimate child has never been proved, although there were rumours of a child called Constanze, who died of small-pox in 1833. He studied music with the composer Dussek without obvious success, then at twenty-two, enrolled himself for a compo-sition course at the Milan Conservatoire on his own initiative. His mother suggested he should give it up in case he proved mediocre. She had less inhibitions about Franz Xaver, whom she regarded as talented but lazy. Poor Karl Thomas heeded her advice, for after the early apprenticeship to a business in Leghorn (Livorno) he became a civil servant. He survived his younger brother by fourteen years and died at the age of seventy-four; by all accounts a disarming, gentle and modest man who spent his last hours gazing at a portrait of his father.

1785   *12th February* – Leopold visits Vienna to hear Mozart's subscription concerts. After the performance of three of the six string quartets dedicated to Joseph Haydn, Haydn turns to him and says: 'Before God and as an honest man, I tell you that your son is the greatest composer known to me in person or by name.'

1785   *27th July* – birth of Nannerl's first child in Salzburg. Leopold Alois Pantaleon Berchtold zu Sonnenburg was the only one of her chil-dren to reach adulthood. He survived his mother by eleven years and died on 15th June, 1840 in Innsbruck at the age of fifty-five. He was adored by his grandfather Leopold, but despite living with his grandfather for the first two years of his life, showed no lasting signs of musical talent. He became a conscript during the Napoleonic wars and ended up as a Bavarian civil servant in the Tyrol.

1787   *28th May* – Leopold dies in Salzburg, age sixty-seven.

1789   *22nd March* – birth of Nannerl's first daughter, Jeanette – christened Johanna Maria Anna Elisabeth Berchtold zu Sonnenburg.

1790 *23rd September to beginning of September* – Mozart journeys to Frankfurt.

1790 *22nd November* – birth of Nannerl's shortlived third child in Saint Gilgen – christened Maria Barbara Berchtold zu Sonnenburg.

1791 *29th April* – death of Maria Barbara at five months in Saint Gilgen.

1791 *26th July* – birth of Franz Xaver Wolfgang, sixth child of Mozart and Constanze, later known as Wolfgang Amadeus. He was five months old when his father died. The names, Franz Xaver, were also those of Süssmayr, the composer who completed Mozart's Requiem at the request of Constanze. Franz Xaver Mozart gave his first public concert at Schikaneder's theatre in 1805 and was well received by people anxious to support the name. His teachers in Vienna were Hummel, Salieri, Albrechtsburger and the Abbé Vogler. It was eventually Salieri who wrote a testimonial on his behalf and helped secure his first teaching appointment in Poland.

He was never rapturously praised for either his compositions or his performances, although he was popular in Poland. He began a long affair with Josephine von Baroni-Cavalcabo, who as well as being the married mother of two of his pupils, was a fine singer and, according to Constanze, the chief reason her son was reluctant to leave Lemberg where he lived for most of his adult life. (Josephine's younger daughter was Franz Xaver's star pupil at the keyboard). In Vincent Novello's diary of his travels in 1829, he records: 'Young Mozart's mistress in Poland is a countess who is, unfortunately, married to a man she does not esteem. He is so much attached to her that his mother feared he would never leave Poland for any length of time without her as he cannot take her with him on account of the husband. Madame Mozart begins to despair of his ever establishing himself in Vienna or other large capital where his parts might be better known and appreciated.' In 1819, Franz Xaver began a musical tour of Europe without his mistress, before returning to Lemburg in 1822 and resuming teaching, performing, conducting and inevitably, their affair. It was during this tour that he first met Nannerl in 1821. She wrote in his album how so many 'delightful memories' of her brother were stirred by her nephew when he played for her in her seventieth year. But by now, F.X. was composing less and less and felt unable to escape the shadow of his father's genius. This vulnerability and his physical resemblance to his father made him sympathetic to Nannerl. Their affection for one another was strong and whenever he was in Salzburg, (usually every three years), he made a point of visiting her. He claimed he learnt more about his father from his aunt than he had ever discovered through his mother. He moved with the Baroni-Cavalcabo family to Vienna in 1838 and later died in Karlsbad on the 29th July, 1844 at the age of 53. Death was caused by liver failure – he had been plagued by stomach troubles and depression for some time before. His most attractive characteristic seems to have been his capacity to love others – love for his mistress, whom he wished he could have married, for her daughter Julie, who was his pupil, and his genuine, lasting affection for his brother and his Aunt Nannerl.

1791   *5th December* – Mozart dies in Vienna at thirty-five. Constanze is only twenty-nine.

1797   Constanze lives openly with Georg Nikolaus Nissen.

1798   Constanze arranges for Karl Thomas, her older son, aged fourteen, to become an apprentice in a business in Leghorn.

1801   *26th February* – Johann Baptist von Berchtold zu Sonnenburg dies in Saint Gilgen. He is sixty-four.

1801   *28th October* – Nannerl is fifty when she returns to Salzburg with her two children and four of the five surviving step-children. She lives in the home of the Barisanis, friends of the Mozarts. Although she was well provided for in old age by Sonnenburg, she takes on a few piano pupils.

1805   *1st September* – Nannerl's sixteen-year-old daughter Jeanette dies in Salzburg. Her brother Leopold is twenty at the time and living in the Tyrol.

1806   Joseph Maria Cajetan Berchtold zu Sonnenburg dies in Salzburg, aged twenty-nine.

1806   Karl Thomas Mozart enrols at the Milan Conservatoire to study composition, but gives it up on Constanze's advice.

1807   Franz Xaver takes a teaching position in Galicia, Poland – his reference for the job came from Salieri.

1809   *26th June* – Constanze marries Georg Nikolaus Nissen, although they have been living together for twelve years.

1810   In September, Constanze and Nissen move to Copenhagen.

1810   At twenty-six, Karl Thomas is appointed to the Civil Service by the Viceroy of Naples. Later he served as the Imperial and Royal Court Clerk when Lombardy was taken over by Austria after the Congress of Vienna.

1813   Franz Xaver Mozart settles in Lemburg as teacher and performer. It marks the beginning of his intimate relationship with the Baroni-Cavalcabo family. He is twenty-two years old.

1818   Towards the end of the year, Franz Xaver begins an extensive concert tour of Europe.

1820   *21st August* – Franz Xaver visits his brother Karl Thomas in Milan for the first time since they were separated.

1821   *21st May* – Franz Xaver visits Nannerl in Salzburg for the first time.

1821   Later in the summer, Constanze and Nissen return to Salzburg after an absence of eleven years. Nissen begins his biography of Mozart.

1822   Franz Xaver returns to Lemburg.

1825   *7th May* – Salieri dies, paranoid and suffering from the delusion that he poisoned Mozart.

1825   Nannerl is effectively blind, having already lost the use of her right eye several years before.

1826   *24th March* – Nissen dies and later in August of that year, Franz Xaver conducts his father's Requiem in a memorial service for his step-father.

1828   Constanze publishes an edited version of Nissen's unfinished biography of Mozart.

1829   In mid-July, Vincent and Mary Novello visit Salzburg to meet Nannerl and Constanze, bringing a substantial gift of money to Nannerl from her admirers in England:

THE PRESENTATION TO MOZART'S SISTER
                              London, Wedy. June 24th, 1829.
The undermentioned Persons, who are enthusiastic admirers of the
delightful compositions of Mozart, have formed (quite privately
among themselves) a little Collection amounting to 60 Guineas,
for the purpose of offering a small present to the Sister of Mozart,
as a trifling token of their respect for the memory of her illustri-
ous Brother, and of their cordial sentiments towards his estimable
Sister, Madame Sonnenburg.
    They have confined their little present to the care of Mr V.
Novello, in order that he may place it in Madame Sonnenburg's
own hands, in any way which he will find most agreeable to herself.
Whatever mode will afford most pleasure to the Sister of Mozart,
will be that which will also afford the greatest gratification to her
cordial friends, whose names will be found subjoined.

Mr Stumpff *£10*
Mr V. Novello *£10*
Mr Stevens *£5*
Mr Attwood (pupil of Mozart) *£5*
Mr Braham *£5*
Mr Capel *£5*
Mr Trueman *£2*
Mr Potter *£1*
Mr Moscheles *£2*
Mr J. B. Cramer. *£2*
Mrs Haddon *£2*
Mrs Doxat *£5*
Mr Cazenove. *£5*
Mr Horsley *£1*
Mr Dampier *£2*
Mr Holden *£1*

With the most heartfelt gratitude I acknowledge in the name of Mozart's sister the receipt of the sum mentioned, herewith-signed: — Constanze v. Nissen, Mozart's Widow.

(J.A.Stumpff, one of the benefactors, translated the statement by Constanze. The list was returned to Novello).

Vincent Novello was the founder of Novello Music Publishers. The travel diaries which he and his wife kept in the year 1829, were published a hundred years or more later under the title 'A Mozart Pilgrimage.'

1829 *29ᵗʰ October* – Nannerl dies at the age of seventy-eight in Salzburg. Her son, Leopold Alois Pantaleon, and the remaining step-children – Maria Anna, Andra Averlinus and Karl Franz – are by now middle-aged.

1835 Franz Xaver travels to Karlsbad with his pupil, Julie Baroni-Cavalcabo and meets Robert Schumann.

1838 Franz Xaver moves to Vienna to live with the Baroni-Cavalcabo family. The relationship with his mistress, Josephine Baroni-Cavalcabo has already lasted twenty-five years.

1840   Karl Thomas visits his brother in Vienna. He visited his mother only once after settling in Italy.

1841   Franz Xaver is made an honorary Kapellmeister at the Salzburg Mozarteum, a post he prized. The 'active' responsibility went to a young theatre conductor from Silesia. This happened despite Constanze's efforts on behalf of Franz Xaver, who may have been passed over because he was lack-lustre or not young enough.

1842   *6ᵗʰ March* – Constanze dies at the age of eighty from collapsed lungs. Her last years were spent on the third floor of an apartment in Salzburg, which she shared with her younger sister, Sophie. She was rich enough to leave substantial legacies to both her sons and to Sophie.

1844   In June, Franz Xaver travels to Karlsbad for the spas and dies there on the 29ᵗʰ July, aged fifty-three. Just before he died, he willed everything he had to his mistress, Josephine, whom he regarded as his wife in every way except fact.

1858   *31ˢᵗ October* – Karl Thomas is seventy-two when he dies at his country estate in Caversaccio which he had purchased in 1853 for his retirement. Just before his death, he declared that sons of famous fathers should never share the same career because even if they revealed more talent than the parent, they could never match up to expectations. He was probably thinking about his dead brother, Franz Xaver, whom he regarded as more talented than himself. Described as a modest and gentle person without any illusions about his musicality, he enjoyed accompanying friends on his father's piano when they visited him in Italy. He was the last known, direct descendent of Mozart.

No More of Love

for soprano & clavier

by A. M. Bauld

A. M. Bauld

Printed in the United Kingdom
by Lightning Source UK Ltd.
109512UKS00001B/163-186